# Maria's Trail
## The First Adventures of Señora Chica Walsh, Hero of
## The Mule Tamer Trilogy

John C. Horst

For Jimmie D. Flanagan

Be kind, for everyone you meet is fighting a hard battle

# Contents

# Chapter I: Curanderas

The child watched the curandera work on the old woman. The hovel was dark and hazy with smoke from the old healer's cure. She leaned close to her patient as she spread the mixture of ointment and dirt and saliva onto the woman's chest. In a little while the invalid would be resting again and the girl was hopeful as she watched the witchdoctor gather up her belongings. She followed her out into the little yard.

The curandera was even more frightening in the daylight and she stank of her treatments. Her breath was bad. It reeked of the various things she smoked and blew onto her patients. The little girl looked at the medicine woman scratching her backside as she pointed to the remaining chickens. The girl complied. She didn't need to be told, she knew that the payment would be dear. The sick woman had no earthly possessions, money, jewelry or any goods of consequence. The little girl didn't know what they'd do without chickens as now there'd be no eggs.

"She is beyond my help." The curandera eyed the chickens doubtfully. The little girl wondered why, then, she was being paid. The curandera looked at the child and wagged her head slowly from side to side. "There is another, in the next village, who will help her but it will cost more than chickens."

"How much?"

The healer tipped her head toward the hovel. "More than she has in the world."

"How much?" The child was precocious and the healer gave her a weak smile.

"Let her die, child. Let her die."

"How much?"

"Ten centavos."

The little girl kept her face stone-like. She calculated in her head. She'd never heard of such a sum.

She thought hard and replied without thinking. "Will you fetch her here? I will get the money."

The curandera became severe. "I will, but if the payment is not made, it will not go well for you or anyone who lives here. You understand, child? You understand that if the debt is not paid, it will not go well for anyone here?"

"I understand."

The other one would be here in three days, she promised, as she tied the chickens together by the legs. Now, added to the curandera's odor was the stench of chicken manure. She was gone.

The little girl prepared the last of the eggs while the old woman slept covered in the strange thick paste. She'd begun stinking from being ill and the treatment made her nearly unbearable. The child was diligent in keeping her clean but now this seemed impossible. The curandera gave no instructions on how long the unguent must stay. Would it dry and peel off, would it continue to stink? The little girl did not know.

The old woman stirred momentarily, but drifted off again and the little girl began taking an inventory. She dug up the treasure the old woman kept hidden. She had her dowry necklace. The little girl put it on. The old woman used to pull it out every so often and put it on the child and now she looked down at it, hanging low. It was big and the child was very small. It was supposed to be hers one day. It was made from old coins and they'd be worth something.

She dug some more. There was a gilt mirror and hairbrush. The bristles were mostly gone and the gold had mostly worn away, only a metal color showed through on the high spots and sides. But it was beautiful and one could still see a reflection in the glass. It must be worth something as well.

Then there was the old woman's work. She'd made some good baskets before she'd gotten so ill and they must be worth something.

She thought about the amount she needed. There were the two goats. They'd make it all up but then they'd have nothing. The chickens were gone and if the goats were gone there'd be nothing left. She thought about this. If she didn't get rid of everything, the old woman would surely die. But if she did get rid of everything, the old woman would perhaps live but they'd have nothing to live on. It was a significant problem.

"What are you doing, child?"

The little girl looked up. The old woman was awake. She took the string of coins from around her neck and moved over next to the old woman. She gave her a drink.

"Wash this from my body, hija."

"But it is the cure."

"Bah. Take it off. It stinks of shit."

The little girl complied and the old woman did not stink so. Her breath was still horrible, not like the curandera's, as the old woman did not smoke, but of some kind of dreadful odor that the little girl did not know. It was the smell of impending death and there was no way to take it away.

"But you will perhaps die."

"When?"

She laughed a little at her own joke until she saw the effect it had on the girl. She reached up and touched her gently on the face. "What are you doing with these things?"

"The curandera cannot heal you but she can bring in another. They need payment to heal you."

"Hah." She thought of how to break the news to the girl. She was already weakening from the little bit of talking she'd done. She breathed deeply and her chest rattled. She coughed and spit into a rag. "You keep them safe, child. Keep them safe." She looked at the mirror and brush and asked the child to bring them to her bed.

The old woman looked them over as if she were trying to remember them. She held up the mirror and looked into it. She then looked at the child. "See this, hija, see what is in there?"

"Me."

"You remember this, child. There is no one else in the world. No one else will take care of you in the world. Only this one." She pointed at the little girl's reflection. "Never forget that, child." She pointed again. "This is the only one who you can rely on and trust. You remember that, child."

She fell back and rested her hands by her sides. The little girl took the mirror and brush; she covered up the old woman and hid the treasures. Gathering the water jars, she walked outside.

It was getting late and a few people in the little settlement milled about. The mean man was there and he saw her. He sauntered up to her and looked her over dismissively.

"Is she dead yet?"

The little girl didn't want to answer, but he was important in the little settlement and she wanted no trouble.

Before she could speak the important man's wife interjected. "Don't talk like that to the child."

"Whore's spawn."

"Stop it." The mean man's wife was not so mean and the little girl could not understand why she was with him. The mean man's wife walked up to the girl and regarded her. She brushed back her long black hair and put her hand to her cheek. "How is your old mother?"

"She's not her mother. She's an old woman." The man spit tobacco juice as he spoke. "She's the whore's spawn," he pointed, accusingly and self-righteously at the child.

The wife took the girl away from the mean man and they walked a little way to the well. The girl worked and the woman watched her. "What did the healer say?"

"To let her die." The little girl filled the jars. "But I told her to get another healer. She's coming in three days."

"I see." The wife sat down and looked at the child. She was smart this one. She'd survive, but it was sad to see that she'd have nothing when they'd finished. The old woman would be dead in a week, probably, and then the girl would have nothing and the woman's husband would not let her live in the hovel alone. The child interrupted her thoughts.

"Where can I sell some things?"

"What things?"

"Just some things. I need the money for the second healer."

"Nuevo Casas Grandes would be best. There is a man there. He has a store. He would buy some things I guess."

The little girl turned and slowly walked away. She was thinking of all the things she needed to do. She was soon back at the shack. She'd never been to Nuevo Casas Grandes but knew it would take a whole day to get there and a whole day to get back.

She thought about the old woman being alone for two days. The mean man's wife would not help her. She couldn't help her as the mean man would not allow it. She decided she could make up food for the old woman and leave it nearby, within easy reach. That would not be a problem. She'd likely soil herself though. She'd have to lie in her waste for two days.

She looked outside and reasoned that it was too late to do anything now. If she worked late into the evening, she'd have everything prepared and could leave before sunrise in the morning. She'd be back in time for the healer and have the payment. It would be enough, it had to be enough.

She worked and the old woman slept.

Nuevo Casas Grandes was overwhelming. She'd never seen so many people and she soon realized that she was not dressed anything like them. She wore, literally, rags and was barefoot. She knew well enough that she'd not be taken very seriously in her present state.

She spotted a stable. She washed in the trough and braided her hair. She adjusted her rebozo to cover the top part of her dress and carefully cut away the ragged part of the skirt. She could do nothing about her feet but wash them the best she could. She pulled out the mirror and looked herself over. She didn't look so bad now. At least she was clean.

She surveyed her treasures. The goats traveled well enough and she could not believe that all of it would not be enough for the amount needed. She decided to hide the necklace and looked around.

There was a spot at a corner of a building with loose rocks and earth. She looked to see if anyone was watching her and saw no one. She dug a little hole and hid the necklace there. If worse came to worst, she could always try and sell it to make up any shortfall.

She was ready now but a bit shaky. She wasn't hungry, but the thought of going into the grand and fancy store and talking to a stranger, selling her pathetic goods, made her shake. She resolved to eat a little and drink from the trough. That helped the shaking to stop. She looked at her reflection in the water and thought about what the old woman had said. She took a deep breath and let it out. She was ready now.

She tied the goats to the post outside and entered the store. It immediately made her shaky and dizzy again. It was more than she could take in; the odor of the fresh straw from new brooms mixed with finely dyed fabric, new leather and chemicals, coffee and candy and so many odors she'd never known. She looked around at dresses and fabric for rebozos and fancy hats. It was the most beautiful place she'd ever seen.

A man was behind the counter. He looked at her and smiled. She did not expect that. She expected someone like the mean man and he wasn't anything like the mean man. She suddenly felt a little fluttery in her stomach. The man seemed to be good and kind.

"Well, young lady." He looked behind her and all around for an adult and realized she was all alone. This made him even friendlier. "How may I help you?"

She looked at him and hesitated, she couldn't seem to find her voice. He looked like a nice man. He had a big smile and good teeth. They weren't stained or black or missing anywhere. He wore a white high collar around his neck made from a material she'd never seen before and a colorful cravat protruded from the collar. He wore a vest that matched his trousers and his sleeves were clean, everything was clean. He looked through little oval glasses and he had no hair on his face at all. His face seemed as smooth as a lady's. She was very impressed with all of this.

"I have things to sell and was told to see you."

"I see." He beckoned her to the back of the store, to his desk where she could sit down and not have to reach up high to the counter. This made her fluttery again; she knew this part of the store was not for customers. He was a very nice man.

She sat and pulled the items carefully from a sack. She then laid the sack down, as it too was for sale. She'd have no use for a sack if he would buy the other things.

He looked them over carefully.

"And two goats." She turned her head, then pointed at the front of his store.

"I see." He picked up the useless items and turned them over in his hands, as if he were regarding some great heirlooms. He did not look up from them but asked her, talking toward the items as if they'd give him the answer to his questions, "Why do you need to sell such things, child?"

He finally looked up, looked into her eyes with a tenderness she'd never known.

"The old woman, eh, the woman who cares for me." That sounded silly because she'd been caring for the old woman for more than a year now. "She's sick and I need money for the curanderas."

"I see. And your mother or father, cannot they do this? Cannot someone else help you in this?"

She answered automatically. "There is no one else."

"I see." The man became animated. He was excited and suddenly sat back in his chair. "Well, let's see," he stroked his chin and regarded the items. "I have no use for goats, so I can give you nothing for them. He picked up the brush and mirror. "The bristles are gone and the finish is gone. The mirror needs to be re-silvered. So, I am sorry, but no, they have no value."

He watched her face fall. She was about to tell him about the necklace when he continued. "How much do they need?"

Te...twenty centavos." She didn't know why she lied to the nice man, but thought it would be better to start high. He laughed as he could see her little lie, and then grinned a fatherly grin at her.

"Twenty centavos! A king's ransom!" He stood up and held out his hand. "Little girl," he stopped himself and walked away. She watched him as he retrieved a box and opened it. She could see great piles of paper money and coins. He laid out ten centavos before her. He went back to the box and gathered more coins. He placed another pile of coins next to the first one. She could not understand why. He smiled and continued.

"The pile on the left is ten centavos, little one. The pile on the right is one hundred." He stood up again and walked to the front of the store. He turned the sign around and locked the door. He returned and picked out a pretty blue dress hanging on a rack and held it up to her, under her chin. "Lovely, lovely. And just the right size."

She suddenly felt weak again, like her legs were made of lead, like something had happened to them and she was afraid that she would not be able to move them when it was time to leave. She didn't like this and wanted the man to stop. She found she could not speak; blood pounded in her chest and ears and was giving her a headache. She could only watch him, wait and see what he was going to do next. He sensed this, too, and continued.

"Little girl." He held up his hands ever so kindly. "I will not harm you. As God is my witness, I would never harm you. I, I lost my little girl and my wife and, I, just want to be nice to you."

She relaxed and he continued. "I will give you all the money on the desk," he looked at the two piles of coins, "and this lovely dress and some shoes if you'll just be nice to me." He patted her gently on the cheek, "And you can keep all your treasures."

She regarded him. He *was* nice. She did not understand his kindness. It was confusing, but she'd known some kindness like this before. Wasn't the old woman kind to her for the same reason? The old woman took her in because she'd lost all her children, and her husband was dead. Wasn't this the same thing?

She felt the flutter again. It was going to be all right. He'd even picked the dress that caught her eye when she'd first come into the store. It was as if he knew what was in her mind. Then she thought of the money. A hundred and ten centavos! And she could keep the goats and the mirror and brush and the necklace.

It was overwhelming and she was more than a little proud of herself. She'd make the old woman well and they'd be fine. They could buy extra goats and more chickens and they'd be good through winter and beyond. She smiled at the man and thanked him.

He jumped up and patted her gently on the knee. "This calls for a celebration, my little one. A celebration!"

He looked about, not certain what to do next. Then he remembered and, pushing the dress on her, pointed to a little room. "Go, go change, child."

She did and when she returned she looked very pretty. She was quite pleased with herself, despite the fact that she was still barefoot. He'd laid out some things on the desk, a fancy drink of yellow liquid and some candy and a cake. She'd never tasted anything so wonderful in her life.

He chatted constantly but she couldn't respond. She listened and ate and drank. She looked down at the pretty blue cloth covering her legs and she became dizzy with the excitement; overwhelmed and happy, warm and tingly all over. She wanted, for some reason, to sleep.

# Chapter II: Alone

She awoke; it was hot and nearly dark. Something wet was splashing her and, as she looked up, whatever it was splattered into her eyes. It burned terribly. Whatever was being thrown on her had gotten into her mouth and it tasted horrible.

She squinted and saw the man. She could tell that she was in the desert. He was ranting and speaking so quickly that she couldn't make out what he was saying. She cast her eyes about to see who was there for him to speak to but there was no one else, just his horse hitched to a wagon.

He was wetting her down with coal oil from a metal can and it was getting everywhere. She looked down and saw that she was wearing her old dress. She wondered at that, as she remembered having the pretty blue one on before she fell asleep. Her old outfit was now getting soaked along with the rest of her.

He backed up and tripped, spilling coal oil down his front. He brushed at it as if he could wipe it away. He no longer looked happy and friendly. Now he was feral, like an animal she'd once seen with hydrophobia and it scared her very much.

He turned and put the coal oil can in the wagon and then came back. He picked at his vest pocket and found some matches. She knew he was going to burn her up. She desperately thought about what to do. She couldn't run, he'd catch her. Her legs were full of pain and her feet hurt.

He was striking the match now. It would engulf her. Suddenly she knew what to do. She learned from a young age how to throw things with precision. She'd killed rabbits and chickens in the desert this way since just about the time she could walk and she knew this was her only chance. She picked up a fist-sized rock and threw with all her might, striking the man in the forehead.

He fell as the match ignited and lit his soaked matching vest and trousers. He was suddenly a giant torch and he screamed and ran in circles nearly running toward her then changing direction. He ran into the desert and finally, after a hundred or so feet, dropped and continued to burn. He was finally dead.

The horse pulling the wagon panicked and also ran wildly into the desert and after a time she realized that she was all alone. It was fully dark now. She did not recognize this place so surmised that she had to be somewhere other than southeast of the town as that was the route she knew and she'd never been on the road nearby.

She slowly got to her feet and stumbled to the burning corpse which was by now devoid of most of its flesh, the face gone, now nothing more than a red burning skeleton. She realized that this did not scare her but actually made her feel good. He was a bad man and he was the first of his kind that she'd seen get what he deserved. She couldn't help being a bit proud of the fact that she'd made it happen to a certain extent. No one could say that she'd killed him or burned him up, she just stunned him with the rock. But he was dead now and he'd died a fittingly horrible death and she was partially the reason it happened.

She sat down next to the corpse, upwind because she didn't want to smell like greasy burning human, but she was suddenly very cold and the corpse gave off a fair bit of heat.

She warmed herself as the coal oil dried from her dress. She became sleepy and slept next to the shopkeeper until morning.

When she awoke it was full daylight and the corpse was burned out. Nothing much was left but a skeleton and she regarded him again. She could recognize him. His nice teeth were recognizable.

She needed to urinate and did and had to push extra hard as things were bound up down there. Something popped or tore and she looked down to see that her urine was reddish. She realized then that he'd been up to no good but that she'd been so sleepy from what he'd given her to drink and eat that she didn't know.

She was glad of that and looked down to survey her dress and saw blood on it and further surmised that she'd been bleeding at some point. What he'd done to her made her bleed and made her very sore. He was a wicked man and she looked on the corpse again and was glad to see him in such a state. She was glad that he was dead.

She got her bearings and began walking toward town. She was famished and had nothing but her soiled dress. She needed to get her things. She wondered if the goats were still tethered to the post in front of the burned man's store.

She found some water and drank until she was full and washed herself. It burned and stung very much and she felt down there. She could feel that her body was torn and that it would scab over then open up whenever she urinated and wondered how it would ever heal.

She soaked her dress where it was bloody but the stain wouldn't come out. The blood had dried and was fixed. She'd have cut it away but her knife was gone, so she resolved to continue walking in her bloody dress. There was nothing more that she could do.

She arrived at the town at midday and the goats were gone. She checked the store and it was locked. She tried the windows and could not open them. She sat down and was shakier than before. She started to doze when a man on a horse rode up and dismounted. He tied his horse to the post she'd used for the goats the previous day. He wore a uniform and had a sword which bounced about on his side. He walked past her and pulled on the store's door, then peered in and knocked. He turned and regarded her.

"What are you doing here?"

"Waiting."

"For what?" He looked around. "Where's Sanchez?"

"I don't know. I don't know who that is."

"The shopkeeper."

"He's...I, he's not here, but he has my things. I need my things."

The rurale regarded her. He looked at her dirty bloody dress. "What have you gotten yourself into?"

She realized that she might not want to tell him much. "Chicken blood."

He shrugged and shook his head. "Big chicken."

He began to walk away and she decided that he was her only hope. She called out to him as he mounted up. "That man, Sanchez, he has my things. I need to get inside."

"You, peon, have no business with Sanchez. He's a respected shop owner. You come back when he's here. Don't bother me with such things, child."

"But he took..." she thought better of it. "He has my things, it is my right. And my goats are gone."

"Hah!" He sneered. "You have no rights, child. Go back to your hole in the ground, go back home." He was gone.

She did as she was told and by sundown was nearly home. She walked without thinking and was so hungry that her stomach ached constantly. She drank a few times through the day and that helped a little. By full dark she was just too tired to go on and resolved to lie down for a while. She thought that she would only rest for a little while and then go on.

But she didn't wake up and it was full daylight by the time she got moving again. She worried over the old woman and wondered and hoped that she was okay. She did not know what she'd tell the curanderas. She wanted them to treat the old woman but now had nothing to give them. She decided that she couldn't worry about that now. She decided, after all that had happened to her in the past two days, that she'd not worry about things that she could not control. She resolved, from now on, to control as many things as she could. She also decided to trust no one, as the old woman had told her, except herself. She could rely on no one in the world and that was the way things would be from now on.

She saw smoke off in the distance, in the direction of the hovel, and she hurried on as best she could. Such a large fire made no sense to her. She finally arrived to find the hovel burning, the mean man and his wife and the curanderas looking on. The mean man sneered. "You are late."

"Where's the old woman?"

The mean man's wife pointed at the hovel and the girl looked at them. "Why?"

The mean man spit tobacco at her feet. "She was dead when they came to treat her. They said it all needed to be purified and we burned it. She's gone, child."

The little girl watched it burn alone. The curanderas left and the mean man and his wife went about their business. She watched the little shack fall apart and looked on as the foundation was revealed. She remembered everything she could about her time there. She could not say that any of the times were really good, but they were her time and the old woman's time, and sometimes she was a little happy when she made the old woman smile. She never went hungry and the old woman was good to her, better than any other human being had been and now she was dead.

She thought about crying but didn't. She lay down in the shade and fell asleep until the mean man's wife nudged her awake. The wife was nervous and looked back at her own hovel often. Her husband would be cross if he knew that she was helping the whore's spawn, but the woman was good and she could not help herself.

She had food for the girl and sat beside her as the child ate. She reached over to touch the girl's hair and the child recoiled, pulling away and putting several feet between them. They were both shocked at this behavior.

"Take these things, child." She gave her a bundle of old clothes wrapped in a rebozo along with a knife and a flint and steel. At least the child could make a fire. She gave her a sack of tortillas and some dried beans and a water gourd.

The little girl looked the things over and then gazed into the woman's eyes. "May I live with you?"

The woman looked away, at the burned remains of the hovel. "No, child. You may not and you must not stay here. He won't allow it." She regarded the child's dress and the bloodstains. The bastard missed nothing, she thought, looking back at the hovel where her husband was likely eating, gorging himself while this little one suffered. His mean, beady little eyes saw everything.

"He says you are no good, that you are the product of a whore and now you've been spoiled." She looked away and the little girl saw that she was crying. She felt sorry for the woman even though she was not going to help her beyond the little bit that she had. She stood up and brushed her skirt off. She looked down on the woman's head, grabbed her new kit and walked away.

She walked back to the town because she remembered the necklace she'd hidden. She needed to get it as it was the only thing she had left in the world, other than her kit and her clothing, which was of any tangible value. She at least was not hungry and this helped her progress a good deal.

She killed a rattler with a rock on the way and made a fire and cooked it. If she could do this regularly, she could save the tortillas for when she was in the town as she did not know how long she'd be there or even what she'd do after reacquiring her necklace.

She had reached the area just outside of town by dusk and decided to bed down in the desert. She felt safe in the desert and vulnerable in the town. That puzzled her. She thought a lot about her short time in the town and the shopkeeper and rurale who were not good to her. It seemed that the desert was safer as it had no people in it.

She made a fire and found water and filled her gourd and settled down for the night. She'd made her camp in an arroyo so that her fire would draw no attention. No one taught her this but it was reasonable to think that it would be best to remain invisible. She found an armadillo and killed it with a blow from a stick and ate it. At least she wasn't hungry and she was safe. She was alone and she missed the old woman, but the thought of being alone did not bother her as much as she thought it might.

Before going to sleep, she had to urinate. It still hurt but not as bad as before and she no longer bled. Her wound was healing. She went to sleep.

# Chapter III: Juana

She made it to the corral and the water trough and remembered the building well. She looked left and right; there was no one around. She had begun to dig when a voice called out. She jumped and tried to hide what she was doing.

"What are you on about there?"

She looked up and saw a child peering at her, trying to see what she was digging at. The child was about the same age as the little girl, no more than ten. She was about the same height but she was quite round and the little girl thought that she must be from a wealthy family to be so fat.

"Nothing."

The fat child pushed her aside and began looking at the spot. "Oh, you are looking for something. What is it?"

The little girl pushed her back and placed her body between the hole and the fat girl. And now the fat girl, with a good deal more force than one would expect, struck the little girl along the side of her face, knocking her to the ground.

She was suddenly furious. Tired of so much injustice, tired of being mistreated by so many and now this fat little girl, someone akin to her size, had attacked her. The little girl jumped up and began beating at her attacker, smacking her over and over, like a wild beast. The chubby girl recoiled, not expecting such an attack. She retreated and held her nose which was now freely spouting blood.

"God damn you! You didn't need to do that."

"I'm sorry." She wasn't really but knew that she'd won. There was no reason to be cruel and she had a kind heart.

"Jesus!" The girl pinched her nose to keep from bleeding all over herself. She spit a gob of blood onto the ground. The two sat together for a while and the little girl kept an eye on her buried treasure. The fat one looked her attacker over. "What's your name?"

"Maria."

"Where'd you come from? I've never seen you before."

The little girl pointed southeast. "Back there." She looked over at her nemesis who had by now staunched the bleeding. "What's your name?"

"Juana."

"I'm sorry for making you bleed." She regarded the girl and thought that she might perhaps live with her. "Do you live in this town?"

"Yes."

"Where?"

"Here, there, everywhere." She shrugged and smiled.

"You have no home?"

"No." She grinned, she could read the girl's mind. "I know, I am too fat to be a vagrant."

She regarded the girl again. "Maria."

"What?"

"Nothing. Just saying your name. Named for the Virgin."

"Who's that?" She suddenly had an urge to urinate again and ran behind the trough as Juana looked on.

"Oh, you're in a state." She watched the little girl wince as she peed. "Let me have a look."

"Where?"

"Down there."

"No!" She stood up and straightened her skirt. The fat girl was appalling.

"Who did that to you?" She suddenly had a thought. "I know!" She grinned and then stopped grinning. "That pig Sanchez, the shopkeeper. Didn't he?" She leaned over the trough and washed the blood from her blouse. "He's missing, you know."

"Yes. I know." She watched the fat girl for a while and decided it would be safe to dig up her necklace. Juana watched and nodded approvingly. She took it from Maria and washed it in the trough for her. "It's pretty." She handed it back.

"Who is this virgin?"

She giggled. "You really don't know?"

"No."

"Do you know of Jesus and the church and heaven and hell?"

"No."

"But you're named for her. The Virgin Maria. Except you aren't one now."

"A what?"

"A virgin." Juana was getting hungry. "Come on, I'll take you to the whores. They'll help you down there." She pointed at Maria's midsection. "They'll know all about it."

"What are whores?" Maria was feeling very stupid around the chubby girl. She said words and talked of things that made no sense, things Maria knew nothing about.

"Are you serious?"

"Yes."

"They do it for money."

"What?"

"It, what Sanchez did to you."

"I don't know what he did. I was asleep. He gave me something and I don't know what he did."

Juana laughed and then thought better of it. She became serious. "Did you ever see animals doing it..., you know, breeding, dogs or cats?"

Maria understood now. "Oh, goats, I've seen goats breed. Yes."

"That's it! That's what the whores do for money, what Sanchez did to you. He mated with you. He stuck his thing in there, but you're too small. The whores said that about me. I'm too young to be a whore. I'm not big enough yet."

"I see." Maria thought she was going to be sick. It made sense now and it made her feel ill. She thought back to her time with the shopkeeper. Some things she kind of remembered. Juana brought her from her reverie.

"Come on, Maria, it's okay, the whores will help you."

They made it to the far side of town, to the end of the street where there were three saloons and a bordello. Juana escorted Maria through the front door. Maria had never seen such a place. The walls and door were painted red. The carpet was red, the drapes were red and red shades covered all the lamps. A woman greeted them. She was wearing only underwear. Her breasts were exposed and Maria turned her head away. The prostitute was kind to her, though. She had a kind face and when she smiled it revealed an incomplete set of teeth. She was an Indian, yet she had yellow hair.

"What's this, Juana?"

"A new girl. Maria. She needs help down there. Sanchez got her and made her sore."

"Oh." The whore lit a cigar and regarded the little girl. The child was a beauty and the whore's face reflected a deep twinge of regret. She reached down and patted Maria on the head, then took her by the hand. "Come with me, Maria. I'll help you."

She took her into another red room with a sagging bed that was pushed against the wall. It stank of sweat and dirty bodies and things that Maria had never smelled before. The woman told her to lie back on the bed and Maria complied. She handed Maria an ointment and told her what to do. She left the room so that she was alone.

Maria did as she was told and immediately felt better. She was not certain what to do and stayed in the room. She rested on the soft bed. The pillow was nice.

She'd never felt such a thing in her life, it was the first bed she'd ever lain in.

She thought about the mean man from the village. He called her a whore's spawn. She now knew what a whore was and what a whore did, but she did not know what it meant to be a spawn. She considered it. She'd only ever known the old woman and knew well enough that the old woman was not her mother. The old woman had always made that clear to Maria, and she'd never thought much about her mother. Perhaps her mother was here. Her mother was a whore, according to the mean man. Maybe the woman with the yellow hair was her mother. Probably not. She soon fell into a deep sleep.

She awoke to find food next to her bed. Juana was sitting nearby, puffing on a cigarette. "Feeling better?"

"Yes." She looked around and then heard a party outside the room.

"Go ahead and eat, but hurry. We've got to get out of this room. It's needed."

She complied and ate and enjoyed the food. She could not understand why they were all so good to her. She regarded Juana and regretted hitting her earlier in the day. She spoke without thinking. "I'm sorry for making you bleed, Juana."

"Oh, that's okay." She smiled at her. Juana had a pretty round face. "I deserved it. I shouldn't have been so cross with you." She brightened. "Let's go get your things."

"How?" She was confused. She didn't even know where her things were. If they were in Sanchez's shop, it would not be possible to get them. She needed to urinate again and asked Juana where to go. She handed Maria a chamber pot and turned her back. She understood her new friend required privacy.

Maria urinated and it didn't hurt anymore.

"That medicine is a dream."

"The whores know." She grinned. "They always know and they are good. You'll never go hungry when there are whores, Maria. That's why I'm so fat." She grinned.

They left and wandered through town. It was getting busy because some men had come in from a mine and were letting off steam. Maria saw the rurale from the other day but he paid her no mind, as he did not remember her. She got Juana's attention and pointed him out. "Who is he?"

"Pedro, the rurale. He's a real pendejo."

"What's that?"

"Oh, Maria." Juana bobbed her head from side to side. "You are the most ignorant bumpkin I've ever known. I'll tell you all the words, but later."

They were interrupted by some excitement. A little man had been drinking with some friends and now they were humiliating him. They all took turns holding his head as the man swiped at them, flailing about and falling to the ground. One man became angry at him and began kicking him. The little man became enraged. He screamed at the top of his lungs and the bully laughed at him. The bully spat on the little man and then pinned him to the ground. He ground his face into a pile of horse manure and told the man to go sleep it off.

Maria watched the little man. He was not unlike her, except that he was drunk and to an extent asking for it, but there was no call for pushing him into feces or spitting on him. There was nothing he could do because he was so small.

This is what Maria was thinking about her own situation. There was nothing she could do but take it. Take it and be quiet because the more the little man squawked, the more the bully man mistreated him.

Finally, mercifully, the bully became tired and relented. He was becoming a little embarrassed in front of his friends. They all knew the little man well enough, knew that when he got drunk it was best to just leave him alone. He'd be better when he'd sobered up. He never really caused any harm.

Juana wanted to move on, but Maria wanted to see how this little drama played out. She watched the little man. No one seemed to notice him, only Maria, as they were all too busy with other things. She watched as the man brushed himself off, rubbed the feces from his ear and cheek, then walked away to his mount, still saddled in front of the biggest saloon. He pulled something from the saddle and walked up to the bully man, got his attention and, when the bully man turned, the little one shot him through the head. The bully man was dead.

This is what Maria wanted to see. It *was* possible. She needed only to learn how.

"Come on, there'll be trouble when Pedro, the pendejo gets here. He always makes trouble."

Juana grabbed Maria by the hand and pulled her down the street. Soon they were at Sanchez's store. It looked different to Maria now, all dark, and the outside did not look so nice. She noticed that the building was not painted and bare wood showed through, two steps were broken and one looked rotten. She looked at Juana.

"What are we doing here?"

"Getting your things."

Maria recoiled. "We can't."

Juana grinned and tipped her head, "Come on, I'll show you."

They walked to the back of the place and Juana deftly dropped down to a place beside the rear steps. She slid her body under the stairs until Maria could no longer see her and now Maria was alone, waiting for the mean rurale to show up. Suddenly the back door opened and Juana was standing there with a big grin on her face. "Come on, Maria, hurry." She whispered in a low hiss as she looked about.

"How did you do that?"

"There's a trapdoor. I learned about it a while ago. I come in here sometimes in the middle of the night to get candy. He never misses it."

They were inside and Maria remembered the good smells. She looked over at the desk, the last place she remembered being during her time in the store. Juana casually walked about and grabbed some pretty candy sticks for them both. They began eating.

Juana smiled. "The asshole's missing, you know."

"I know."

Juana looked at her sideways. "How do you know, you've only just got into town?"

"I know where he is." Maria suddenly wanted to tell her new friend everything. Juana sat down and opened two bottles of beer for them. They drank and Maria liked the beer. She'd never had it and it made her feel a little dreamy.

Juana grabbed some cigars and lit two. Now she was drinking beer, eating candy and smoking. She looked very funny to Maria who smiled for the first time.

"He tried to catch me on fire out in the desert and I hit him with a rock and he caught himself on fire. Now he's dead."

"Really?" Juana grinned. "A rock?"

"Sure." Maria tried the cigar and liked it. She blew smoke at Juana's smoke. "I'm good at rock throwing. I can kill a rabbit from all the way over there." She pointed to the far end of the room.

Juana picked up a fancy glass paperweight from Sanchez's desk and handed it to Maria. She didn't doubt the child, but she wanted to see what Maria could do. "Hit that hat over there."

Maria threw and easily knocked the hat down.

"Ay, chingao, you *are* good."

Maria smoked and finished her beer. She was getting sleepy. She looked around a little nervously. "Should we leave?"

"No, let's just stay here tonight. Sanchez, I heard from the whores, didn't have family nearby. The rurale captain's been notified and the pendejo, Pedro, is guarding it. No one will come in here. He's too lazy to do anything but check the doors, and they're locked.

She began wandering around the place and soon found a box with Maria's stuff. She showed her new friend and it pleased Juana to make Maria happy. She looked at the items doubtfully. She picked up the mirror, then the brush. "This stuff's junk."

Maria looked hurt and Juana regretted her comment. "Why not take some new ones?"

Maria considered the girl's suggestion. She looked around. She'd not thought about it until now.

"The son of a bitch owes it to you, Maria. He took away," she pointed at Maria's midsection, "you know, that."

"We should take the money, too." Maria was emboldened by Juana's comment.

"You're right." Juana searched and found a money box. She handed it over to Maria.

"You take half, Juana."

"No, it's yours. The dirty devil owes you." She looked around. "We should get new clothes."

"Someone'll see us with them, that'll never do." Maria thought about the pretty dress she wore briefly. It looked and felt nice on her.

Juana suddenly had an epiphany. "Let's take it all." She smiled at Maria.

"How?"

"Sanchez has a wagon. His horse and wagon showed up this morning. The wagon's outside and the horse is at the stable, where we met."

Maria considered it. Her mind raced. If they took everything from the store, certainly it wouldn't all fit in one wagon, and it would take all night to do this.

"We'll be caught and what do we do with a wagon full of stolen things anyway?"

"No, no, Maria." Juana put up a hand. "That man who got killed, that'll keep pendejo Pedro busy most of the night. No one'll be around here until morning. We can take the stuff that we want, stuff we can easily sell. I know of a man by the sea. He is a fencer."

"A what?"

Juana smiled at Maria's continued ignorance. "A fencer. He buys things, no questions asked. He'll buy our things. We'll be rich."

Maria was beginning to sober up from the beer and now she had a headache. She looked at Juana and then all around at the store. "Okay."

By sunrise they were plodding west. Just as Juana thought, no one caught them; no one even came down the street while they were cleaning Sanchez out. By midmorning she'd counted all the money. They had nearly three hundred pesos. They also had three outfits each, two hats each, five shotguns, six rifles and half a dozen six shooters. They had many boxes of ammunition. They had ten dozen bottles of beer, five cases of whiskey and ten boxes of cigars.

This was all Juana's idea. She had considered very carefully what the men liked most at the whore house, other than the whores, and it was always whiskey, beer, cigars and guns. She was certain the fence would pay them well.

Maria regarded the horse. He was a fine animal and she'd regret giving him up. She loved horses though she'd never known or even ridden one. He was a nice horse and Maria had a way with him as she had with all animals. Goats, sheep, dogs and cats always loved

Maria. Now she could add horses to the list of animals she could control, mesmerize, and she didn't know why. She was just good with animals.

They had candy and beer for breakfast and afterward smoked a couple of cigars. It was getting hot and they put their new hats on. Maria was now having a little fun, driving the wagon as Juana fiddled with their treasure.

In short order, she emerged with a six shooter and began looking through the boxes of cartridges to find a match. She finally found the right ones and loaded the gun.

"Do you know how to shoot?" Maria looked on as Juana pointed the gun at her own belly. Maria turned the muzzle away.

"Sure. You just pull on this." She pointed to the trigger and suddenly blew a hole through the carriage floor between their feet. "Oops."

"Juana. You're going to kill us." Maria stopped the wagon and got down. She took the gun from Juana and remembered the little man shooting the bully through the head. She gripped the gun. It felt right. She turned away from Juana and the wagon and spotted a rock on the ground. She pointed and fired, shattering the rock and throwing pieces of it into the air.

"Ay chingao. You are good!"

Maria tried again and repeated her performance. "You did this before."

"Never." Maria was proud. "Here, you try."

She helped Juana and the child fired, actually missing the ground in front of them. They looked at each other and shrugged. They got back in the wagon and rode on.

Maria handed Juana the gun but she pushed it back. "You take it, carry it, we might get robbed." She laughed. "Robbers getting robbed."

"Are there bandits around here?" Maria scanned the horizon around them, doubtfully.

"Maria, there are always bandits around here. Everywhere. This is a poor country and bandits are all over."

They would not reach the man who'd buy their goods for at least another two days and they decided to camp. Maria took them off the road for a good distance and drove into an arroyo. They'd not be seen now and they settled in for the night. They decided to eat better and left the candy and beer alone. They found canned peaches amongst their booty and had them with a chicken and rabbit Maria killed with one of the rifles. She liked shooting the rifle better than the six shooter. It was great sport.

Juana looked up at the sky and then into the little fire Maria had made with her flint and steel. Maria did not think to use the box of matches as she'd only ever used the flint and steel. No one in their little village was rich enough to own matches. Maria and the old woman were even too poor to have their own flint and steel, they just kept a fire going all the time. The nice woman with the mean man used to loan them the flint and steel if they let the fire go out.

"What are we going to do with the money we get from the fencer?"

Maria considered this as she stared into the fire. She hadn't thought about it. "What do you think we should do?"

"Let's start our own whorehouse."

Maria thought about that. She didn't want to have a whorehouse. Somewhere in the recesses of her mind, in her heart, in the pit of her stomach, she knew she didn't want to have a whorehouse.

"No. I don't want that. No."

Juana shrugged. "Okay. What then?"

"How about goats?"

"Goats?"

"I've kept goats. I know them. We could have goats. We could buy some and breed them. Soon we'd have many and then we'd sell them. We could sell the milk and make cheese, too. I know how to make cheese."

"Okay." Juana sat back and pushed herself into one of Sanchez's nice blankets. It was getting a little cold and she moved closer to Maria. They were soon sound asleep, tired from their night's thievery and long journey to the sea. They held each other and it was a good feeling. They had dreams of canned fruit and good cigars and brightly colored candies.

They rode for another day and slept another night in the desert. By midday of the third day they came upon a settlement and the people were friendly. They traded for a hot meal and learned how to get to the little shop by the sea. They'd be there by midday next. It was exciting and as they slept in the barn, under a carriage, Maria could feel something moving under her head. She looked up and saw Juana sliding a six shooter beneath her makeshift pillow. She smiled into Juana's eyes.

"Just in case, Maria, just in case."

The store was not unlike Sanchez's store, but it backed up to the Gulf of California. The girls thought it must be the ocean as they did not know of such things. It was beautiful and they'd never seen such water.

The shop owner was a kindly looking man who was really a snake, but a wily snake who had learned to survive among thieves by treating them well—all of them, even if they were of the diminutive variety.

He was famous throughout the land and this is how Juana knew of him. She'd learned a great deal from the whores and their clients. Bad men liked to talk and brag, and what better place to brag in than a brothel?

He walked out of his store with his little customers and eyed the goods. They were high quality and he knew where they had come from. He looked the horse and the wagon over as well. He looked at the girls and surveyed their clothing.

"I'll take it all and trade with you for some burros and clothes. You don't want to be caught in any of that."

He pointed at them and they looked down. Maria was a little disappointed, then disappointed in herself for not thinking of it. It would take a lot of thinking and planning to be a successful bandit. She was glad she'd be out of the trading business once this transaction was completed.

Now it was Juana's turn to be clever. "Mister, here is what we need." He looked at her and listened intently.

The man liked the girls and he turned out to be a good man, despite his trade. There was so much wickedness in the land and the man, by one set of circumstances or another, found himself in the business. It was essentially easy, as the government was corrupt and he need only pay tribute to the local authorities in order to ply his trade.

He had an assistant, a young woman who was very pretty and she too was kind to the girls. It was as if she'd known what they'd been through up to this point in their young lives. She invited them to dine with her and the man and to sleep inside. There was a little room in the garret and it had windows on either end. The sea breezes made sleeping comfortable.

They slept together and Maria felt good again, just as she had in the whorehouse bed, but this one was even better. It did not stink or sag and the covers weren't red. They were white and bright and clean and smelled good because the fence's assistant hung them out in the ocean breeze to dry.

The pillow was the best, though. Maria had never felt such a pillow. It was made of good goose down and cradled her head and neck. She wondered if maybe they should just stay with these people. They could work and help out and let the people keep all the money from Sanchez's goods. Then Maria would not really be a thief because she hadn't profited from the goods. She'd just transported them and the fence took them and let them stay as a favor. She fell asleep dreaming of this as Juana snored softly in her ear.

But it would not do for them to stay there. They ate breakfast and listened to the man as the pretty assistant moved about, completing various tasks. The man held court and lectured them on being bandits and on the various dangers they would encounter. The girls sat, wide-eyed, as they'd not considered the many things the man spoke of to them. They could not begin to imagine how much danger was involved and it made Maria wish she'd never done any of it.

The assistant sensed it and moved up behind Maria's chair. She stroked her head gently and Maria got a flutter in her stomach like she'd never known. She sat, frozen. She didn't want the woman to stop stroking her head. She started to ask why they couldn't stay here forever when the man started speaking again.

"You two could go up north." He lit a cigarette he'd just finished rolling and then regarded the assistant who was becoming too attached to the girls. The fence was not an old man and he didn't want the assistant distracted with young girls. Besides, he'd grown up in a house full of girls and didn't want that right now. He continued. "With the money you two have, you could go up to Texas or even Arizona or California and live well for a while. No one will try to find you."

Maria could see it in his eyes. She and Juana were not wanted or welcome here. She glanced over at the pretty woman, now keeping busy with something at the stove. She looked back at the man smoking. It wasn't his fault. He wasn't like the mean man at the village, and he wasn't like the rurale, Pendejo Pedro, and he wasn't like Sanchez. He was just a man who did not want to take in two girls and she couldn't fault him for that.

"Gringos are all assholes." Juana looked at the man and then at Maria. She was pleased with herself for such a bold declaration. She sat smugly finishing the food on Maria's plate.

"What are gringos?"

Juana laughed and looked at the man. "Maria is from the country. I think she lived under a rock. She knows almost nothing."

The man nodded, knowingly. "The Americanos, the ones up north. They're not all assholes, just most of them."

The pretty assistant came back and wanted to know what they were talking about. She blew air between pursed lips. "No, this is not a good idea. They would not do well up there. They have no English and they are too dark. The Americanos don't like Indians. Look at what happened with Custer."

The man ignored her and stood up. "Well, maybe so." He was not really interested in what they would do next, as long as they were not living with him. He wandered outside and left the three of them alone.

The assistant took them down to the shoreline and they swam in the big water for the first time in their lives. Maria loved the saltiness and they stayed in the surf for the rest of the day. The pretty woman watched them.

"You two are very lucky young girls."

They stopped and looked at her. They wondered if she meant because of the money and it was if she read their minds.

"You have each other and that is a good thing."

They pulled themselves out of the water and sat down next to the assistant. She had something to tell them and they respected her. She was a kind young woman and they wanted to please her.

"What will you do?"

Maria spoke up, automatically, before Juana could open her mouth. She was not convinced that Juana had given up on the brothel idea and didn't want her to tell the assistant about it. "We're going to get goats."

"I see." She liked this idea. Maybe they'd go into a village and out of the path of the bad men. She continued. "I want you two to remember some things."

"Yes?" She had their attention.

"You both have a big fortune now, much more than children should have. Guard it. Don't flaunt what you have. Don't buy fancy things: clothes, or jewelry or even guns. Don't show the money you have when in public, don't eat in fancy places."

Juana thought this very silly. "Why have so much money if you can't enjoy it?"

"Because it wasn't really for you to have, little one. This is not your money, really. It is not money for a poor Indian to have, and you will be found out. You'll be found out by the rurales or other bandits." She looked at her hands and then out to the sea. "My girls, you've known many hard things, but the worst of all the hard things is not having enough to eat. You know this."

Maria nodded solemnly.

"You now have enough money to ensure that you will eat well for many years. You have enough money to live in a comfortable home for many years. Do this, girls, and keep quiet. Be invisible."

Juana looked up at her. "Be invisible?"

"Yes, invisible. Don't attract attention. When you are old enough, perhaps in six years or so, find men. Find good hardworking men, not bandits. Put the money to good use. Get a farm or buy horses or cattle," she smiled at Maria, "or goats. Make certain your family never goes hungry." She stood up and stretched her back into a beautiful arch. Maria had not, until now, realized just how beautiful the woman was. She now knew and also knew that she was a good person. She was happy to have met her and resolved to take her advice.

"How long may we stay here with you?"

"Not long." She pointed in the direction of the house up on the hill with her head. "He's not a bad sort, but he doesn't want you here. No offense intended, but he likes to be alone."

Maria suddenly had a thought and it made her nervous. "He is good to you?"

The assistant smiled. She knew what Maria meant and it upset her and made her sad to know that the child had knowledge of such horrible things. She put a hand to Maria's face. "He is, child. He's good to me."

That night they lay in bed together but were not sleepy. They'd eaten well now for three days and Maria was no longer exhausted all the time. The sheets smelled good and she hoped that it would be okay to buy a bed and sheets with the money. The assistant didn't say anything about that, but surely buying a good bed and sheets would not be flaunting. She thought it would be okay. She looked over at Juana who was looking up at the ceiling, forming words with her mouth.

She smiled at what the assistant said and felt happy to be with Juana. Maybe they'd be friends forever. She didn't see why not. She spoke automatically. "Juana, we should leave tomorrow, but I don't know where we should go."

Juana stopped forming the words and looked over at Maria. "I have an idea. Back near the town but outside of it, there's an old settlement with caves where the old people used to live many years ago. No one lives there anymore and we could live in the caves. There's good grass and things up there. I think goats could live there."

Maria liked this idea. She could get goats from where she used to live. There was a man who would sell them goats and if it was close to the town, it would not be far from her village. "Juana, that nice lady, she was right, you know."

"I know."

"I know you like nice things and I know you want to buy good food and things."

"It's okay. She's right. Anyway," she turned on her side to face Maria. "in a couple years, I'll be bigger and then I'll just look like a rich whore. I can dress and wear what I want and go where I want. No one will know it was Sanchez's money or from Sanchez's things. They'll think I made it on my back."

Maria suddenly felt ill. She didn't want Juana to be a whore. Without thinking she began to speak. "Juana?"

"What?"

"Don't talk about that anymore. Don't talk about being a whore."

# Chapter IV: Going Home

They were on the road and Juana looked at Maria a little doubtfully. She looked down at her peasant clothes and was disappointed. The dress she got from Sanchez's shop was so much prettier. They rode along in silence, both thinking the same thoughts. Maria was sad to ride the burro. It was a nice burro and it listened to her well, but she wanted—dreamed of—a beautiful horse. She even had it picked out in her mind. It would have a fancy saddle with a big wooden horn and conchos all over it.

It was better this way, of course. The big prize was secreted in a pack under Maria's seat; a pile of money, a king's ransom. The fence and his assistant took good care of them and they knew doing it this way was right, it just seemed so ordinary. But they had three days to travel and they were, for all intents and purposes— thanks mostly to the lady—quite invisible.

Juana was chatty. She rode up next to Maria and pulled out the cross on the necklace around her neck. "It was nice of her to give us these." Maria had one to match.

"Yes it was." She wondered at it. It was a pretty pewter cross with a little man attached. Maria pulled hers up and looked at it as well.

"You don't even know what it is, do you, Maria?"

Maria looked on. "No." She didn't mind. It didn't bother her when Juana spoke of Maria's ignorance anymore. Juana wasn't being mean and Maria knew that she wasn't stupid, just ignorant. Ignorance could be cured by knowledge and she was resolved to learn many things. She had a good mind.

"That's Jesus." She nodded her head like a donkey when she said his name.

"Why do you do that?" She mimicked Juana's nod.

"You're supposed to do that whenever you say Jesus's name." She nodded again and Maria found it very amusing. She nodded to herself and it felt a little silly.

"So, teach me of Jesus."

Juana laughed. "I cannot believe someone doesn't know of Jesus." She grinned and moved her head from side to side and Maria realized that she'd forgotten to nod. But all this nodding would likely knock one off balance and she didn't want Juana falling from her burro, so she didn't say anything to her about forgetting the nod.

"He is the son of God and his mother is Maria, like you. But she's the Virgin Maria, not like you."

"Can you not talk of that?" Maria felt sad when Juana brought it up and it made her feel funny and hurt a little down below.

"I'm sorry, Maria." And Juana was. She'd been so casual about the act for so long, living around the whores, that she didn't realize how hurtful it was to talk of such things, especially to a person like Maria, who'd been abused. Juana had seen many bad things in her young life and known much depravity, but she'd never been abused.

She tried to change the subject away from the virginal properties of the Virgin Maria. "So, God and Maria had Jesus and he is the son of God and he was made into a man, but he was still God and he did a lot of nice things and then he died for our sins by being nailed to a cross."

"Oh, that's terrible."

"Yes. You can see it at any church. They have big statues of Jesus nailed to the cross and he got stabbed in the breast and he had a crown made from thorns and it was pressed into his head so the blood ran in his eyes. It was really quite terrible."

"Why'd they do such a thing to him? Was he a bandit?"

"No, no. He was good and nice."

"And they did that to him?" Maria was confused and wondered if maybe she didn't want to wear the crucifix anymore. She didn't know if she wanted to be named after the poor woman Maria whose son was so terribly abused.

She didn't want to talk about it anymore and looked off in the distance. She pointed at some high hills a few miles away. "Let's camp there." She looked up at the sun and reckoned they'd be there with an hour of daylight to spare.

She was pleased that they had good food to eat and she wouldn't have to hunt. She didn't have a rifle now because the assistant told her it would not be a good idea. It would not be normal for young girls to have a rifle so they didn't keep one. She did have a little six shooter tucked under her rebozo but that was supposed to be used only if she had to defend herself or Juana. The assistant told her that she shouldn't fire the gun as that would also make them not invisible.

Maria thought a lot about the assistant. She was so good to them. Maria decided to start remembering every person who was ever good to her. She'd remember them and keep them in her mind and someday she'd go and visit every one of them and do them some kindness. She'd buy them a gift and visit them.

So far, she had the nice woman with the mean husband in her village, the whore with the yellow hair in Nuevo Casas Grandes, Juana, of course, and now the assistant. This made her feel good.

And there was the man. The fence. He was good to them. She didn't know why she didn't think of him right away and she thought it was queer that she didn't think of him as nice. Maybe she'd known so few men who were nice that she didn't think of any man as being nice. But they could be nice. He was and she thought she'd add him to the list.

It wasn't really his fault that he didn't want them to stay there, by the beautiful sea with the beautiful lady assistant. She thought about that some more. Well, actually, it was his fault, but he was not to blame. There was a difference in that. He had his own life to lead. He couldn't take in every poor person or child. That would not do. So, yes, she would add him to her list.

Then she had another thought. Should she have a list of people who did her wrong? Should she get back at them? Should she take revenge? That didn't seem a good use of her time and she resolved that she would not have such a list.

Anyway, the only ones who would be on it were the mean man from the village and the pendejo, Pedro, the rurale. But they were just rude to her. Of course, had he lived, Sanchez would definitely be on the list. But he was dead and she wasn't sad at all about that. It actually made her feel better to know he was dead. He could never make her dreamy and sleepy and do that to her again and, more importantly, he could never do that to a child again. That was the best part of it and she was again pleased with her performance. She was pleased with her rock throwing ability.

All this thinking got her to the hills. It was time to stop. Maria pulled up ahead of Juana and then turned to the south. She rode a ways until they hit a gully and were out of sight, invisible.

She slid off her burro and Juana settled the beasts down as Maria made a fire. She then took their treasure and hid it some distance from the camp. If anyone attacked them, they'd likely take the burros and leave them alone. At least they'd have their money. She thought of this on her own and was pleased with herself for being so careful and clever. She kept her gun tucked in her rebozo. She had it with her always, even when she was asleep. No one would get them as long as she had her gun.

They ate and settled down under the blankets and stared up at the clear night sky. The stars were so tightly packed together and brightly lit that it almost hurt their eyes. Maria was feeling very happy now.

"Tell me the bad words, Juana."

Juana was pleased at the thought. "Okay, let's see." She concentrated. "What do you want to know?"

"I don't know. How about pendejo?"

"A pendejo is a big jerk, a dumb ass, an asshole."

"Oh."

"What do you want to know next?" Juana felt important. She was the great professor now.

"I don't know any others."

"Hmm, let's see." She stroked her chin. "How about cagada?"

"That's shit." Maria was pleased with herself for knowing cagada.

"Yes." She smiled. "Okay, how about mierda?"

"That's shit, too."

"How about hijo de tu puta madre?"

Maria did not know.

"Son of a bitch." Juana liked that one. "How about boca de pedo?"

Maria did not know.

"Fart mouth."

"Really?"

Juana laughed out loud. "Yes, fart mouth, especially when someone has stinky breath. You call them boca de pedo."

Maria laughed now. "That's not nice. Some people cannot help if they have stinky breath. I wouldn't ever say that to someone."

Juana grinned and snuggled under the covers. She was getting sleepy. She rested her head on Maria's shoulder. "You are too nice, Maria. Too nice." She slipped off to sleep.

By midday they could see the hills off in the distance that held the cave dwellings where the old people lived. Maria was happy as they were far away from the town and far enough away from her village that no one from there would ever run into her.

Juana was riding steadily along, dozing, not paying attention when Maria saw him. He was alone and on a horse sitting on a rise about halfway between them and the caves. She watched him but didn't say anything to Juana. When they were hidden from his view by another little rise she slid off her burro and let the animal plod along following his companion carrying Juana. She ran up alongside her burro and pulled the bag of money from under the blanket. She scurried off into the brush and hid it there.

Juana was brought out of her trance by the man's deep voice commanding her.

"Alto."

She stopped and looked at him. He was an older man with dark skin and long moustaches. He wore a rurale's coat and striped vaquero pants. On his head was a smallish sombrero made of straw with a fancy band all around it. He had a six shooter stuck in his pants. He did not have a gun belt or holster and his knife was smallish and stuck in the top of his boot.

Juana looked him in the eye and waited.

"Where's the other one?"

Juana looked behind her and saw only the burro. Maria was gone but Juana pretended to not be surprised. She looked back at the man and shrugged her shoulders. She did not speak.

"Don't shrug your shoulders. Where is she?" He was angry and rode close to Juana, rode around her and the other burro, surveying them, calculating what they'd be worth. He didn't wait for her answer but instead ordered her off the beast. Juana complied.

The man dismounted and grabbed Juana by the forehead. He pushed her face all around to look her over. He looked down at her poor dress and grunted, then turned his attention to her animals. They were good burros. He dug around the blankets and found her food and water. He took the bags of food and threw them over his saddle skirt and then turned to her once again.

"How old are you?"

"Ten."

"And the other one?"

She shrugged and he hit her hard across the face. She fell to the ground. She lay there for a few seconds and then struggled to sit up. She waited for him to strike her again and then the rock sailed from the brush and hit him in the eye, right where a cluster of ugly moles grew like a bunch of grapes on his cheek. It was his turn to drop to the ground and he lay next to Juana. She wasted no time and hit him soundly on top of the head with a flat rock that was lying nearby. He lay there senseless.

Maria ran up. "I'm sorry, Juana. I should have thrown sooner. He wouldn't stay still long enough."

Juana grinned and rubbed her cheek. "He didn't hurt me." She looked him over. "Should've shot the son of a bitch bastard, though. Let's shoot him now."

Maria thought about it. She looked at the man. He was out cold. Blood ran freely from the wound she'd given him and a big lump was forming where Juana had hit him. She found her six shooter and pulled it out. She pointed it at the man's head and looked at Juana.

"I don't want to. He's out. He's can't hurt us now."

"I'll shoot him. Give me the gun." She held out her hand and Maria complied. Juana gripped the pistol and pointed it at the man's head. She waited. "Oh, to hell with him. He's not worth a bullet, and besides, the shot might attract his friends." She handed the pistol back to Maria.

"I've got an idea." Maria began pulling the clothes off the man. In short order, his boots, trousers, hat and shirt were gone. He lay in the dirt wearing nothing more than faded long underwear. He looked very silly. She grabbed his things and made a sack with his rurale coat, tying everything into a ball. This she threw on his horse's back and tied it down securely.

"Come on."

They rode quickly in the opposite direction and retrieved their fortune. Along the way they scattered his clothes. They turned back and rode past the unconscious man and, grabbing the reins of the man's horse, rode on to their destination. When they were a mile away they removed the horse's saddle, tossing it into the desert. They rode on another mile and removed the bridle and turned the horse loose. The man would have a lot of work to do to retrieve his traps. Hopefully, it would be enough to keep him occupied and no longer interested in the girls. Maria was particularly happy until she saw Juana's face, swelling like she'd stuck a ball between her cheek and gum on the left side.

"You're hurt, Juana."

Juana grinned and rubbed the swollen cheek. "Oh, that's nothing." She was proud of Maria and as far as she was concerned, it all went off very well. Maria constantly surprised her. She was smart and nervy. She could throw a rock better than most men could shoot a gun. She was deadly accurate.

"I didn't mean for you to get hurt, or make you bait, I just didn't know what he wanted and we couldn't change direction or run away from him. A burro can never outrun a horse."

Juana smiled at Maria's guilty conscience. She was the most caring and selfless person Juana had ever known.

"I knew you weren't tryin' to save your own skin. It's okay." She put a hand on Maria's shoulder and patted her. "It's okay."

By late day they arrived at the ruins and Maria was mesmerized. The ruins were high up in the side of the mountain and here and there walls and buildings could be seen peeking out from the honeycombed face. It was as if the people had just walked out the day before. Maria stood, jaw hanging. "Where are they?"

Juana chuckled. "Dead."

"How? Were they attacked? Did they get sick?"

"No, Maria, they've been dead a long long time. Millennia."

"What's that?"

Juana shrugged. "I don't know, the bad priest said it. It's a long time."

They wandered about and found an entrance. A little further on, they discovered a box canyon which would be a good corral for the burros. Maria put them there and cut some mesquite to make a fence to insure they stayed. She hobbled them for good measure. They were content; there was much for them to graze on. She found Juana and they went to the nearest cave.

"Whew. It stinks of bat shit in here." Juana held her nose.

"It's not so bad." Maria peered at the walls which were still good. This would be a perfect home for them. She sat down and made a fire and soon had a good blaze going. Juana dug through their kit and prepared a meal. She wasn't much good at helping because she was used to talking and listening to the bad men at the brothel, she wasn't used to doing chores. Maria didn't mind. She liked working and she enjoyed Juana's company and constant banter as she watched her new partner work. Maria was always working it seemed, it is what made her happy.

They got their oil lamps and lit them. It was time to explore. Maria was enthralled and Juana bored. They found the place with the most guano and surmised that the bats used that part of the cave. The rest would be cleaner and smell better and it wouldn't be bothersome when the bats flew in and out. This is where they'd make their home.

Further up, they found by walking a steep incline of narrow steps, a beautiful high fortress-like structure. It offered a commanding view of the entire valley below. They would be able to see any intruder for at least a mile away. This is where they'd sleep.

Next, they moved down another set of steps, a steep decline into a dark and narrow passage. Maria heard movement—water, and in short order they came upon a fairly swift moving stream, flowing from under a deep crevice in the rock. She tasted the water and it was good. It was clear and cold; they would be good here indefinitely as they'd never want for water.

Before Juana could say anything Maria had dropped down into the swift current and was wading her way across to the other side. She held her lamp up high to illuminate her way. She eventually reached the far side and was soon perched on a narrow ledge, up high and invisible from Juana's side.

"What are you doing?"

"We'll hide our money here. No one can see it and they won't think to wade and carry a light like this. They won't ever think to look here."

She waded back and was shivering. They hurried back and sat close to the fire to warm up. Juana threw a blanket over Maria. They ate and stared into the fire.

They soon fell asleep and stayed there until morning. Maria was up first and started the housekeeping. She moved their traps up to the fortress where she began kicking the debris away and, to her pleasant surprise, found a neatly laid stone floor. The people were very handy who lived here so long ago. Next, she hid their treasure and came back by the fire to dry off and get warm. Juana finally stirred.

"Sleep good?"

"Uh huh." Juana stretched and ate a tortilla left from the night before.

"Well, tonight we're going to sleep better. We're going to make pine needle beds up there and sleep in comfort."

Maria was happy and excited about her new home. It was safe and warm and had plenty of water and no one could bother them. She couldn't wait to make it a proper home. Juana watched her and shook her head from side to side. "Bumpkin."

By afternoon, Maria had made a broom and a big bed. She had covered the bed with their blankets and fashioned pillows from some empty sacks. Everything smelled of fresh pine. She'd collected grasses and was working on a basket when Juana finally sauntered in. She sat and ate and watched Maria work.

"You need to learn to make baskets too." The old woman had taught Maria well and she could make many baskets in a day.

"For what?"

"To trade. At that little village we passed. The people will trade food for them. We can keep from spending our money that way and no one will wonder how we got money in the first place. They won't care if we have baskets to trade. That's expected."

Juana picked up some grass and half-heartedly mimicked Maria's actions. She soon sliced her hand and stopped. "That hurts."

"You get used to it."

Juana began fidgeting around.

"Is there anything you know how to do, Juana?" Maria wasn't cross with her friend. She was just teasing her a little.

"Oh, sure. I can sing." She began singing very badly and Maria stopped her.

"You sound like a trampled puppy."

"Hmm!" She thought for a moment. "I can burp words."

"That's handy."

"Oh, it's funny." She took in a deep breath and burped. "Ma-ri-a." And smiled. "I can burp a lot better with beer. I wish we had some right now."

"What else can you do?" Maria liked the sound of her name burped.

"Well, I can make farting noises with my hand and my armpit." She reached under her arm with her hand and began flopping it at the elbow, emitting fart-like sounds. Maria smiled and held her nose.

"You're stinking up the place."

They giggled. It was the first time the walls had echoed giggles in many years. It sounded happy in there.

Juana stood up and surveyed the place. "Poor pagans."

"What's that?"

"Pagans. People who didn't know Jesus. They're pagans. All the savages, like you, who don't know of God and Jesus. You're called pagans."

Maria kept working and wondered if Juana wasn't making such words up in her head.

"How do you know?"

"A priest. He was a drunk and took up with the whores. He used to talk a lot when he was only half drunk."

"What did he do when he was all drunk?"

"Fall on his face."

They both giggled at that.

"And he told you about the people here?"

"Oh, sure. That's how I knew about it, about the caves and the people. But I thought he was lying. I didn't know we'd really find it." She looked around and regarded their handiwork. "Too bad they all went to hell." She sighed and regarded Maria. She liked to hold court and leak out little bits of information to her friend. It made her feel very intelligent.

Maria was intrigued. She'd heard of heaven and hell, certainly, but never gave it much thought. She figured hell was for very bad people like bandits and cutthroats and that everyone else just automatically went to heaven when they died. She didn't know that one must know of and believe in Jesus to avoid hell. This didn't make much sense to her and she figured she'd probe Juana a little. She liked Juana and was entertained by her, but was not completely certain that Juana knew as much as she let on. She'd probably gotten much of this information wrong from this priest, or maybe the priest was wrong or addle-brained or drunk when he was telling it and told Juana a lot of bad stories. She decided to get her new friend to talk.

"So, what is this priest, then?"

"Oh, he's the man of God. He usually wears all black and he lives in a church and performs the miracle at mass."

"What's mass and what's a miracle?" Every new concept made Maria even more confused and Juana sensed this. She huffed and sat down.

"Okay, let's start at the beginning."

Maria put her partially completed basket down and looked Juana in the eye.

"Okay, Maria. Many years ago an angel came down from heaven and found the Virgin Maria. The angel told the Virgin she was going to have a baby, but she wasn't going to have relations with a man. You now, they wouldn't do it."

"Yes."

"So, then Jesus was born. He had the Virgin for a mother and God was his father. But he was God too."

"I see."

"So, in order to go to heaven, you have to know Jesus and go to church whenever you can and eat his body."

"What?" Maria looked, confused. "What do you mean?"

"Well, it's not really his body. Well, it is, but its bread, and the priest does a magic trick and turns bread into his body and wine into his blood."

"Now you're just being silly." Maria started to resume work on her basket, then thought of something. "So why did these people have to go to hell?" She looked around as if she could see them peeking out from the various crevices in the rock.

"Because they didn't know Jesus."

"Well, where was he?"

"He lived many years ago in another land, longer ago than even these people, and there were no priests then. No one could tell them of Jesus."

Maria shrugged. This was ridiculous. How could anyone be sent to hell when they couldn't know about Jesus which was required in order to go to heaven and not be sent to hell? It was stupid. She looked at Juana who seemed just as confused. Maria decided to change the subject.

"Tomorrow we take stock of the land around us and see what there is to get us through winter." Juana nodded and finished a tortilla. She stood up and brushed the crumbs from her lap. She was ready for bed.

In another week they were settled in and preparing for winter. Maria knew what winter was like in the country and she was resolved to have a good one in the cave. She poked and prodded and got Juana to store wood every day. She'd made many baskets and visited the people in the village to trade. They now had enough for all the tortillas Juana could eat through winter. Maria also hunted and made snares like one of the old men in her village had taught her before he died. They worked and she felt confident that she'd be able to get enough meat for them. She surveyed her little settlement and was pleased until she looked on at the distracted and sour-faced Juana.

"What's the matter?"

"Bored."

"Why?" Maria genuinely did not understand. There was plenty of work to fill the day and it was good work and made Maria happy.

"I don't like this bumpkin living."

Maria shrugged. She knew what Juana was thinking and realized she wanted to go to the brothel. Juana grew up there. It wasn't reasonable to expect her to like the country, just as it was unreasonable for Maria to like the brothel. She thought hard about this.

"Maybe we could go there before the weather is bad. We need an axe."

Juana brightened, then thought of all Maria had done. She looked around doubtfully. "I don't think we should leave everything. Someone might come in and take it. Or move in and we'd be out of luck."

She sat resting her head in her hands, poking every now and again at the fire. She suddenly brightened. "I'll go!"

Maria thought about it. Juana was right. Someone had to stay behind. They couldn't just leave everything, and their fortune needed guarding. They did need an axe and more coal oil for the lanterns. They needed some extra blankets as well. And candy.

Juana was excited now. She skipped around the cave and thought about the fun she'd have. She'd take some money and spend it. She'd visit the whores and they'd be happy to see her. They'd probably given her up for dead by now. She was ready before sunrise and sat on her burro as Maria worried over her.

"Stay out of sight. Spend the night in an arroyo, don't let anyone see you." Juana nodded and waved her off.

"It's only a day and a half. I'll be fine." She smiled and rode off. "See you in five days." She was gone.

Maria was alone now, really for the first time in her life. She was always with the old woman and then she immediately met Juana. She thought about this as she worked. She used to work constantly with the old woman but now it felt different. She used to work, really, *for* the old woman. The old woman would tell her what to do and when to do it and for how long. The old woman ran their little household and she decided when things were to be done and it seemed, somehow, more like drudgery then. Now it was fun. She decided what needed to be done and for how long and when. It made her very happy.

Before she realized it, dusk had fallen and she had let the fire burn down. She'd fashioned coverings for the old windows, but decided not to use them. It was a bright night and the light from the stars and moon poured in through the windows. Slits of silvery light illuminated her bedchamber. She rested and thought about Juana not being in the bed with her and it didn't bother her too much. Juana had a habit of snoring and flopping about quite a bit and this night Maria would likely sleep all the way through until morning. She turned onto her back and looked at the silver slivers of light. Soon she fell asleep.

Next morning she got cleaned up, ate breakfast and made three baskets. She wandered up to the high place, the lookout, and gazed out over the land as she had her midday meal. It was bright and clear and she thought about Juana's progress. She'd nearly be there by now. She'd taken a lot of money with her and she imagined Juana would come back with fancy clothes and lots of candy. She'd probably forget the coal oil and axe and blankets, but that didn't bother Maria. Nothing Juana did really bothered her. She was a free spirit and did not take much in life very seriously. That was okay with Maria. She resolved that someday she would be more like that; be more happy go lucky. But, then again, it probably wouldn't work. Maria had to always be thinking and working and planning.

She was just about to get down when something moving off in the northwest caught her eye. She stared and then realized it was some creature. It was Juana's burro and it slowly plodded along, back to the cave dwelling and its sibling, Maria's donkey. Juana was not with it. It still had on its bridle and blanket. Maria ran down to intercept it.

The creature was a little skittish and Maria had to talk softly to calm it down. Its mane was covered with dried blood and there were scrapes, long narrow slashes on its rump. She led the animal back to the box canyon and quickly prepared her own burro. Within an hour she was gone, on the trail to find Juana.

She hadn't gone far before she found some of Juana's clothes, also covered in blood. Further down the trail was one of her blankets. It was here she found the remains of a camp. The fire was out and the ashes were cold.

She could make out no direction in which the campers had traveled and she couldn't find any more evidence of Juana. She rode along the most likely trail all day and found nothing. It was beginning to get dark and she was forced to return to her cave. She hadn't brought provisions for an extended foray into the desert.

Maria didn't hold out much hope for Juana now anyway and thought it a worthless endeavor to follow up on whoever had caused all the blood. She ate a little and did not bother with a fire. She got into her bed and finally fell asleep.

After a time, she sensed a presence and sat up. Juana was sitting in her bloody clothes and eating Maria's leftovers. She smiled at Maria. There was something very strange about her. She looked like a dead person, very pale, her round face appearing to glow in the dark; her raven tresses were almost too black to be natural against the porcelain skin. Maria got up and sat next to her. She suddenly felt cold and got a fire going. The whole time, Juana said nothing. Maria watched her eat.

Finally, Juana smiled and, lifting her chin, leaned back and a gash opened wide across the width of her neck. "Look what the son of a bitch did to me."

Maria got closer. She could see it was a fatal blow. "So, you are dead?"

"I guess."

Maria looked at her hands and down into the fire. She felt as she had when the old woman died. She looked back at Juana. "Why are you here, then?"

"You need to sew this up for me." She pointed at her throat. "I can't go around like this. And I need clean clothes. These are a mess."

Maria got her kit out, the one she got from the nice lady by the sea, and began working on Juana's throat. Before she could start, Juana stopped her. "Use blue thread, Maria. I like blue."

Maria changed the thread and worked on Juana's neck. She got some water and a rag and wiped the dried blood from her neck and face and arms. She got her a new dress and handed it over. Juana stripped down and threw her bloody outfit on the fire and, as it burned, the whole room lit up and got very warm. "Are you in heaven, Juana?"

"I guess so." Juana looked herself over and then looked around the room. She found Maria's old mirror, the one the old woman had given her. She looked into it to survey the work Maria had done on her neck and was satisfied. She turned the mirror over to Maria and regarded Maria's reflection as they both gazed into it. "This is the only one you can rely on, Maria. Remember that."

"Did the man who attacked us do this to you?"

"I don't know."

Juana stood up and brushed the back of her dress off. "Thanks, Maria. Your sewing looks good." She looked as if she was preparing to go somewhere and Maria didn't want her to leave. She suddenly thought of a question.

"What's it like?"

"Oh, it didn't hurt. I just ..., just died."

"No, no. What's heaven like?"

"Oh, I don't know. It's nice. I don't know, it's more of a feeling, not like the world. I haven't seen any people and I'm not tired or hungry. Just nice."

"You've not seen Jesus then?"

Juana laughed out loud, as if it was a silly question. "Oh, no. None of that." She began to drift away, away from the firelight and then stopped. "You can't stay here, Maria. You can't be alone. You'll go mad."

Maria looked at her. She felt desperate to say something, but she was becoming very sleepy and she couldn't think of anything to say. She finally came up with some words. "Where will I go?"

"Go to the whores, Maria. You don't have to be one, but you need them. You need them." Then she was gone.

Maria woke late. She awoke to hunger pangs as she'd not eaten since early the day before. She looked around the room for Juana but she wasn't there. She missed her and wanted to cry. She'd never cried before, even over the old woman, but she wanted to cry now. She suddenly started crying and the tears ran down her cheeks and into her mouth and they tasted salty. Her nose was running and she got tired of crying and stopped. She wiped her face and blew her nose.

She occupied herself with chores and thought about Juana some more. She kept looking for Juana but she was never there and all the looking made her exhausted. She had to lie down. She never went to sleep during the day but she had to now. She was so tired and had a horrible headache. She awoke near sunset and climbed up to her lookout and watched as the sun went down.

Maria felt a little better because the sky was clear and the sunset beautiful. She watched as shadows were cast on the land and daylight slowly turned to darkness. The sky became a beautiful deep purple and, eventually, black and the stars were out again. Way off she heard coyotes crying and it was a comforting sound.

She thought about Juana when the coyotes cried. They were together, the coyotes, it was always that way. The animals, most of them, liked to be together. She had thought at one point, before Juana became a ghost, that she could always be alone, that it wouldn't bother her, but Juana's words were haunting and she was suddenly lonely. She'd never been lonely up to this point in her life but now she was and it was a sad feeling. The ghost of Juana was right. She could not stay here, in her lovely cave, all alone. When Juana wasn't a ghost it was all right. She didn't need a huge clan, but she needed another human being. Juana's ghost was right.

She ate and got ready for bed. She had no companionship and decided to bring the burros into the cave. They were such good burros, they always did what she wanted, and as long as they were together, they didn't mind where they spent the night.

Soon they became acclimated to their new sleeping quarters and lay down like a couple of oversized dogs, at the foot of Maria's bed. She felt better hearing other beings breathing, living, nearby and this let her fall quickly to sleep. She hoped that Juana would visit her again as she missed her desperately.

Halfway through the night, Juana was there. She was eating again and the burros didn't stir. She waited for Maria to sit down across from her at the fire ring before addressing her.

Juana looked at the burros. "It stinks of these beasts in here, Maria."

"They're not so bad."

"Why'd you bring them in?"

Maria shrugged.

"I know and so do you. You're lonely. You're going to go mad, Maria. You've got to leave."

"I'm ..., I don't know the way."

Juana ate crumbs from her skirt. "It's easy. Just follow the road north. It'll take you right to the town. Once you're there, go to the whores. It's going to be okay, Maria. See the one with yellow hair. You remember her."

"What's her name?"

Juana shrugged.

"You don't know her name?"

"I've forgotten."

Maria looked at Juana's neck and the sutures of blue thread were gone. She was surprised at this.

"I know." She tilted her head back to give Maria a good view. "All healed." She stood up and smiled at Maria. "I've got to go now, Maria. And you do, too. Go before the rains come. It will be good. I promise it will be good." She looked around the cave and then at Maria. "This is no place for you, Maria." She was gone.

For the next few days, Juana didn't visit her and Maria spent her time making baskets and talking to the burros who were very companionable. They'd now become familiar with the new routine and would let themselves in and out of the cave as they pleased. Every evening, just at sundown, they returned to Maria's bedchamber and settled in for the night. Maria mucked out the cave every day and added it to her list of chores. She didn't mind as it kept her occupied.

She awoke to heavy rain and thought how nice her cave was now. It kept her dry, not like the hovel she shared with the old woman. Every time it rained there, it was miserable because the structure had a horrible roof and all their things would get wet. She'd have to lie under a wet blanket and it was so hot and steamy that it would make sleeping impossible. The cave was not like that at all and she fell back to sleep listening to the rain and the sound of rolling thunder off in the distance. Every now and again a lighting flash would light up the cave, but not even the burros cared one way or another. They were all safe and dry.

By morning the rain was still coming down and Maria regretted disappointing Juana. She was certain she'd get a visit from her, admonishing her for not going to the whores by now. She couldn't say that she actually liked Juana's visits. They were scary and she didn't like talking to the dead. It was not natural for Juana to be roaming about as a ghost, but she did enjoy the conversations with her. She liked, even perhaps, loved Juana very much and missed her terribly. Now she'd have to wait for the rain to stop and this gave her some time. She didn't have to worry about what to do as she could do nothing until the rains were gone.

Maria heard a great rushing sound and decided to investigate. Suddenly she started to run as she realized her treasure cache was in danger. The water under the cave had become a great rushing river and had risen above the height of her secret ledge. She arrived to see the water steadily rising and, without giving it any thought, jumped in. The current was horrendous and she found herself being swept away.

Maria fought with all her might and made it across. Everything was gone. The ledge was empty. She held onto the ledge and looked back at the other side. She didn't want to try to get back. A wave of panic hit her and she clamped onto the ledge, frozen, unable to move.

Maria knew she had to move, knew she could not stay where she was. The water was cold and she was getting numb. Soon she wouldn't be able to make her legs move and the water was getting steadily higher. She thought about what she had to do.

If she didn't get back across, the water would soon press her against the roof of the cave and she'd drown.

Taking a deep breath, she pushed off with all her might. She felt herself being sucked downward, down as if the river was running into a giant drain. She wondered if she would soon be dead, would she join Juana. They'd be together, but perhaps not. She was a pagan and Juana was not. Maybe she wouldn't go where Juana was and then she'd be alone again.

Maria was becoming lightheaded and she wasn't certain where to swim. She was fading. Finally, looking up, she saw a light and could see Juana standing in a little doorway at the foot of the steps. She was reaching for Maria.

Maria found the bottom and pushed off, using the last bit of energy she had. Finally, she was there, on the other side and could pull herself out of the water. She was safe and Juana was gone.

She made a fire and warmed up as she considered her situation. Now she had no money. She had plenty of food and the burros, but no fortune. She couldn't wait it out until she was old enough to find a man and settle down like the nice lady by the sea told her to do. She was back to square one and she thought she might just have to stay in the cave indefinitely. At least she was out of the elements and could survive. She had enough to keep herself alive.

She thought about all this until she fell asleep and Juana woke her again.

"Well, you've done it now." Juana was eating.

"I know."

"You should have left before the rains. I told you that."

"I'm sorry."

Juana smiled, like a parent scolding a child. "Oh well. At least you're alive."

Maria sat and wondered what to do. Juana continued. "You still need to go to the whores. You've got the burros and your lamps and blankets and things.

You can sell all that and live. You can find work with the whores. You don't need to be one. You can do the washing and you're a pretty good cook."

Juana continued to give her advice but Maria didn't hear her. She was too tired and drifted off to sleep.

After a while the rains finally stopped. During this time Maria did a lot of thinking. She still wouldn't go to the whores. She didn't like the brothel and there was something about the mean man calling her a whore's spawn, something so hateful in his voice that she resolved not to be with them. She didn't want to be a whore and, despite Juana's declarations that this would not happen, she was sure it would be only a matter of time. She knew, already, at a young age, that she was remarkably beautiful and she'd grow into a beautiful woman and the whores and the whores' customers wouldn't leave her alone. She was certain of this, knew it in her heart and she would not take such a path. She would never, no matter how bad things got, become a whore.

She thought a lot about the pretty assistant by the sea. The sea was the most beautiful place she'd ever seen, even more beautiful than the desert at sunset and she thought that, even if the fence wouldn't let her live there, she'd have enough money to live somewhere by the sea. Maybe she'd find a cave there, like the one she had now and she'd live in the cave and she could find things by the sea to eat and sell. She could make baskets and the pretty assistant would buy them from her to sell in the fence's shop.

Suddenly she had a great deal of energy and she resolved that she would do this thing. She would travel back to the fence's shop and sell all that she had back to him and the pretty assistant and she'd live next to them, nearby so that the man would not be cross with her or feel like she was a burden to him, but she'd be near the pretty assistant and they'd be friends.

She thought hard about this and decided that she'd not tell Juana of her plan. She didn't want to disappoint Juana. She knew Juana had the best intentions and that she loved the whores because that was the only life she'd known. The whores were good to her and she'd not had anyone do it to her yet, like the bastard Sanchez did to her, so Juana didn't think it was such a terrible thing. But Maria knew differently.

# Chapter V: Padre

Maria didn't know why, but she could not resist the pretty gold candle holders on either side of the alter. She looked around. No one was in the church. She looked up and saw the likeness of Jesus nailed to the cross, just as Juana described it. It was horrible and she wasn't sorry that she'd not known of Jesus before. She was not certain any of this could be right. What kind of God would let his son be tortured and treated in such a way? It made no sense.

She took the candles out of the holders and set them carefully down on the big table. She'd not need them as they wouldn't fetch a good price and they'd be cumbersome to transport to the fence. She turned and nearly ran into the tall man.

"Where do you think you're going, little bitch?" He grabbed her by the arm and squeezed hard, hard enough to hurt Maria and leave a mark. This made her angry and she clubbed him across the head with one of the sticks. He stumbled but didn't let go. He was a tough one.

She raised the holder high. She'd do a proper job of it this time and knock him senseless. Someone grabbed her arm from behind. She could do nothing now but wait to see what her captors had in store for her.

"Well, now." She looked at the man behind her. He had a funny accent, one she'd never heard before. He was dressed all in black so she figured he must be a priest. The other was dressed in peon clothes. He was a worker in the church. He was bleeding profusely from the blow to his head and he was very angry at her.

"Padre, let me take her, I'll give her to the rurales." He sneered as he blotted the wound on his head.

"No, no." He looked down at Maria and gave her a kind smile. "If she promises not to fight or run away, I won't let the rurales have her."

Maria stopped fighting and stood still. She could only think of pendejo Pedro, the rurale, and did not want to be anywhere near such men. She looked up at the priest, into his strange blue eyes and nodded, promising not to fight or run away.

"Good, good." He looked up at the peon. "Go on back and have Agata look at your head, Paulo. I'll take care of this little one."

Maria watched the man stride away. The priest turned away as well and began fixing the candles, putting them back in place. Maria thought for a moment and started to drift toward the front door of the church. She could get away.

"Hungry?"

She stopped and looked back at the old priest. He was not like any of them. He had pale skin and tan hair with a good amount of gray on the sides. He had pale blue eyes and he was tall, more than six feet.

"A little." She wasn't really. She'd been eating well enough but thought it sounded better if he thought she was starving.

He stood back and regarded his work. The candles were now back in their proper place. "Come with me."

She followed him and was soon in a kitchen with an old woman and the man she'd clobbered. He looked at her, then away. The old woman grinned.

"Agata, this is..."

"Maria." She looked down at the floor.

"Maria. She needs something to eat." He patted Maria on the head and walked away. Paulo soon followed and she was now in the church's kitchen, alone with Agata, the cook.

"Will he be all right?"

Agata snorted. "Oh, you hit him on the head. Everyone who knows Paulo knows his head is full of rocks. You didn't hurt him any." She grinned and winked at Maria. "Just his pride."

Maria looked at the food being prepared for the evening meal. There was pie. She'd never had pie in her life. She was suddenly hungry and looked up at the old woman. She was afraid to be so bold as to ask for some of it. She thought of another question. "Is he your husband?"

"Hah!" The old woman startled Maria with her energetic response. "No, child, my goodness no." And at that, as if on cue, another old man came in. He was holding his hat and some work gloves. He kissed his wife on the head and smiled broadly at Maria.

"Ah, a visitor." He bowed to Maria as if she were an important, grown up person, which gave Maria a little flutter in the pit of her stomach.

"Yes, Maria. She wanted to know if Paulo was my husband."

The old man smiled broader. "Hah, little Maria. In his dreams. He wanted her but I got her." He pinched his wife on the cheek. "I got her."

They were nice people and Maria was feeling good. Maybe she would stay here and not go to the sea. She blurted out, "What's to become of me?"

The old people shrugged. They weren't certain. The padre said nothing to them.

"You'll have to ask the padre, my girl. But not now. He's busy. At dinner."

By the third day the padre was still busy and it seemed that Maria was just absorbed into the family. She was one of them, as if it had all been arranged. She didn't ask about it again. She liked the old people and she liked the place. They'd given her a little room with a bed. It was clean and bright when the window was not shuttered and nice and cool and dark when it was. It was quiet there and even at night, in bed, she could sense people around, not like at the cave. Juana's ghost didn't even bother her.

She felt safe there and had her little gun that she didn't tell anyone about. She hid it under her pillow but didn't really feel the need for it. She slept soundly and didn't even try to bar the door.

She took to doing chores for the old woman; she thought it would be a good idea to be useful. She'd earn her keep and, since it was getting along toward winter, she didn't find traveling by burro all the way west so attractive now.

Anyway, there was a lot to do and she found herself in the church more and more often in her free time. She looked through the hymnals and the bibles. They had all sorts of writing in them. Maria knew well enough that it was writing but couldn't read. She quickly decided to learn how to do this over the winter. She also saw gringo words thereabouts and decided she wanted to learn to read them, as well. One day she'd go north to the US and she planned to learn the lingo used up there.

When she was finished with the books, Maria would examine the decorations in the church. It was a simple, yet well-appointed country church. It had several statues, of course, of Jesus being crucified, but also of the Virgin. She liked that one. She liked the Virgin's blue rebozo and the kind look on her face. She was pale like the priest so she thought that the Virgin must be from the same stock as the priest. She certainly was no Indian.

All around the church there were little wooden plaques made up with what Maria later learned were depictions of the crucifixion. These were called the Stations of the Cross and Maria found them sad and intriguing. She was fairly caught up in all this when she saw the old priest standing at the back of the church, watching her. He beckoned for her to sit beside him.

"Do you like the church, Maria?"

"I do."

"Is it like yours?"

Maria was a little confused. "I don't have a church. I don't have religion."

"Oh." He was shocked and realized now that she must have been very isolated, likely from one of the poorest of the villages.

"Have you been baptized?" He could tell by her expression that she had not. He smiled at her. "Would you like to be?"

"I don't know what that is. What is baptized?"

He grinned. "When you take Jesus into your heart. When you become a Christian."

"Oh." She sat quietly for a while. She wanted to ask the padre a thousand questions but didn't really know where to begin. Finally, she decided to ask him one.

"Are you a gringo?"

"I'm an American. From Chicago."

"Why are you here?"

He nodded. "I don't know."

She looked at him, deep in his eyes. What a strange answer to give. He did not know? How could a grown man not know why he was in Mexico?

She decided not to pursue that and, instead, reached over and picked up a hymnal and opened it. "Would you teach me to read this? And to read in your language? The language of the gringo?"

He smiled at her and patted her hand. "I will."

"And, may I stay here? You can sell my burros and have my things and the money they will bring if I can stay here."

"You may."

It appeared to Maria that he would cry and she wondered at his sadness. He continued. "You will keep the money from your things, little one. You will keep them for your dowry."

He smiled again because he could tell that Maria did not know what a dowry was. "For when you are grown and get married and have a family."

He stood up. He had things to do. "Agata says you do the work of two men, anyway. I think you will earn your keep."

He patted her gently on the head and it felt good to Maria. It gave her a warm feeling deep in the pit of her stomach, much like when the fence's assistant touched her hair. It was the best feeling she'd known in her life. She watched him walk away and then looked back at the hymnal. She wasn't stupid, just ignorant, and she could make the ignorance go away. She felt a little bit of happiness.

She stood up and wandered around again, since she was alone. She liked the smells of the church, the candles mostly, and the hint of the incense that was burned during special occasions. She did not yet know of all the grand celebrations, but she liked the odors. She wandered to the baptismal font and looked it over. It was empty now but she could tell it held water and she wondered what was in store for her when she got baptized.

Her daydream was interrupted by a tug on her hair and Maria wheeled, instinctively striking as hard as her small fist would allow. The boy fell backward onto the stone floor of the church and held his eye. She stood over him, glaring, determining what he was about.

He got up slowly and she pulled her fist back, ready to strike again. The boy backed up and put up a cautionary hand. "I, I, don't hit me again!"

He was a nice looking boy, well dressed in a grey suit. He wore a tie and nice shoes, not boots or sandals. His collar was stiff and his hair had been neatly combed. He was a head taller than Maria and a bit older. He had thought he'd have some fun with the new peasant worker of the church but now stood as if he were before the padre himself. He looked her over and Maria stood a little straighter. She had him now.

"I, I was just having a little fun. You didn't need to hit me."

"I don't like to be touched." She regarded him. He was a handsome boy, almost as pale as the priest. "What's your name?"

"Crisanto. You are Maria."

She felt funny that he knew her name. "How old are you? Why are you dressed this way?"

He grinned. He liked that she was interested in him. "I'm thirteen."

He looked at his clothes and realized how differently they were dressed. "I, my father makes me wear these clothes. He is the shop owner of the town. He, we have a station to represent." He blushed a little as he regarded Maria's bare feet.

"I'm eleven," she lied. She wouldn't be eleven for several months. She wasn't certain why she said such a thing. She instinctively turned her back on him, pretending to do some work, moving away just quickly enough so that he'd follow her.

She began moving the hymnals from one end of each row of pews to the other and Crisanto began to help her. There was no purpose in this, but Maria wanted him there and this would give them a chance to talk while they worked.

"Where are you from?"

She shrugged and did not look up. "Just around."

"Where's your family?"

"Dead."

"Oh." He began rubbing his eye as it was swelling. It would be purple by morning and Maria regretted hitting him.

"Are you going to live here, at the church?"

"I guess." She looked at him and liked the look on his face. "What do you care?" She didn't know why she said that to him either.

"I, I don't, I just..."

He was interrupted by a terse call from the back of the church. "Crisanto!"

"Yes, father." He cringed and turned away, to the rear of the church toward the man who was standing there, arms crossed, looking severely at them.

The man was remarkable in that he was a taller and older version of the boy. He wore a matching outfit. They looked very odd in this respect and Maria wondered at it. How did they get everything to match so well? He waved his hand, gesturing for the boy to come more quickly.

"This is the new girl, Mar..."

"I see well enough who it is. Come away." He looked at Maria with obvious scorn and ushered the boy out. She could hear him as they walked through the vestibule. "You stay away from that. Damned country Indians. Don't know why they let them in here, and barefoot. Savages."

They were gone.

Maria sat at the dinner table and was surprised to find her six shooter on her plate. She knew it meant something bad and waited. The old man wandered in and looked at his wife. They looked at Maria who kept her eyes fixed on the gun.

"My girl, your six shooter was cocked, under your pillow." He grinned a little devilishly. "If you'd a flopped a little hard, bang, no more Maria!" He picked up the gun and regarded it. It was a good one and he wondered how she'd acquired it. "Do you know how to use this, Maria?"

She looked up at him. "Oh, yes."

"And you were taught? By whom?"

"Oh, no one. I just figured it out."

"I see."

The old woman shook her head from side to side.

"I'll show you." He sat beside her and opened the latch. This Maria already knew but she was gracious and allowed him to show her as he loaded cartridges into each of the cylinder's chambers. He got to the fifth one and stopped there. He held up one of the bullets. "Only five, Maria."

"But it's a six shooter."

"Ah, and how many toes does my little Maria have?"

"Ten."

"If you load six bullets in the gun, you might end up with only nine toes." He laughed and closed the latch on the revolver. He handed it to her as he wagged his finger from side to side. "And don't cock it until you are ready to fire."

She nodded.

"Now, go put it back."

The old woman harrumphed. "Under the pillow is no place for a gun."

The old man sat down and waited for Maria to return from her room. He continued. "All little girls should learn guns. Then no one can bother them."

With that, he placed a leather bag on Maria's plate. She opened it and looked at the pile of coins. It was nearly as much as what she and Juana had originally been paid by the fence.

"For the asses." He grinned. "The padre is a good burro trader, Maria. You must thank him for that." He nodded at the fortune before her.

It was more than she ever imagined they would bring. She put the money back in the sack and they ate. The old folks were so good to her. She loved mealtime because they talked and laughed and there was always plenty of good food to eat.

Afterward, the old man helped Maria with her numbers, then they played cards.

The old woman didn't much like it as he was teaching her all the bad games, the ones played in the saloons and gambling houses. It was not for a young girl growing up in a church to know. But the old man liked numbers and cards and saw no harm in it. He grabbed Maria's bag of money and poured it onto the table. He counted out half for each of them and slid her pile in front of her, he took the other one.

"Now, my girl, I am going to show you how to make some money without breaking your back."

He started out with the old standard, veintiuno. Maria was a good student and by bedtime they each still had half the money. Maria neither won nor lost. The old woman was impressed, the old man was a good player and he was not patronizing the child. Maria was holding her own.

When it was finally time to go to bed the old man put the money back in the sack and handed it to Maria. "Is there anything you want to buy with your fortune, Maria?"

She looked herself over. Her clothes were good enough. The old woman had taught her how to use the fancy soaps to keep them clean. She finally had a thought.

"I'd like shoes." She got up and let the old woman kiss her good night. It made the woman happy and Maria obliged. The old woman became serious.

"No more secrets, child." She hugged Maria a little tightly. "And be careful with the gun. We finally found you and don't want to lose you." She nodded. She suddenly looked strange, as if she might cry. She sent Maria off to bed.

Maria lay in bed, staring at the ceiling and thought about what the old woman had said. They finally found her? What could she mean? They didn't know her. They could not have known her or known her situation.

She grew sleepy and thought of the boy in the suit and the priest and veintiuno. She thought of the six shooter under her pillow. That was a stupid thing to have it cocked just under her head. Sometimes she felt very stupid. But she was ignorant and not stupid. She could learn. She learned the veintiuno and now how to keep the gun and later she'd learn to shoot properly. Tomorrow she'd go to the fancy store and let the boy find her shoes that fit and she'd wear them in the church from now on. She'd never go barefoot in church again.

# Chapter VI: Crisanto

Two winters passed and Maria no longer thought much about traveling to the sea to visit the fence's pretty assistant. She'd grown nearly ten inches during this time and was blossoming into a beautiful young woman. The boys in town had difficulty concentrating on their work whenever the pretty church girl was around. The old woman and old man were constantly by her side, teaching her, nurturing her and, perhaps, even overindulging her a little from time to time. She still dressed simply, but Maria had a way of making the most humble outfit look beautiful.

She'd taken to keeping many animals and had a knack for it. The old man even arranged for her to have a horse, something Maria had dreamed of possessing ever since she could remember. He'd let her go off into the desert alone and she'd ride and ride. Sometimes she'd ride for so long that it was well after dark before she returned home, much to the consternation of the old woman.

Maria loved her horse as much as she loved the people of the church. The old man said that when animals loved a person it was a sign that the person had a pure heart and it seemed that all animals loved her.

She learned many things from the priest including how to read and write in both Spanish and English. She wasn't the best student but now she could easily get by in el Norte. She let the priest baptize her and she took her first communion. She learned about confession, and told the priest most of her sins. Not all, as she had difficulty really believing most anything she'd ever done much of a sin.

She even made peace with Paulo, the man she had clobbered with the candleholder. He was gruff and grumpy but she won his heart. It was the way of it with Maria; she had found her voice, lost her timidity. She was blossoming into a fine young lady and she turned heads and hearts constantly, wherever she went.

And none of this was lost on Crisanto or his father. They were both attracted, in their own way, to Maria. One was falling in love and the other was continuously revolted. Maria enjoyed it all thoroughly.

One day Maria was working with some horses when shots drew her to the back of the fancy store. The old man was teaching Crisanto to fire a six shooter. This amused Maria very much, as Crisanto was inept at just about anything that required dexterity.

They'd set up bottles on a fence and Crisanto stood, one hand on his hip and the other pointing a big six shooter. He fired and missed, fired and missed, fired and missed. He was disgusted as he reloaded and Maria sauntered up beside him. She waited and let him fire and miss again before she picked up a rock and hurled it at one of his targets. She smashed it easily. He looked at her, humiliated, then turned his attention to the next bottle. He fired and missed. Maria threw again, shattering the next bottle.

"Maria, we're going to run out of bottles."

"Someone needs to break them." She grinned.

"It's easy enough to throw a rock. Shooting a gun is entirely different."

She shrugged. "No it's not."

"It is."

"No, it's not." She turned and ran to the church, retrieving her own gun. She nodded to Crisanto. "Go on, try again."

He fired and missed. Maria fired and shattered the target. The boy turned and looked at the old man in disgust. It wasn't the teacher, since the old man had taught Maria, too, at least rudimentarily. Maria could shoot a gun as naturally as she could throw a rock.

"How do you do that?"

Maria shrugged. "I just do it."

He was completely frustrated now and fired wildly and too fast at the bottles, missing every one. He opened the gun and tore at the empty cartridge cases.

Maria smiled, "That's even worse."

"You do it, you're so smart."

She fired quickly and killed four more bottles. She deftly reloaded and fired again and killed five more. She looked behind them and spotted a rifle propped against the trough. "Oh, with a Winchester it's even easier."

She grabbed the rifle and began shooting again, this time shattering the pieces of the broken bottles until there was nothing more to kill down range.

"That's a nice rifle." She handed it to Crisanto and picked up her gun. She walked, a little too provocatively, back to the church and the shooting lesson was ended for the day.

They played cards that night and the old man laughed and told the old woman all about it. Maria had by now added faro, Mexican Monte and poker to her repertoire. She beat the old man constantly and he was proud of her.

She just finished taking all his beans, as now they played strictly with the old woman's foodstuffs instead of with real money which was safely in the town bank, when the old woman spoke up.

"Easy on the boy's heart, Maria."

Maria grinned. "Oh, I won't hurt it too badly. I just want him to make his father take it back."

"Take what back?"

"Calling me bad things. Calling me a savage." She spoke to her cards and did not look up. She laid out another winning hand.

It was the first time the old woman had heard of the insult, though she was not surprised. Now, she grinned at the humiliation of Crisanto, though it really wasn't the boy's fault that he had an ass and bigot for a father. In fact, Crisanto wasn't anything like his father. He was sweet and kind and just a little frail. He was a good boy and they all loved and felt a bit sorry for him.

The old woman looked back at the work she was doing, and continued. "Crisanto's father has an idea that he is superior. He believes he has Spanish blood." She pretended to spit. "He's no more Spanish than the Pope."

And the old man interjected, to add weight to the old woman's statement, "He's Italiano, you know."

Maria smiled. Everyone knew the pope was Italiano.

"And he's a shop owner." The old man picked at a bean and did not look up. "Shop owners and church girls do not mix, Maria." He smiled at her with love in his eyes. His Maria was better than the owner of the grandest shop in Mexico. He shrugged. "Some people are very small, Maria. They think that having us broken into castes makes them bigger."

He got up and headed for bed, kissing his two favorite girls on the head. "You keep at him, Maria. He might finally learn some humility one day."

Maria dreamed a little of Crisanto that night. He was a good boy, just as the old woman had said, and she liked him very much. She felt a little guilty for showing him up with the shooting, but she couldn't help herself. She liked the way he looked at her when she shot the gun so well. She could feel his eyes on her when she walked away, swaying her hips like she'd seen the women do at the brothel. It made the men very funny. She fell asleep thinking of these things and slept until morning.

She awoke earlier than usual. She felt that she was wetting the bed. She'd never wet a bed in all her time that she could remember and she jumped up to use the chamber pot. When she was finished she looked in it and there was blood.

She got cleaned up and went back to bed. It was very early and she needed to think. What was this? She'd not experienced this, not bled, since the bastard Sanchez, the shop owner, had abused her.

She wasn't in pain this time, though. It didn't hurt. She jumped up again and there was more blood. She'd not be able to go out like this. Her dress would be ruined.

She considered her situation. Did a man come in and abuse her in the middle of the night? She looked around and her door was secure. The old folks had made her bar it now that she was older. They were just too afraid of something bad happening to her. It was still barred. No one had been in her room.

She thought about the Virgin Maria. Could this have happened? That was preposterous. She could not be another Virgin Maria. She was not a virgin, as Juana so annoyingly reminded her many times. But it seemed the only logical explanation. A man had not abused her, yet she was bleeding, just as she had when she'd been abused those many years ago. So, did an angel do it? Or God Himself, or Jesus?

She was a good girl, there was no doubting that, and now she was a good Catholic. She took the communion every Sunday, even if she didn't really believe she was eating flesh. And she went to mass all the time and she was good. Did Jesus want to start a family and he'd chosen Maria? She was an Indian. The real Virgin Maria was very pale, so that did not seem to make sense. But the Virgin Maria was poor and from a lowly family, the priest told her that. Maybe the Virgin

Maria was like an Indian in her land. So, maybe it wasn't preposterous.

She looked through the cracks in the shutters and could see the day was dawning. She sat on the chamber pot again and bled. She got cleaned up and made herself a bandage. She had to go see the priest.

He was worried when he saw her at his door. She did not look well. She was very pale. He got her to sit down.

"What is it Maria?"

She did not know what to say to him. Her theory seemed ridiculous now that she was sitting before him. "I, I , no. Nothing padre."

She got up to leave and he stopped her.

"Maria, tell me." He was so kind to her. She loved the old priest and now he looked especially sad. She felt it was her fault that he'd start the day so sad. He usually started the day fairly happy, then got sad as it progressed. There was no telling now how sad he'd be at the end of this day if he started out badly.

"I, I think that God or Jesus or an angel has visited me in the night, padre."

He nodded. "I see. And how, what form did this visit take, Maria?"

"I think I'm going to have a baby, padre. I think, they did, you know, that."

"Why do you think such a thing, child?"

"Because, padre, I am bleeding, down there. And it happened only once, a long time ago. When I..." She looked away, said nothing.

"What is it, Maria?"

She'd never told anyone about the time she'd been abused. Only Juana and the yellow-haired whore knew of it. The priest knew nothing of her past. She wondered how he would react to this news. She was committed now and had to tell him. "I, a man did that to me, padre. When I was ten and I bled, so I thought perhaps..."

He stood up and grabbed her up in his arms. He held her for a long time. She could feel him crying. She pulled away and looked into his eyes. "Why are you crying, padre?'

"This is such a wicked, wicked world, Maria, and what you have told me makes me very sad. I love you very much, Maria, and I did not know such wickedness happened to you. I am sorry, child. I am sorry."

This caused Maria to be confused. It wasn't the padre's fault and there was no reason for him to apologize. "But what of the visitation, padre? Did this happen?"

He finally smiled. He took her by the hand and led her back to the old woman. "No, no Maria. You are a good girl but you are not the next Virgin Maria." He called to the old woman and spoke into her ear, in a hushed tone so that Maria could not hear.

The old woman smiled and nodded to the padre and turned her attention to Maria. She waited for the padre to leave and when they were alone, the old woman hugged her and kissed her on the forehead. "My darling little girl. Today you are a woman."

"Come on, Crisanto, catch up!" She rode hard in her vaquero outfit, Crisanto lumbering along behind her. They were chasing mustangs and Maria was catching up. This was the best sixteenth birthday a girl could have and Maria was pleased with her new outfit, much to the chagrin of the old woman. The old man had bought it for her.

She was splendid in her trousers. She had not had trousers and this made riding difficult. She now wore trousers and tall boots and a lovely print blouse. She wore a short vest and a straw sombrero. The old man even got her a gun belt and big knife. He promised her that one day he'd get her a Winchester. He called her his beautiful vaquero.

She looked on from the top of a cliff, down at the valley below as the beasts ran off in a cloud of dust. Crisanto finally made it to her side. He was winded. "See that one, see that one, Crisanto?" She pointed at a black filly with a white diamond between her eyes. "That one is magnificent. If you catch that one for me, I'll marry you!"

She was joking but the words struck the young man through the heart, like a thunderbolt. He looked at her smiling at the herd of wild horses as they ran off. His heart pounded in his ears and he felt that he might fall over. He was more in love with Maria now than he'd ever been in his life, and he'd loved her since the time she'd given him the black eye in the church those many years ago.

She pulled her sombrero off and shook out her hair, letting the raven tresses fall onto her shoulders. She knocked the dust away from her hat. She'd become more beautiful than any young woman in the village. She was more beautiful than even Crisanto's mother and his mother was famous throughout the land for her stunning features and lovely hair.

He handed her his canteen and she drank and let the water run down her front and onto her breasts. He was nearly incapable of speech as he stared at her, until he blurted out, nearly incomprehensibly, "Maria, marry me."

She looked at him. She knew the day would come and knew what her answer would be. She smiled coyly at him and gave her reply. "Crisanto, you know that is not possible. You know that your family will not have this. It cannot be."

It was easy for her to say this because, though she liked Crisanto very much, she did not love him and did not care to be the wife of a shop owner.

He dropped his head, dejected. "I cannot please you and I cannot please my father. I cannot please anyone." He miserably turned his horse toward home. He was a good boy, a young man, really, since he was now nineteen years old and Maria felt sorry for him.

"Crisanto, stop. Wait."

He slowed and then stopped. He had no will when he was with Maria. She could wind him up and make him do whatever she wanted. He awaited her command.

"Come here, Crisanto. Sit for a while."

They dismounted and sat and watched the sun move across the sky. It was a lovely day and Maria was happy. She knew she had to break his heart and now was just as good a time as any to do it.

"I do not love you, Crisanto, and that was mean to say to you what I did about the horse. I am sorry."

She extended her hand and he took it and this only made him sadder because now he was holding her hand and everything, everything about Maria, made his heart ache until he felt it would burst.

"Your father is very proud of you, Crisanto. He just doesn't say it right. He thinks you are a very good man."

He lit up at her using the word man to describe him. She was lying, of course, she knew Crisanto's father didn't really like Crisanto at all. The young man's father was a monster and an ogre and he didn't like his own kind-hearted, sweet son and that was terrible, but Maria didn't want to say this to him. She'd never say this to him.

"He called me an alfeñique."

Maria suppressed a laugh because it was true, he was an alfeñique. Crisanto really was not at all manly. Poor Crisanto was the opposite of manly.

"Oh, I don't know. I bet he'd have all respect for you if you brought in one of those mustangs. He'd think differently of you then."

He snorted. "That will never be, Maria, you know that. I cannot ride or rope. I am not one tenth the rider that you are. That is impossible."

"What if we worked together? What if I helped you and your father didn't know?"

He smiled weakly. "You'd do this for me, Maria?"

"Crisanto. You are like a brother to me. I love you," she held up her hand, "but not in that way, Crisanto. Not in the marrying way. I love you like a brother and I will help you." She looked him in the eye, "But be clear on this, Crisanto. I will never love you like a wife. I will never marry you."

They hatched a plan to do this thing in a week.

The old shopkeeper came to see them of an evening, just as Maria and the old man were starting a game of faro. They were all kind to him as he was very anxious. Crisanto had gone for a ride the day before and had not returned. He was hoping Maria would know something about it.

She didn't, at the time, think much of it and only as she got into bed did the realization hit her. He must have gone for the horse on his own.

She awoke extra early and was in the desert by sunrise. If Crisanto had gone down, after two days, he'd likely be dead if the accident or whatever'd befallen him hadn't killed him outright. She did not hold out much hope for him.

By noon she was scanning the valley below. This is where the horses ran. She saw a glint, way off in a distance. It was something metallic and she decided to check it out.

Sure enough, it was the young man. He'd fallen from his horse and his leg had become lodged between two boulders at the knee. From there down was now black; the boy was dying.

He smiled uneasily. "Hello, Maria." He was delirious and happy to see his love.

She gave him water and pulled a blanket off her saddle skirt. She made a little tent over him. He'd been baking in the sun, hatless, for more than two days. He slept most of the time and his face was burned and blistered, his lips cracked and bleeding. He could barely see.

Maria poured water on him and he felt a little better. She thought about riding back and getting help but that wouldn't do. She studied the situation. The boulders could not be moved and his leg was now doubled in size. It was dead below the knee and she could detect the odor of rotting flesh. It had to come off, and quickly.

"Crisanto, tell me." She pushed hard on his thigh, just above the knee. "Do you feel this?"

He smiled weakly. "No, Maria. No." He gazed on her and smiled. "You are so beautiful, Maria."

"Shush, Crisanto." She pulled out her big knife. She looked him in the eye. "I have to cut your leg off, Crisanto."

He looked down and didn't care. He didn't care about anything anymore. "Okay, Maria. Okay."

She cut the material of his trousers away. The blackness had not yet made it above the knee. She held out some hope.

She breathed deeply and began carefully cutting the flesh, fileting the skin and muscle back until the joint was exposed. She thought about the old woman and how she had taught her to separate the joints of animals they would eat. Maria'd gotten good with swine. She decided that this was not the leg of Crisanto, her childhood friend, but just another leg of a hog for the table.

She worked deftly and, with a sudden pop, Crisanto became separated from the boulder and his lower leg. He fell back and bled profusely. Maria could now get a good tourniquet on his thigh and stop the flow of blood. He smiled at her and then down at his leg. He still felt nothing.

Crisanto was not big, but he still outweighed her by forty pounds. She couldn't put him on her horse. She thought quickly and decided to pull him up, with a rope around his chest. She got him to stand and pulled and got him to hop and help pull himself up. He was finally in the saddle and looked very strange with a good part of his leg missing. She jumped on behind him and tapped her mount's sides, kicking him into a full gallop as she held onto the young man.

As they rode, Crisanto mumbled and babbled. He spoke to someone and seemed to be having a conversation about horses and women and Maria. He said that Maria was the only one he'd ever love, but he couldn't have her and, therefore, he'd be alone for the rest of his days. Eventually he slumped forward and lost consciousness.

She took him to the church as she didn't know what to expect at the store. The old woman and old man and priest would be better suited to help. They came out and eased him off the horse and placed him on the kitchen table. The old woman worked fast, pouring mescal liberally on the wound. She then took a big drink herself and handed the bottle to Maria. It was the first time she'd offered the girl spirits and now Maria knew for certain they were in for a rough time.

Maria swallowed deeply and it warmed her to her toes. She looked at her hands covered in Crisanto's blood and expected them to be shaking, but they weren't.

She was excited and keyed up but she was calm, too; this was the way with Maria. From the time of the bastard Sanchez catching on fire, to her own near drowning in the cave and now this, she was always calm under stress. She never got scared or shaky or cried.

The old woman dumped cup after cup of water on Crisanto's wound. It would be as clean as she could get it and she was nearly ready to remove the tourniquet. She bound the stump tightly, winding it round and round with a cotton sheet until it looked like a great turban on the end of the boy's leg. She removed Maria's scarf tourniquet and the bandages held. No blood seeped through. The wound was clean.

They removed his boot and sock, cut his trousers away and removed his shirt. They bathed him and made him comfortable in Maria's bed. If he survived the night, he had a chance. They turned to leave the room when the old woman drew in a deep breath. She sniffed the air near his leg and waited as if she were trying to remember something. She shrugged and looked at the old man and the priest. "Just the slightest hint, but that might be left from his clothes." They walked out and everyone had a big shot of mescal.

The shopkeeper was there. He was frantic and they let him look in at his son. He was crying now and looked each of them in the eye. He looked at Maria, wanting to thank her, but he could not. He couldn't bring himself to stoop so low. He turned and walked out. This would break the boy's mother's heart and he was glad she was away just now.

When they were finally alone, the old man reached out for Maria. He hugged her and kissed her cheek. He held up his fists, clenched together in victory. "Even if the boy dies, Maria, you are a hero. You are my best girl and I am so proud."

He had tears in his eyes and now Maria had to comfort him. She smiled and patted his shoulder. "He was trying to get a mustang for his father. He was trying to prove to his father that he was not an alfeñique."

She slept with the old woman that night and awoke alone. The old woman was in with Crisanto and she did not look happy. She lifted the blanket and Maria could see the bandages were bloody. His leg was now black beyond the knee, halfway up his thigh. "That smell, Maria. Gangrene. It is what I smelled last night. He is doomed. Poor Crisanto is doomed." She dropped her head and walked out as Maria changed the dressing.

Crisanto smiled weakly as she worked. "Maria." She looked up and smiled back at him. He was trying to focus and realized where he was. "I've always dreamed of being in your bed."

She grinned at his naughtiness. He was dying and knew it. He didn't care if he was embarrassing himself. He wanted to make Maria smile.

She stood up. "I'm going to get the priest, Crisanto. I'll be back."

The padre gave him Last Rites and now Crisanto was parchment pale. He wouldn't last long and wanted to be with Maria. He asked the padre not to tell his father. He didn't want to see his father now.

They stayed together for the rest of the night. Maria watched as lights went out under her door. The old woman and old man left them alone and Maria was thankful for it. Even though she didn't love him, she thought, it was a good thing for her to spend his final moments with him. She had cast a spell many years ago, and it was the least she could do. It was the greatest kindness she could give him and she sat close and kept his head cool with wet rags. She brushed his cheek gently. He smiled up at her.

"I love you Maria. You know I love you."

"And I you, Crisanto." He brightened. "I know I told you that day out with the mustangs that I did not and could not love you, but I was wrong. I love you."

With that she stood up and, gently, noiselessly barred her door. She stood over him and slowly removed her clothes. With all his will he moved aside, making room for the love of his life as she climbed into bed with him. She pressed her naked body against his and then, gently, lovingly made love to him, his first and last and best time. He was dead.

# Chapter VII: Rosario

Maria thought a lot about Crisanto after he died. She wasn't in love with him but she did love him and was sorry to see him die. She enjoyed making love with him because she wanted to make him happy. He did die happy and she thought that it might very well be the best death for a human being; to die after making love to the one person he loved more than anyone or anything else in the world—and she liked it, too.

She enjoyed the act and was relieved because she'd worried over that for a long time, off and on over the years, ever since that bastard Sanchez had abused her. She often wondered if that would put her off it and now she knew that it wouldn't. She had liked it; it made her all tingly and she felt a little convulsion deep inside. She thought it would be good to do again.

She knew it was what the padre called a mortal sin. She knew the Ten Commandments and she knew that the act was supposed to be between husband and wife. But there was no time for that as Crisanto was dying and she really was too young to marry. She didn't much care, anyway.

The more Maria learned about the faith and the church, the less inclined she was to follow it. It was all just too much and she'd already done things that were against the Ten Commandments. She didn't feel bad for doing them and she was not sorry for anything she'd done. If any of it kept her out of heaven, well, that was God's problem and not hers. She'd just as soon go to Limbo. It seemed that all the interesting people were in Limbo anyway. She knew she'd never ever go to hell. That was out of the question because she was good, deep down she was good and pure and pure of heart and she knew she'd never go to hell.

After a few weeks she became ill and did not know why. She'd not given any thought to becoming pregnant. Of course, she knew that having relations could result in such a thing, but she'd known men and women who'd been married a long time and had not gotten pregnant. The old man and old woman had been married for more than fifty years, yet they had no children. She knew that doing it would not result in pregnancy every time and just didn't give it much thought.

But along about the tenth week, she felt a bulge and she knew. She was most definitely going to have a baby. She looked at herself in her old mirror, the one the old woman had given her, and could see a bit of a bulge. It was going to get bigger. She thought hard about when to tell the people who cared about her.

This was all very queer because she wasn't in the least unhappy about it. She was quite pleased. She knew the old priest would become sad, but he was always sad anyway. The old man and old woman would probably be happy. They loved her and they loved children. It would just be another child to love. There would be room for the child and she'd be happy to give up her fortune to help raise the baby, but they probably wouldn't take the money. They'd let her keep her money and they'd all raise the baby together.

She was suddenly excited but still wanted to keep it a secret. Somehow, she had a feeling in the back of her mind that this might not happen. It might not come to pass and there was no reason to bring it up if it wasn't going to result in a baby. It would be easier on the padre and the old people if they never knew that it almost happened, so she kept it to herself.

She'd known of that, too. She heard of women in the village and back in the poor village where she grew up that lost babies all the time. They'd be pregnant just long enough to be sick and feel terrible, then the baby would come out dead. She thought about that and hoped it wouldn't happen. She worried about it a bit too and decided not to ride horses or do anything strenuous that might hurt the baby.

The old man was starting to wonder because Maria rode as much as she could but now, strangely, she didn't. He started to ask her about it one day and then decided not to, almost as if Maria had telepathically told him not to ask the question, told him she was in her confinement and was not to be bothered. He didn't ask.

After a time she swore she could feel a fluttering and this made her feel very happy. The baby was alive and moving about and she felt a little giddy. At night she'd talk to the baby. She didn't know the sex of the baby, of course, and resolved to call it Rosario. That could be the name of a boy or a girl. She didn't know if she'd name the baby Rosario when it was born but, for now, it worked. She did not want to presume the baby's sex and call it by the wrong name.

She thought about all the things she'd do with the baby. She didn't care if they called it a bastard. She didn't care that she wouldn't get a man once she had the baby. It didn't matter to her. Nothing seemed to matter now but the baby and she thought about going to the sea, to show the baby the beautiful water and the fence's pretty assistant. The fence's assistant would like Maria's baby, she was certain of that. She'd take the baby in the sea and hold it and bathe it in the salty water and then lie on the beach in the sun and love her little baby.

It went on like this for four months. By now she was bulging a bit and she had trouble hiding it because she was so slender. She pulled her skirt up pretty high and puffed out her blouse and then wrapped her rebozo in such a way that it hid everything well.

The old woman was strange about it all, though. She said nothing and made no comment on Maria's change in behavior. She seemed to be feeding Maria often, as well. She put food in front of her constantly and Maria was glad for it. She was ravenous these days. She figured she was hungry because she was eating for two. The baby took a lot of her energy and that was also a big change for Maria. She slept well until daylight most days. She seemed always to want to sleep.

And now, as if all these changes weren't enough, her breasts began to grow again, and now they leaked. Sometimes she'd have to change her blouse halfway through the day. She found this amusing. It didn't bother her very much because she had a magnificent bosom already. Now her breasts became downright tremendous and leaky and itchy. She knew it was all for her little Rosario and at night she'd tell the baby of her adventures; all the details of her day and how her body was changing and preparing for when the little one was ready to come out.

But as with everything in Maria's life, nothing ever seemed to go as planned and on an early Sunday morning, just as a cock crowed, she awoke to strange goings on down below. She had pains that rolled over her in great waves and she felt again as if she were wetting the bed.

She managed to sit on the edge of her bed and thought about calling out to the old woman. She waited and the contractions came again. She gave birth to a little, half-sized Rosario. Her little precious one was dead.

She bundled the babe up in a sheet and climbed back into bed. She remembered what the priest said about babies born and dying before baptism, that even someone who was not a priest could baptize a baby, so she did. She wetted her fingers with her saliva and made a little sign of the cross on Rosario's forehead. "I baptize you in the name of the Father, and of the Son, and of the Holy Ghost. Amen."

She looked at every inch of her baby. She was beautiful with tiny hands and fingers and toes. She looked as if she was asleep and Maria didn't even feel like crying. The baby had been baptized and now wouldn't be stuck in Limbo. Maria had been baptized, too, so they'd both meet up in heaven. She couldn't wait.

She finally fell back to sleep and slept until late morning.

She awoke and, for a moment, forgot that little Rosario was dead. She thought maybe she wasn't, that she was just sleeping and she'd be able to feed her little baby from her breasts. They were paining her so much and leaking terribly.

But she was wrong; her baby was dead.

Maria got up and cleaned herself. She bundled the baby up tightly. She kissed her one more time and took her out to the desert. She resolved to bury her near the mustangs where her father had gotten his leg trapped. Maria thought it was a fitting place for little Rosario to rest. She dug a small hole and lined it with stones. Rosario was so tiny. Her baby didn't need much room. Maria rewrapped her snuggly in a rebozo.

Maria held her to her breast and kissed her cheek then gently placed her in the stony crib and looked at her. She thought about how long they'd been together and knew it wasn't long enough, just enough to break Maria's heart.

Her little sleeping angel. "Sleep well, my darling, I will be with you soon." She found a large flat rock to seal the tomb and fashioned a cross from some mesquite branches. She spelled out her name with little pebbles. She would never tell anyone of little Rosario for the rest of her days.

That evening the old man left right after dinner, which was very strange because he never did this on a Sunday. He always stayed with them and played cards with Maria. Now she was alone with the old woman. They sat quietly for a while. The old woman warmed some milk and they drank it together. Finally, when it was time for bed, the old woman stood up and touched Maria on the cheek. She smiled at her and there were tears in her eyes. They spilled down her wrinkled face and the old woman kissed Maria on the forehead. "We are sorry, child." She turned and went to bed.

# Chapter VIII: The Virgin of Guadalupe

They were going to Mexico City and the old priest seemed a little happier. They had a good wagon with two horses to pull it. It would be a fairly fast journey as the roads were good.

Maria was not certain why he'd chosen her to go, but he had. They rode together and she handled the horses for most of the way. She was a good companion and he was falling in love with his little charge, not in a biblical way, he just loved her as did everyone who knew Maria.

She'd just had her nineteenth birthday and had matured into a fully grown young woman, likely, the most beautiful in the land. No man could resist her charms and everyone, everywhere wanted to do things for her.

She regarded her city clothes as she rode and worried over the dust kicked up from the desert roads. She didn't want to look a mess when they arrived and the priest sensed this. He rummaged around and found a long rebozo and threw it over Maria, wrapping her to the neck.

He'd taken his vows of poverty and did not want for worldly things. He wasn't concerned in the least about his own appearance, but Maria was different. She was not of the church; nothing he could do or say or teach her would ever make her wholly of the church and he did not regard this as a bad thing. She'd certainly never be a nun. He was delighted, just like a proud father would be of his lovely daughter coming out to the world as a woman. He wanted to show her off a little.

"And padre, tell me again, why are we going to this place, the big church?"

"To visit a friend, Maria. Just to visit a friend." He smiled and looked at her. "And to show you a glorious city. Mexico City, Maria. It is a jewel. We'll go to see some sights. We'll go to the Archaeological Museum."

"Thank you for the city clothes, padre." She smiled at him and he patted her arm.

"My pleasure child."

They rode for a long time and eventually arrived at their destination. Maria could see immediately what it was and it made her feel very strange. They were shown to their rooms. Maria offered to spend the day in hers but the old padre wouldn't hear of it. He insisted that she accompany him and, reluctantly, she complied.

They went to see a nun about the same age as the priest. She was sitting in a chair in a dark room with shuttered windows. She was reading a Bible and was dressed in her nun's garb. She looked as if she were dead except for her eyes. They shone with life. She was very glad to see him.

He introduced Maria to the old nun and the woman touched Maria's face and then patted it. "Beautiful, beautiful."

Maria smiled and said nothing. She didn't know why she was there and she didn't want to see the priest look any sadder but this was making him look that way. This was why they'd come to Mexico City.

Maria tried hard to think of a way to extricate herself from the meeting. Let them be alone together. She had just come up with a plan when the priest turned to her and asked her to help him with a special mass, just for the nun.

She was disappointed because she found these little masses to be tedious and she hated going through every ritual: making a little alter for the priest and setting up the chalice, the water, wine and wafers. She thought it all somewhat silly and redundant as the nun likely already attended a mass that day. Now she'd have another and Maria didn't want to do it.

But then she saw the look in the nun's eye and, just as funerals are not for the dead but for the living, her ministrations and her assistance at the mass was not for her to endure or be bothered by, but for the happiness and peace of mind of the old woman who was dying.

When they finished, the old nun was exhausted and the padre was also very tired. A nurse soon came and guided the old nun away. The priest and Maria went to their rooms to rest and recover from the exhausting trip and the even more exhausting meeting with the dying nun.

At dinner time Maria looked in on the padre. He was lying in bed and there was a half empty bottle of American whiskey alongside him. Maria knew he was drunk. This made her feel very sad as she knew the priest did not normally drink, except for the holy wine and that he mostly watered down. She came into his room and looked at him until he acknowledged her. He'd slept the worst of it off and was no longer so drunk that he couldn't talk. He sat up and threw his legs over the edge of the bed and beckoned Maria to sit down.

He'd been crying and Maria decided that she should get him to talk about it. She began.

"Did you love her a long time?"

He looked at her and then looked away. "It is so obvious, Maria?"

"Yes. To me it is."

"Now she is dying. She no longer has the church and she doesn't have me. She's alone in the world, Maria, and she will be dead soon."

Maria thought about what to say, thought perhaps she would be going too far, then went ahead anyway. "Is life not hard enough, padre, that you must heap on sin after sin, so that it is impossible for you to live?"

He smiled cynically at her. His Maria. He saw it the first day, back when he caught her stealing the candlesticks. She had the wisdom of the ages about her. "It is not so simple as all that, Maria."

She harrumphed. "I am an ignorant girl, padre. But I am not stupid. There is a difference." She looked him over, looked into his sad eyes and continued. "My life has been very hard, padre. I know this, and I don't know why God has made my life like this. But it is the only life I have and I will live it the best I can. But you, you make all this too hard. You make sins where there are no sins. You make sadness where there doesn't need to be sadness. Does Jesus really want us to go around with sour faces all day, all day looking so sad that you could make a baby cry?"

He smiled at her and was embarrassed. "I..., I'm sorry, Maria."

He looked out the window as if seeking out someone waiting for him in the courtyard below, someone who could perhaps give him the answers to her questions. "She and I met when we were young. I was a new priest and she a new nun. We fell in love. I was going to leave the church for her, but she could not. She said that she could not leave the church and that she could not be with me."

"I see." Maria thought hard about it. He was the poor Crisanto and the nun was Maria. "So, this terrible thing, this sin, will it make her go to hell when she dies?"

The priest grinned and looked up at her. Maria was so wonderfully black and white. There were no shades of grey with the girl. He shook his head from side to side. "I don't know, Maria."

"Well, you need to let her go. You need to be with her when she dies and you need to tell her that she's forgiven and that she'll go to heaven. If you don't know then you have to tell her the best possible outcome for her. It might be that she goes to heaven and it might be that she goes to hell, but if you do not know, then you need to tell her it is heaven. She'll find out soon enough, but she needs to think, believe right now that it will be heaven."

He loved her simplicity and her kindness. She was a thoroughly good person and he smiled at her. "If only a fraction of my parishioners were so good and wise as you, Maria."

She stood up and looked out the window. She picked up the bottle and took it with her.

"No more drinking for you, padre. It does not suit you." She held out her hand and helped him to his feet. "Now, go to her and tell her. Tell her to expect Jesus at the gates of heaven and that you will meet her there one day." She thought for a moment, because she loved the padre, "But not too soon."

On the ride back to their village, the priest was happier than Maria had ever seen him. The nun was dead and that made him sad, but her last hours had been good and it was because of Maria's advice.

Maria saw him regarding her out of the corner of her eye and decided to ask about the old nun. "Was she from Chicago, padre?"

"Oh, no Maria. She was from Mexico. I met her in Mexico when I first came to this country." He didn't know why but he began to speak freely of her. "She was as beautiful as you, Maria."

"Oh, I see now." She gave him a sly grin. "That is why you have always been so good to me. I remind you of your lover."

He blushed. Then smiled. She was teasing him a little and he didn't mind. "No, Maria. I took you in because of the wonderful light in your soul."

"Oh?" It was her turn to blush.

"I saw it the moment I met you, the day you clobbered poor Paulo with the candlestick."

She grinned. "I have always been sorry for that, padre."

They rode on and the priest decided to bring up something that had been bothering him for a long while.

"Maria, what do you want to do with your life?"

She smiled and looked at the road. "I, I just want to do what I am doing, padre. Be at the church and be with the old woman and the old man. They are getting along in years, padre. It is my turn to take care of them. I will do this thing, I will take care of them and make them comfortable and happy until they die."

He decided to drop it. She was one of the brightest young people he'd ever known and she had a good and curious mind but now he realized his scheme was a stupid one. Maria was not studious, she'd be miserable doing any kind of formal study. He smiled a little broader, admiring her for what she'd just said.

"You are a genuinely good soul, Maria. A genuinely good soul."

# Chapter IX: Metamorphosis

Paulo met them on the outskirts of town. His head was bandaged and Maria couldn't help but wonder what he'd gotten into to get himself clobbered again. She didn't like the look on his face. When he saw them he began to wring his hands. His sorrow turned to tears.

"What is it, Paulo?" The padre got down from the wagon to better look at the man's wounds.

"A.., I..." He looked up at Maria and cried harder. He ran to her and grabbed her hands, crying into them.

Maria pushed him away and slapped the reins against the horses. They broke into a run for the church.

The old man and old woman were dead. Maria looked at them, laid out in the church awaiting burial. They looked like they were asleep.

She waited for the padre and Paulo to catch up. She was too calm for the circumstances. "What happened, Paulo?"

He was blubbering and she couldn't get a clear answer. She looked at him and demanded, "Paulo, get hold of yourself. What happened?"

"Bandits. They came in the middle of the night. They were stealing from the church and Decio discovered them. They shot him and when Agata tried to help him they shot her."

He went back to crying inconsolably. The padre fussed over him and looked at Maria. There was nothing he could do.

She went to bed that night and listened to the nothingness of the little home. She used to hear the old people snore and cough and pass wind. She used to listen to the old woman clang around in the kitchen early in the morning; the old man would tap out the dottle from his pipe and blow his nose. She used to hear the old man laugh. He laughed a lot and he was always kind to Maria. He never, not once, said a mean or angry or cross word to her.

She dozed off thinking of these things and fell into a deep sleep. She was awakened by a strange light that appeared under her door. She went into the kitchen to investigate. Juana was sitting at the kitchen table eating some beans and tortillas. She didn't look up from her meal as Maria seated herself across the table from her. "These beans and tortillas are old."

Maria looked at Juana. She hadn't changed. She was still a child and this confounded Maria. "Where have you been?"

"Oh, here and there." She took a drink of water and regarded Maria. "You got big." She pointed with a piece of tortilla. "Your tetas are muy grande."

Maria looked down at her breasts.

"What are you going to do now that they are dead?"

"I don't know." She didn't like the casual way Juana was speaking of the old people.

Juana looked around the room. "This is nice. You could take over what they were doing for the church, get a man and raise a family here."

Maria became angry. It was a mean and insensitive thing to say and Juana seemed to sense it.

"Mind you, that's not what I'd do."

"Oh, what would *you* do?"

"I'd go track those bandits down and cut off their cojones and make them eat them with a plate of beans." She was pleased with that thought. "Beans with beans." She smiled at Maria and then looked at her a little seriously. "Oh, you don't think you could do it?"

"I didn't say I couldn't do it."

"You don't have a good look. You have a look like you don't think you could do it."

"I could do it."

"Then do it." Juana stood up and brushed the crumbs from her lap. She kicked the crumbs far under the table out of sight. Maria looked at what she was doing, then at the clock on the mantle, then back at Juana. The girl was gone.

She suddenly felt cold and went back to her bed and pulled the covers up to her chin. She soon fell asleep but it didn't last very long.

Awaking again, Maria realized she wouldn't be able to sleep anymore. She sat up and lit a lamp. For some reason she didn't understand, she got the mirror the old woman in the hovel had given her and looked into it. The old woman was right again. There is no one else in the world. No one else in the world will take care of you. Only this one.

She looked at herself in the mirror and regarded her face. She thought hard about what to do next. She got up, even though it was the middle of the night, and began her preparations. She would not sleep another night in this house.

The priest watched her as she rode up to him. He could tell she was leaving. She had packed for travel with a war sack tied onto her saddle and several canteens. She'd been to the bank to retrieve her fortune and then to the store where she purchased a Winchester. This she had in a fancy leather scabbard tied to her saddle, as well.

"Good bye." She began to turn away.

He called out to her. "Maria, stop."

She waited.

"What are you going to do?"

"I'm going to get them."

"And this is the right thing for you to do?"

"Yes."

"They wouldn't like it, Maria." He pointed to the church, toward the coffins with the bodies of the old woman and old man inside. "They'd say, let it go, they'd say that Jesus would tell you to forgive and move on. Please, Maria. Please help me bury them, give them a good funeral and stay and do the work they've done so well. Please, Maria."

"They're dead."

"And it is terrible, but it's God's will, and more killing won't bring them back. It's God's..."

She became furious and hissed at him. "God, God! Goddamn your God. Your God has brought me nothing but pain. Your God has pulled down his trousers and shit on my head all my life. Your God can go to hell, padre. Your God's a fool."

He looked at her, pain and sorrow in his eyes. He wanted to speak, but nothing he could say would mean anything to her now.

"I will be the justice now because your God is nothing; he is, like Crisanto, he is an alfeñique. He is a nothing and I am finished with him. Goddamn your God."

She thought of something and jumped from her horse. She walked up on him. "Give me a Bible!"

He stood, dumbfounded and a little afraid of her. She grabbed him by the arm and pushed him ahead of her into the church. She found a Bible. "Let's see." She paged through and found the book of Exodus. "Here." She tore a page from the Bible and held it up. She read through it and looked at the priest.

"I will break every one of these a hundred times over. I will taunt Him and do the opposite of Him. I will make every bad thing that I can think and I will make things right in this world. No more bandits or cutthroats. No more children starving or men abusing little girls. No more! No more! When I find them, I will kill them. This is better than your God. Goddamn your God, padre."

She stormed out and, jumping back on her horse, wheeled around and was gone.

She pushed her way into the saloon at the end of town. The old man would come here of an evening now and again, to play some cards and beat the locals and make money for Maria's vaquero outfit. He was well known and respected by them all.

The men acknowledged her at once. Everyone knew Maria even though the old woman had not allowed her in this place. She walked up to the bar and ordered mescal. She drank it quickly and ordered another. One of the men walked up to her and handed her some money. "Your father, he won this from me. He, he'd want you to have it."

She looked the man in the eye and then back at her glass. "He was not my father." She poured again and handed the man at the bar the money and told him to keep giving her and everyone drinks until the money was gone. They all stood up and toasted her and the memory of the old woman and old man.

She looked at them.

"Who were these bandits?"

No one spoke up.

"Come now, boys," she sounded odd calling the men boys. "Come now, you must have seen them. You must know of them. Tell me where to find them."

"Let it go, little one." A kind old man touched her arm and she recoiled.

"I will not let it go!"

Suddenly a voice came from the back of the room. "I'll tell you."

"No!" several men responded in unison as the man stepped forward. He was a vaquero and a tough man. He was not old like the other men. He wore a six shooter and carried a big knife. He looked harsh but his eyes were kind.

"Yes, I'll tell her." He gestured for her to sit down. She complied. He got two more drinks and offered her one. He looked her over carefully.

"These men don't want you to go after the bad men because they are afraid for you, Maria." He drank and continued. "But I know you are not afraid. I know what you can do, and you should do it. Avenge them, Maria."

"I will."

"The men are from a band headed by a man from further south. He's called Sombrero del Oro because he wears a big gold hat. He's a bad one, Maria." He looked at her with intensity.

"He trades in humans and he kills without consideration. But Maria, dying would not be the worst thing that could happen to you if they should catch you. You are beautiful and they would do many bad things to you. You know what I mean?" He nodded when she didn't change her expression.

"I know."

He nodded and took another drink. "I didn't think that would dissuade you."

"And these men. Why did they do this thing to the old woman and the old man?"

"Because they could." He shrugged. "No reason. Because they could. You see, Maria, these men, they are not people. They are not human beings. They are some horrible creature, even worse than a loco bull or rattler. They kill for malice and for fun. No creature in the animal kingdom acts like this. And Maria, don't hesitate. Show no mercy when the time comes. Kill them. Do not show them mercy."

She stood up and felt a little dizzy. She'd never had so much mescal. She held out her hand, as one man would to another and he took it. He shook her hand gravely and nodded. "God be with you, Maria."

She turned and walked away. "No thanks. I don't need Him."

On her way out of town she rode up on Paulo shuffling between home and church. This was the second time in his life that Agata had broken his heart and it was uncertain he'd endure. Maria stopped next to him. He looked up at her with tears running down his craggy old face. He didn't try to hide them from anyone, especially not Maria. She leaned over and handed him something.

"This is Agata's necklace, Paulo." He held it in his clenched fist and pressed it to his forehead. He shook and cried and cried out. He desperately needed her to get down, hold him and comfort him, but that was not Maria's way. It never had been and it certainly wouldn't be going forward. She reached over and patted him gently on the head and rode on.

She rode straight through to Nuevo Casas Grandes, the place the vaquero had told her she was most likely to find the bad men. She lived on cold coffee and tortillas and the cigars she'd gotten from the fancy store. She liked the cigars because they took her appetite away and kept her alert and awake. It would be her way from now on. When she was traveling she'd travel hard and fast and unrelenting. She wanted to get to the bad men before they moved on. She knew that such miscreants drifted. It would be easy to lose them in the big land.

The town hadn't changed much in the ten years since she had been there. She rode past the bastard Sanchez's shop. It was no longer a shop. It was boarded up. Enough boards were missing that she could tell it was nothing more than a shell.

She rode to the far end of town where the saloons and brothels were located and decided to visit the brothel first. It was still red and still well staffed with many sporting girls. Some of them sauntered out to regard her as she tied her mount to a rail. Several of them ooh'd and aah'd at Maria. She was beautiful despite the thorough coating of dust that covered her from the long ride.

"Come on in here, Chiquita, we'll get you nice and clean." They were not taunting her. Many of the girls would be delighted for the company of a delicate and pretty woman rather than the coarseness of an ugly vaquero or field hand. She smiled at them and removed her hat. One of them handed her a beer and she drank quickly. She bowed her head in thanks and regarded the one who'd given her the drink.

"Señorita, tell me of one of your women here about ten years ago. She was dark but had yellow hair."

"Ah, Lupina." The woman put an arm around her. She reached over and kissed Maria on the cheek. "Come with me, little doll, I'll show you." She stopped and regarded Maria. "Now, don't be upset. She is not well. She's old and she's a little addled."

The woman took her to the very room Maria slept in those many years ago. The bed, mattress and even the covers seemed to be the same.

The old prostitute was sleeping when they walked in and Maria's escort led her to a chair. Maria sat down and waited, falling asleep for an hour, until the bedridden woman awoke.

Maria regarded her. She was drawn in the face and Maria could tell that she hadn't much time left. She coughed into a rag until it was bloody and Maria helped her sit up.

"Do you remember me, lady?"

She did not.

"You helped me when I was a little girl. Juana brought me."

She brightened at hearing Juana's name.

"The little chubby one."

"Yes, yes."

"Whatever became of her?"

"She died."

"Oh, what a shame." She coughed again.

Maria gave her money, a big fistful of bills. The old woman was confused.

"You were good to me, lady. I vowed to thank you some day and now I can." Maria got to her feet and, reaching over, pulled the woman upright and straightened her in her bed. She patted her on the cheek. "You rest, lady. Just rest."

The other whores were friendly to her. They'd seen what Maria had done for Lupina and knew that she was not like them; they understood that Maria was special. She was not a peon or a bandit or a lady. She was a creature unto herself. Her escort put an arm around her but wasn't crass or mean or seductive. "Come with me, Miss."

She took her to an empty room in the back. It contained a big bathtub. It had been prepared especially for Maria. She stripped down and they took her outfit and cleaned it. She relaxed in the hot water, smoked a cigar and drank some mescal. She'd rest for a while and decided that now would be a good time to interrogate her escort.

"Tell me. Were there two men here in the past day? They would be from the south, wearing black boots to the knee and striped trousers. One had long moustaches and the other no hair on his face at all."

"Oh, yes. They were here. They had a lot of money. They had some things to sell from a church."

"And where are they?"

The woman was washing Maria's back and becoming too friendly. Maria gently pushed her away and the escort blushed.

"I am sorry." She grinned and bit her lip. "You are just too beautiful not to touch."

Maria rinsed off and got out of the tub. "Come now, darling. Pay attention." She dressed quickly so as not to distract the young whore. "Where did the two men go?"

"Oh, the saloon across the way. They've been drinking in there for the past two days. They are trying to gamble but no one will give them a game."

Maria was now dressed in her fresh clothes. She looked at a clock on the wall and then outside. It was nearly midnight. This would be as good a time as any.

She gave the woman some money and kissed her cheek. "You've been good to me. Thank you, darling."

She blushed again. "It was my pleasure, little doll." She smiled and rolled the money up, putting it down her front. "All my pleasure."

Maria walked across the street. She was surprised to be so calm. She'd never killed men before and she figured she'd be shaky or scared; at the very least, excited. She was none of these things. Her heart didn't race and her hands didn't shake. Her vision was clear and her breathing slow and deep. She actually felt good.

She walked through the saloon door and many men turned and looked at her. They'd not seen a woman like this before. None of the peons ever came into the bar and the whores always looked like whores. No ladies would ever come in and, if they had, they'd be in dresses, not dressed like a man.

Maria let them look her over as she lit a cigar and blew a great cloud of smoke at the ceiling. She looked to her left, then to her right. She did not see either of the men she was looking for.

She slowly walked the length of the bar and there they were, in a back corner, sitting together around a little makeshift table that had once been a barrel. Now it had a plank on top. There was a candle on the table. It was lit and there was a bottle of mescal and two glasses.

The men looked very drunk or sick or both. They did not look like ferocious bad men. They looked old and worn out; dirty peons with some fancy vaquero clothes. She did not regard them as much of a threat even though they both wore six shooters and had fancy dagas in the front.

Neither of them looked at her. She stood there for a while until everyone stopped gawking and went back to whatever they were doing before she came into the saloon.

She had gotten two six shooters back at the village when she got the Winchester and she wore one on each hip. She unholstered them, holding one in each hand by her sides. Still, no one paid her any mind and the bandits continued to sit, stupefied, seemingly not looking at anything. She walked up and stood before them until they finally looked up, squinting and trying to focus.

Maria kept the cigar clenched in her teeth. Her hands were full of her six shooters. She blew smoke around the cigar at the men. They looked at each other and finally at the six shooters in her hands, but they still did nothing. They just sat there.

Maria pointed the pistols at the men and fired both guns at the same time, opening a hole in the head of each man. They fell backwards off their chairs and onto the floor, great chunks of brain running down the wall behind them. She stood over them and fired again and again until both guns were empty and the men's bodies were torn open with most of their entrails spilling out of their abdomens.

The rest of the patrons dove for cover. They didn't know that Maria was the only one shooting and they didn't want to be hit by stray lead. Her ten shots smoked up the saloon so badly that there was a thick haze hanging in the air. It was pink in color from the mist caused by the blood sprayed from the slugs from Maria's guns. Everything was deathly still.

Maria looked around but no one wanted to fight her. No one wanted to arrest her or ask her what she'd done or why she'd done it. No one liked the two bastards from the south. Everyone was a bit afraid of them and they were just waiting for them to go away. Maria had done them all a service.

She dug through the men's clothing and found money and some little items from the church. She took their six shooters and dagas and stuffed them in her gun belt. One had a couple of gold teeth and she beat them out of his head with the grip of her pistol. She dumped the teeth in the glass of mescal to clean them and then put them in her pocket.

She regarded the barman and gave him some of the money from the dead men. She wanted to compensate him for the mess. She nodded to him and he nodded back. He seemed to have a just discernible look of satisfaction on his face as he waited for Maria to do whatever it was that she was going to do next. He had no interest in getting her riled. She turned and walked out.

The barman ran around the bar after her. He stopped at the entrance of the saloon and, standing on the long porch, called out to her.

"Miss?"

She turned as she was putting on her sombrero, her raven hair reflecting silver from the moonlight. He thought for a moment that perhaps she wasn't real.

"Yes?"

He slowly raised his hand and pointed with a trembling finger. He suddenly felt cold. "Those are their horses, ma'am."

"Thanks."

She rode hard with her little train of horses behind her. She'd go back to the fence. She was now as happy as she could be. He'd pay her and then she'd go visit the nice woman with the mean husband, the one who'd given her the flint and steel. She needed to thank her and she'd do it with the money the dead men's traps would bring.

This pleased her. She remembered the old man telling her stories on cold winter's nights. One of the stories was of old England, where there was a man who did these things. He was Robert Hood, or Roberto Hood, or something like that, she could not remember exactly, but he spent his days helping poor people and killing bad people. This is what Maria would do.

She decided to stop for the night. She made a fire and fixed something to eat. As she ate, she pulled out the paper from the Bible. She looked at the list of Commandments. She'd violated many of them in the past days. This was good and she looked up at the sky and held up her little fist and shook it at the heavens. "How do you like all that, God?"

She thought about the whore who helped her with her bath. It was curious because she'd not known women who liked women. It was flattering to her and she felt a little sorry for the whore as Maria had no interest in such things. However, she knew how she could break hearts. Now she broke the hearts of women as much as she did men. She looked up at heaven again. She wished she liked women so that she could be carnally involved with them because she was sure that would not please God and it was now her goal in life to anger God and mock Him and do things that would confound Him.

She remembered a time when the old padre talked about carnal things, that such activity was only for married people and it was for the making of children. So she surmised that it must be something that would make God angry, two women together carnally, that would certainly make Him angry because they could not be married and they certainly could not make babies.

She thought on that a bit and now that was another thing to hate God for. Why would God be angry if a woman liked another woman, or a man liked another man? The world was a cruel enough place and Maria thought, good for them if they found some comfort in the arms of another. What did it matter? It didn't and it was just another stupid rule put in place by God to torture mankind.

Maria thought back to her killing of the bad men. She was utterly remorseless. She could not have cared any less for them. She liked it. She liked the fact that everyone in the saloon did nothing to stop her. They knew. They were just not free like Maria. They were bogged down with their own sense of right and wrong. Or perhaps they were afraid or worried over what God would do to them.

They lacked the clarity of mind that Maria now possessed. She was completely free. She was free of fear, as she was not afraid to die. She was free of guilt, as she knew they needed to be killed and she had the guts, the nerve to carry that out.

It was a good thing that she was beautiful and strange in her attire. That was the most misleading thing about her and it would always, always work to her advantage. That would make the bad men hesitate. They'd look at her and think of bedding her or think that she was weak. They would not think of her as the one who was going to send them to hell. It was the perfect arrangement and she laughed to herself and thought about God's big mistake. He made her this way. He made her brave and good at throwing rocks and shooting guns and riding horses and He made her fearless and beautiful. He made the perfect killer and she was certain He didn't mean to do it. This was her joke on God.

All the musing made her sleepy and she slept among the horses and felt good. Tomorrow she'd swim in the sea and sell the traps and visit the pretty assistant and offer her some kind of gift. She'd think hard about that, as it would have to be a good one.

# Chapter X: The Fence's Pretty Assistant

The sea was as beautiful as Maria had remembered. The store looked the same but no one seemed to be around. She tied her horses to the hitching post and wandered around. She saw the house and looked at the window up in the garret and felt a flutter, a twinge of sadness at the memory of Juana and their time together in the nice bed. She remembered that she'd have to find the bad man with the ugly growth on his face and kill him. He would be next on her list.

A woman emerged from the house. It was the pretty assistant. She was still pretty but old-looking to Maria as she'd aged ten years. Maria still had the image of how the woman looked when they first met. She did not recognize Maria, but nodded to her as she wiped her hands on her apron. She wore her hair high up on her head. She had a pretty, delicate neck and Maria didn't remember this about her. She still had the kind eyes and Maria most definitely remembered them.

"I am Maria, lady. I am sure you do not remember me but another girl, Juana, and I came here a long time ago. We sold things from the bastard Sanchez's store.

The assistant smiled. "I remember you." She stepped back and regarded Maria. "Just as beautiful as I thought you would be."

"I have more things to sell to the man. Is he here?"

"No." She walked past Maria and regarded her traps. She looked at the horses and nodded and then at Maria. "He's dead."

"Oh." Maria looked at the woman and did not detect any regret. She decided not to pursue it.

"Do you have anything else?"

They walked inside and Maria produced all the dead men's traps. She pulled out the gold teeth and the woman recoiled. She grabbed a cup and held it out. "I hate teeth, disgusting. Throw them in here."

Maria complied and the woman rolled them around in the cup as if she was going to play craps with them. "They've got a lot of gold in them."

Maria looked up and could not help but notice the woman's eyes fixed on her. She felt like she had around the too friendly whore. She grinned and didn't mind. It would anger God.

"So you are the new fencer?" She laughed. "Fencer. It was what Juana called you and the man. That's very funny."

The pretty assistant didn't ask about Juana. She'd known enough bad things in her life to know that Juana's story was likely a tragic one and the pretty bandit would tell her about it if she wanted. There was no value in asking her such a thing.

"I am."

"Well, we will be good friends. I expect I will be bringing you many more things like these."

Maria stayed and the assistant gave her fancy wine she'd gotten from one of her thieves. It was good wine from France and it had been stolen from a train. The assistant kept it for herself because now that the man was dead, she could do that and did it often. She had enough money and didn't need to sell everything she took in. She kept the best things, particularly the wine and spirits of quality, for herself.

They were nearly drunk by that evening and Maria wanted to go for a swim. They walked down to the shore and stripped naked. Maria did not think the woman so old looking now. She was quite pretty naked and she felt the woman looking at her again and this flattered her. She looked up to the heavens and muttered something. The assistant asked her what she'd said.

Maria stepped into the water and turning over, floated on her back. The sea was so salty that she could do this effortlessly. She was drunk enough to tell the pretty assistant what she wanted to know. She grinned and said, "I was talking to God."

"Oh?" The pretty assistant swam up to Maria and put her hand on her head, leaned over and kissed her passionately on the lips. It was the softest, most tender kiss Maria had ever felt and she looked at the woman, then stood upright and put her palm to the assistant's cheek.

"I am sorry, Bonita, but I am not that way." She watched the woman's heart break and gave her a smile. "I wish I were that way, but I am not. I would like to make God angry by loving women, but it just is not my way. I am sorry."

The woman smiled and walked back onto the beach and dropped down upon the sand and stared up at the moonlit sky. Maria joined her.

"Why do you want to anger God?"

"Because God's a bastard and a pendejo and an alfeñique."

The woman laughed and stretched out on her side, resting her pretty face on her hand. "I've never heard anyone say such a thing."

"Oh, it is the truth. God has done nothing but torture me all my life and he's killed everyone I love. He's taken everything from me."

"I see."

"And so, I..." She looked the woman in the eye. "Do you know the Ten Commandments?"

"I do."

"I will break all of the Commandments to mock Him. And I plan to rob and steal and bring everything to you so that you can give me money. I'm going to help poor people because God is too much of an alfeñique to do this thing. And I am going to kill every bad man I meet. Every one."

"I see."

The woman was very calm and Maria thought at least the woman would try to argue with her or lecture her, but she did nothing but smile at Maria and look pretty in the moonlight.

Maria wanted more wine and walked over to their clothes and picked up the bottle and drank from it. She handed it to the pretty assistant and she did the same.

"Aren't you angry at me for saying bad things about your God?" She liked the woman. She seemed to be wise and kind and treated Maria like a peer, not like she was a young girl who knew nothing.

"Oh, He's not *my* God."

Maria smiled. She thought she was the only one who had not known of God. Everyone she met was a devout Catholic.

"You don't know of God?"

"Oh, sure."

The woman took another drink and was happy to discuss philosophy with the young beauty. She'd spent so much time either alone or with ignorant thieves. It was good to have a conversation like this.

"I grew up a very faithful Catholic. I know all about God and Jesus and the Virgin. I got baptized when I was a baby and I had my first communion and I had confession. I know all about it."

She was getting cold as the sun was down and the sea breezes were picking up. She brushed herself off and dressed and Maria did the same. "But I had my doubts over the years. I've not had such bad things happen to me as you, Maria, but I've had my doubts."

She smiled. Maria had now stopped drinking and was listening intently. She'd not known anyone who doubted as she had. "And then one day, someone brought in a collection of books they'd stolen. Many books that had many ideas in them and I learned about other kinds of people and other concepts of God and I realized that maybe the God that we've known, maybe He's not necessarily *the* God."

"*The* God?" Maria was intrigued.

"Yes." She smiled. "I understand why you are angry at *your* God, Maria. He, or at least what we've been taught about Him, leaves a lot to be angry about."

"What do the others say about Him? The other people?"

"Oh, lots of things. Some believe God is a force, not a human form. There's no God up in heaven that looks like an old man with a beard, and there never was any Jesus or the Virgin. They believe it is a force. And then there are people who believe in reincarnation."

"What is this?"

"It means when you die, your soul goes to another body. If you were good in life, you get a better body, but if you were bad, you get a bad body, and you keep living and dying over and over and over again." She laughed at Maria's expression. She was giving her many things to ponder and Maria was taking it all in, not judging, not telling the woman any of it was preposterous or right or wrong.

"So not everyone is like us, like a Catholic?"

"No, heavens no!" She felt funny saying heavens.

They eventually went to bed and Maria invited the pretty assistant to share the bed with her, provided she understand that it would not involve anything other than sleeping. They opened the windows wide and Maria remembered the lovely odor of the bedclothes. They needed plenty as it was chilly and this made everything all the cozier. It was nice to have another person share her bed and she felt happy. She didn't feel guilty now as the woman did not look so broken hearted and Maria was pleased that they could share a bed as friends and not complicate things. She decided to be a little bold.

"The man, the fence. Was he not your husband?"

"No. We never were. We were lovers. He had a tremendous thing, you know, down there." She grinned and pointed between her legs.

Maria laughed out loud.

"Really?" Maria had only seen one and that was Crisanto's. It seemed neither large nor small to her at the time. She had no real point of reference.

"Oh, my goodness, yes. And he knew how to use it. He was good at it."

"But you like women."

"Both. I like men and women, Maria. Like women better, but like both."

"I see." Maria was learning many things. Many, many very strange and interesting and wondrous things.

# Chapter XI:  Gold Tooth

Maria rode back east. She was getting good at crisscrossing the desert now and she liked it. She had enjoyed the lady's company and the woman had been good to her. She had a lot of money to give to anyone she pleased. She had to get to the nice woman with the mean husband back at her little village first. After that, she had no real plans.

This made her fairly giddy. No plan for the future. She had a purpose and she had a way to make money. It was all very exciting because she didn't have any obligations to anyone: no home, no man or family or children. It was not actually so bad to be all alone in the world.

The whore and the lady fence and the man at the saloon where she shot the two bad men all flattered her, too. She knew she could get a man whenever she wanted one. There was no hurry in any of that, either. She was a free agent and a free spirit and she had a purpose. It was good to be alive.

She thought a lot about being angry at God, especially in light of what the lady fence had to say about faith and this made her think of all those years growing up at the church. She smiled at the memory of her time with the padre. He used to become so frustrated with her. One time, and it was really the only time he'd ever been cross with her, was when she kept asking about all the preposterous things he told her about the miracle of transubstantiation, and the Virgin Mary's Immaculate Conception, and all the miracles Jesus performed. None of it really made much sense to Maria. She was very practical; a sensible and logically thinking person.

"Child!" He fairly shouted at her. "Some things, some things must be taken on faith. There's no explanation for them, you just have to believe!" And with that, she dropped it. She knew he didn't know and she knew she'd never get to the bottom of it. It just made the padre angry and sad and she didn't like him to be that way, so she just stopped asking.

But now, with the lady fence's take on it, it all started to come together for Maria. Maybe no one really knew any of it. Maybe no one ever would. Maybe all this about Jesus and priests performing miracles and the Virgin and even the crucifixion and the dying for our sins was just a lot of stories that people told and retold until they got muddled and no one really knew any of it.

She stopped at one of her favorite spots, settled her horse and made a good camp. The lady fence gave her a couple of bottles of the delicious French wine. She drank one and ate some jerky and beans. She missed the lady fence. She thought about the woman seducing her and it made her feel good and also, sad, because she thought the lady must be very lonely. Maria could not do or be for the woman and it must have been very frustrating as Maria knew how beautiful she was to the woman. She was more beautiful than almost anyone in all the places she'd ever been.

She pulled out her page from the Bible and looked the Commandments over again. They were good rules and necessary for a good society. Maybe there was something to them. Certainly people could not live against them. Was she really living against them? She did steal, but from people who needed to be stolen from. She lied but only with the best intentions. She'd take a man if she wanted one, but not a married one. That would be unkind to the man's wife and she would never hurt a woman or a child.

She killed, but again, it was right to kill the two bandits. She did curse, but was saying God's name in vain really all that bad? She thought about the lady fence again. Was God just a spirit and not an old man with a big white beard floating around on clouds up in the sky, in heaven? If he was just a spirit, or even just a great force, how could you offend Him?

She got sleepy and let the fire die down. She finished the bottle of wine and felt very dizzy. She closed her eyes and slept for a long time until a pine knot flared up and made the fire very bright. She sat up to find Juana across the way, chewing on a piece of jerky. Maria got up and sat across from her.

"You could have left a swallow of wine."

"I have another bottle. Do you want me to open it?" She was pleased to see her little friend.

"No, save it for tomorrow. That woman's right, you know."

"About what?"

"God and heaven and such."

"Really?" Maria was intrigued as she thought that Juana must know, she was dead and in that world. "What of this reincarnation? Is that right?"

Juana shrugged her shoulders and Maria became a little annoyed.

"What sort of answer is that?"

"I don't know, Maria. I don't know." She grinned at Maria. "Look, I'm sorry. I don't know, but she's right, and you don't have to be mad at God so much."

"Oh, so you think I should stop?"

"No. I didn't say stop. By the way, you did good by those bandits. My goodness, you were a wildcat."

Maria blushed. "Oh, that wasn't so hard. They were drunk."

"Doesn't matter. You don't need to have a fair fight with a pair like that. Just rub 'em out."

"Do you know what happened to them?"

"Oh sure." She became distracted and was looking for something else to eat. "How 'bout a cigar, Maria?"

Maria handed her one and lit one for herself and they smoked together.

"So, what happened to them?"

"Who?"

"The bandits I killed."

Juana shrugged.

"Damn it, Juana, stop shrugging. What happened to them? Did they go to hell?"

"I don't remember." She stood up and threw her cigar into the fire. "I've gotta have a pee." She got up and Maria became tired. She closed her eyes while she waited for Juana to come back and soon fell into a deep sleep.

She made it to the little village where she had lived for the first ten years of her life. It was pathetic and very poor and it looked even worse than she remembered. She rode over to where her hovel was. It was all grown over and she couldn't even tell where it had been. She thought about the old woman with the terrible treatment painted on her chest and the old woman telling her to wash it off as it stunk of shit. She smiled and was not so sad now at the memory of the old woman. She was always good to the old woman and she made her happy and the woman lived a long time, so she had a pretty good run of it. No one could ask for more than that.

She remembered how to get to the nice woman's shack and was about to dismount when she thought better of it. She was proud of her traps. Her horse was splendid. She had traded her stuff for a really fancy saddle that the lady fence had. It once belonged to a vaquero who was very fond of tooled leather and conchos. The saddle was very bright and gaudy and it looked better with a woman sitting on it than it did with a man. She wanted to show it to the mean man and watch him look at her. She wanted to see if he'd be a little humble and not so quick to call her a whore's spawn.

She stopped outside their door and called out. Soon a skinny man emerged and bowed respectfully to Maria. She was afraid that the nice lady and mean man had perhaps moved away. Suddenly the nice lady emerged and she squinted up at Maria. The sun was to Maria's back and she quickly dismounted so the woman didn't have to squint.

"Do you remember me, lady?"

"No."

Maria dug in her saddle bag and pulled out the flint and steel and the knife the woman had given her many years ago. "You gave me this."

"You are Maria."

"Yes." She grinned. "The whore's spawn."

Maria looked behind the woman, into the dark hovel. "Is he here?"

"Dead." The woman spoke automatically. She looked at the skinny man who bowed again and smiled, baring rotten teeth. He extended his hand and Maria took it. "This is my new husband."

They welcomed her into their home and the woman prepared a meal while the skinny man sat silently and smiled at Maria. They ate and chatted about the village and what had happened over the past ten years. They asked Maria no questions about her life.

"I need to give you something, lady." She stood up and pulled out a wad of money, rolled into a neat cylinder. She handed the woman the money and could see the confusion in her eyes. "This is a gift. You were good to me and I want to repay you. I want you to have this money, lady."

She looked at the skinny man and they looked at the money in the woman's hand. It was more money than they could make in a year. Enough money to buy ten times the goats they owned. It was money an aging couple could use.

"This... this is too much." She looked at Maria and her eyes were tearing. She looked at the skinny man who stood a little stupidly, not knowing what to do.

"I will not take it back, lady." She smiled and looked around. "How 'bout a little celebration?"

With that, the man found his voice and ran to a shelf. He grabbed a clay jug and poured for them all. They drank and smiled and Maria sat back, enjoying the happiness she brought to them; enjoying the realization that she had the power to do this again and again and she would.

Their celebration was interrupted by a neighbor. He poked his head in, scared and nervous. He was shaking nearly uncontrollably.

"They found her."

The woman began to cry and Maria followed the man out. "What is this, Mister?"

"A bandit." He tipped his head to the south. "He's been here for a week. He won't go away and he took a girl. A little girl. We didn't know what had become of her, but they found her. He, he..." the man began to cry. Maria had heard enough. She knew what to do and she instructed the man to wait with the nice lady and the skinny man.

The bandit had taken up residence in the nervous man's shack and he sat, cooling off and drinking mescal. He was fairly drunk and continuously called out for more food. A frightened, frail old woman was working diligently to bring him more beans and Maria intercepted her. She took the pot from the woman and indicated, with a finger to her lips, to be quiet. She told the woman to go away.

Maria ducked down through the low doorway and regarded the man. He was a fancy bandit, with a frilly embroidered shirt and tight trousers, a big beaver sombrero and he wore his long moustaches in a deep frown. He was a tremendous man, tall and fat and he looked like a bloated pig sitting on a mat on the floor by the fire.

"What's this?" He looked up at Maria and then slowly looked her over. He'd not seen this one before. He liked abusing children above all others, but a good looking woman would do.

Maria moved a little too quickly and pretended to trip. She fell toward him then caught herself, but not before dumping the pot's hot contents into the man's lap. He howled in anger and pain and looked at her with hate in his eyes.

Before he could say or do another thing, Maria was on him, the little gun she kept in a sleeve pointed at the man's head. She fired and the lead ball slowly did its work on his brain.

He looked up, pondering what had just happened, tried to talk, tried to move, but nothing would work. Maria casually sat down beside him and watched him die. She leaned in close and regarded him. He mouthed words and she could see gold teeth. This one would bring some good cash.

They sat this way for a long time. The man still looking about, ponderously, stupidly, mouthing words that had no sound, wondering what was happening. Maria lit a cigar and smoked and blew smoke at his face. His nose wrinkled and he leaned his head back and sneezed. A great gout of blood flew out of his nose and blood and clear fluid ran from his nostrils and soaked his long moustaches, dripping onto his bean covered lap. He still said nothing.

And then, when Maria could tell he was about to die, she regarded him. "Hey, Mister." He looked up at her, into her eyes, trying to figure it all out. "I'm going to cut your goddamned head off when you die. You know why?"

The man didn't respond and she continued.

"So, when you go to hell, your body will wander around and you won't be able to see anything. You won't be able to hurt little girls again, pig. How do you like that?"

He seemed to comprehend, but Maria could not be sure. She was growing tired of all this and it was getting late. She wanted to move on and the bandit was not dying fast enough. She put the little gun behind his ear. She fired again and he flopped over. He was finally dead.

Maria had made inquiries about the man with the ugly growth on his face who she was certain had murdered Juana and decided to stay in the region a little longer. People did remember the man, but they'd not seen him for many years. The trail was cold. But, as she had plenty of money now, she felt compelled to stay around. Perhaps something would turn up and she'd have the opportunity to kill him.

She rode to the caves and wandered there all day then decided to camp a while. It made her feel very strange as many of her improvements remained. No one seemed to ever come to the caves and things would stay the same there from one year to the next.

She found her old bedroom. The mice had torn it up a bit, but it was livable. She put her horse in the box canyon corral and untied her prize. It was leaking a lot and she resolved to soak the head in the nearby stream for an hour or two. It would not damage the head and it would drain all the blood and brain fluid out and make it easier to transport. She was not really sure what she was going to do with the head, but this bandit made her especially angry and she wanted to heap as much shame on the corpse, the memory of the man, as she could. She would, from here on out be especially brutal and merciless to anyone who harmed a child.

She took the head out of the sack and looked it over. She was able to get one of the gold teeth out quite easily as the tooth was dead and could be pulled without much effort, but the other one was a different story and she didn't want to damage the head by bashing the tooth out with the handle of her six shooter. So, it remained and looked odd, reflecting sunlight because the head now had a slack jaw and the mouth hung open as if it were catching flies. She breathed in deeply and spit a great gob onto the face, then tethered it and held it under water with a big rock. This had the desired effect, and when Maria came back several hours later, the head was as pale as porcelain and no longer drained blood or other fluids.

As she shook the head dry, she heard someone coming and stood, one hand on the grip of her six shooter and the other holding the head by its long hair. She looked like Perseus standing there.

The prospector seemed to know the story, as he averted his eyes from the head, looked down at the ground and held up his hands in surrender.

"Howdy, Miss."

"Hello."

He was a gringo and the first one Maria had met, other than the priest. He wore heavy work clothes of canvas and pulled a mule along behind him. He did not expect to find another human being out here, let alone a beautiful female holding a severed head.

Maria returned to her task and wrung out the burlap bag. She put the head in and tied it off.

"That fellar's seen better days."

Maria smiled and liked the little joke. She liked the prospector right away. He had an old six shooter hanging precariously from his waist, but he was obviously not in the bandit trade. He looked as if he was just a hardworking man looking for gold or silver or some other things, anything really, to keep his belly full.

She invited him to eat with her in the cave and he offered some of his own food for the pot. They sat down together and he began muttering words in English. She made out most of the words. He did not cross himself and she thought that was interesting.

"What is this religion of yours?"

He grinned. "I'm a Christian." He began eating and hoped that would be an end to it, but he could tell it was not. Maria had something on her mind.

"You did not make the sign of the cross."

"I'm called a Lutheran, ma'am." He went back to eating.

"What's this Lutheran?"

"Oh, pretty much the same as a Catholic. Just a few changes. It's all the same, really." He grinned. "All the same God."

"I am doing His work." She looked at the head lying near the fire. "When God doesn't do His job, I do it for Him."

"Hmm." The man didn't look up from his meal.

"What's this, hmm?" She demanded. He was giving responses the way Juana had and it was starting to make her a little angry.

"Nothing." He smiled and then became serious. He could see she had a lot of anger and it was sad to see in such a young and beautiful woman. He decided to continue. "It's a cruel world, Miss. It's a cruel, cruel world."

"Yes." She stood up and remembered the last bottle of good French wine. She liked this man and he knew some things she didn't know so she thought she'd loosen his tongue and try to learn something. He still wouldn't talk, so she probed.

"Why do you think God makes such a cruel world, Mister?"

"Oh, He doesn't."

She flashed with anger. "Oh," she pointed at the head, "you know this hijo de puta? You know what he did? He abused a little girl. You say that is not cruel?"

"No, that *is* cruel. I said God doesn't make it cruel."

"Huh!" She got up and poured for him again. He was disarming, this prospector and she was not necessarily angry at him now.

He thought he should clarify. Go ahead and just say it all and get it over. She wasn't going to let it go and his cryptic answers were just going to exacerbate the situation.

"Ma'am. Look at it this way. In the animal world, there is no cruelty. The animals eat other animals, that is true, but it isn't in malice. Only humans can act cruelly. So, if God made all of the universe and the animals, both human and non-human, and He didn't make any of the other creatures of the world cruel, and only humans can be cruel, then how can we say God is responsible for cruelty?"

She'd not thought of it that way.

"But He made that pig cruel." She pointed to the head.

"No, no ma'am. He made the man, but the man chose the cruel and wicked path. God is not like a manipulator of the marionette..."

"What's this marionette?"

"A puppet. You know, puppets, the kind on a string, the manipulator is the one holding the strings, making the puppets dance or whatever they do. That is not God."

She sat quietly and got cigars out. They smoked and she looked into the fire. This man was very interesting. She thought of something else. "So, when a person, when a person has many bad things happening. That's not God punishing them or making them have a bad time? That is what you are saying?"

"Yes, ma'am. That's what I am saying. We have a great gift. We have something the other animals in the world do not have."

"A soul?"

"Well, yes, we have that, but that isn't what I was going to say. We have a thinking, reasoning brain." He pointed at his head. "We have free will."

"Free will?"

"Sure, you know, the ability to pick and choose. You can be good or you can be bad. You can sleep all day and not work or you can get up and make something of yourself, make something for yourself. You," he pointed at her and she suddenly remembered the old woman showing her the reflection in the mirror. "You can make the world as you wish."

He shrugged, "Of course, there are some things out of our control. If I get struck by lightning, or fall off a cliff by accident, or get wiped out by a bandit or an Indian," he smiled, "no offence, I can't help that. But I can control a lot of my life. And that, I think, is God's plan."

He poked at the fire and continued. "It's like, God kicked it all into motion, but then He stepped back, left us alone and let us figure it out. We can make good choices or bad and, of course, bad things do happen to good people and it's not their fault, it's just bad luck, but we need that in order to be really free. We can't have it both ways, we can't be free and then expect God to come in and intervene and make the bad things not happen to us. That's not possible."

She thought a lot about that. The old woman was very wise and now this prospector was saying a lot of the same things. She wondered why the padre was not so smart as them. He had more book learning. It was as if his teaching was a sort of opposite teaching to this: That we were powerless. That only through the faith in the church could we survive. Like we were forever children who just had to sit there and take it and pray to the statues in the church and hope that God and Jesus would be merciful to us.

She liked the prospector's take on it a lot better. She felt grown up, like a grown woman thinking this way. She had free will. She could manipulate her own world as she saw fit. Not be some puppet, a marionette, like the prospector said, with the padres or God or the church holding the strings and making everyone act a certain way.

She suddenly felt energetic, excited. She got up and wiped the dust from her pants. "You are a very smart man!"

He blushed and looked at the fire. "Oh, no ma'am. If I was smart, I wouldn't be out here, in the middle of nowhere with a mule, looking for bits of rock."

"You *are* smart, Mister." She grabbed him by the hand. "Come with me, Mister. I want to show you something very nice."

She took him to a spring she had discovered when she was here with Juana. The water bubbled out of the ground hot and further down there were pools that mixed with cooler water. They formed a comfortable warm bath. She stripped down to her underwear; she did not want to distract the man or give him any ideas and she was not interested in anything more than a warm swim in the pool. He smiled and did the same and they were soon swimming together and soaking and Maria could tell that it was good on his old, stiff joints.

She lit a cigar for him and stuck it in his mouth then one for herself and they smoked together and soaked and tried not to fall asleep.

Maria lay back and blew smoke at the clouds and watched the smoke drift away. "Mister, someone once told me that gringos are all assholes."

The prospector sat up to avoid choking on his smoke. He laughed out loud.

Maria continued. "But you are not an asshole at all."

"Thank you." He got himself under control and stopped laughing. He wiped the tears from his eyes. "Ma'am, assholes are everywhere. No one country has cornered the market on 'em. There's gringo assholes and Mexican assholes and even Canadian assholes. I'm sure there's assholes all over Europe. They're everywhere."

She thought on that. Of course he was right. She reached over and kissed him on the forehead and then regretted it. He was falling in love with her and she felt sorry because she could not, like with the lady fence, oblige him.

He knew it too and resolved to take a deep breath and wait for the flutter to subside. He leaned back against the silt bank and soaked. "Ma'am, I will tell you, this is living."

She sold the head to the prospector as he had a use for it and she was tired of carrying it around. He didn't have much money, so she sold it to him cheap. It did have the gold in the tooth, and that was likely the only gold the fellow was going to get any time soon. He just could not find enough in the region to pay for the expense of extracting it.

She resolved to go and would leave him at the cave. He seemed to like it there and she welcomed him to all she'd done. She smiled at him as she rode away, "Adios, Mister."

It felt good to tell him to be with God, it didn't anger Maria so much anymore and she knew it was because of the man that she felt this way. She looked back and could see he was crying and she wanted to stop. She continued on and then did stop and ride back.

"What's wrong, Mister?"

Tears ran down his face and he rubbed them away with the palms of his hands. He smiled and moved his head from side to side. "Nothing, ma'am, nothing at all. God be with you, ma'am. God be with you."

## Chapter XII: Colonel Charles Gibbs, Esq.

Maria found herself in a lively town that she'd not visited before. She found some Indian women there selling beautiful silver jewelry and decked herself out accordingly. She let them pierce her ears and she got some pretty earrings to go with the bangles on each arm. She looked stunning in her new finery and decided that she would begin collecting pretty ornaments and wear them wherever she went. This would be more confounding to men and would help her maintain the upper hand.

She looked into her mirror and was pleased and thought that she'd better not wear these around the lady fence as that might break her heart further. She felt a little wicked and proud at that thought. Not that she wanted to hurt the lady, but it was a nice feeling to know that someone loved her and desired her so much. She thought about the prospector, too. It was something Maria would have to be careful about from now on. She broke hearts everywhere and she didn't intend to do that. She didn't like making good people sad.

She wandered through town and nearly ran into a stately looking man, a gringo with long white moustaches and white hair. He was tanned dark by his time in the Mexican sun and he was dressed impeccably in hunting clothes. He stopped Maria and arrogantly put a hand to her face, then looked at his entourage of fellow hunters.

"My, my, and my New York friends wonder why I love Mexico so much."

The men all laughed and Maria stood still and looked the man in the eye. She held her face still as he patted her cheek and waited for the men to walk away. She looked back and one of the men sneered and tried to impress his little party by commenting that he didn't know that Buffalo Bill's Wild West Show was in Mexico. That elicited a great laugh and Maria thought that these men needed a lesson.

They were all in the big saloon eating steak, their horses tied outside. They hired a peon boy to guard the horses and he sat in the shade and dozed and waited for the men to return.

Maria walked up on him and handed him a cigar. "How much are they paying you, muchacho?"

"Un centavo, Miss."

"Hah." She looked the horses over and noticed that one had a fancy scabbard with a queer looking rifle in it. It was not like anything Maria had ever seen. She looked back at the boy and smiled and handed him a pile of coins. He looked at them, astonished. It was more money than he'd ever seen.

"Do you know magic, muchacho?"

"No, Miss."

"Well, it is time you learned. I'll give you all this money if you disappear. You know how to disappear, don't you, little one?"

"My mother says I disappear all the time, lady. I know how to disappear."

Maria smiled. "You are a smart boy. She waved her hands in the air, like a magician. "Poof, boy. Disappear."

He stood up and held the money in his hand. He began to trot off. "Lady?"

"Yes, my little one?"

"If you ever talk to them," he pointed at the saloon, "those gringos. Tell them that I said for them to go to hell." He was gone.

Maria surveyed the horses. They were very fine animals. She wished she could steal them all but knew this was impossible. Instead she walked to each and cut the cinches on every saddle. She took the fancy rifle, scabbard and all, and tied it to her saddle. She mounted up and rode down the street. She turned and, tapping her mount's sides, got him into a canter, than a full gallop. She pulled her six shooters and fired through the saloon's windows and kept going. She was gone.

The gringos came after her. They all, every one of them, put a foot in the stirrup and ended up on their backsides in the dusty street with a saddle in their laps. The colonel was red-faced and angry. He'd not yet fired his new rifle, and now it was gone.

Maria rode and laughed and was so happy that she thought she'd burst. The men paid dearly for their little joke and now they'd be paying the harness maker to put new cinches on their saddles. She stopped and pulled out her prize. It was an odd looking contraption. She played about with it and pulled on a handle and made the action open. It had a cartridge in the chamber and she took it out and examined it. It was huge. It was more than twice the size of the bullet her Winchester fired and she wondered at the gun's power. It had a long brass tube attached to the top of it and this, she surmised, must be some kind of sight. But she couldn't see through it and the whole thing just made no sense to her. She put it back in the scabbard and looked through the pouch sewn onto it. It held many more bullets. At least she'd have ammunition for the rifle; she just needed someone to show her how it all worked.

She continued riding south. She knew the gringos well enough to know they'd not let this go. They'd use her as quarry instead of some silly deer and they'd track her and find her and there'd be no telling what their punishment would be. This pleased her no end. She was excited to be the hare for a change. She was never the hunted and she was keen to match wits with this old American colonel.

She was initially disappointed as it took them two days to get even remotely close to her. She left a trail a blind man could find and she watched with satisfaction as they never got within a mile of her. They were constantly stopping and camping and she was growing bored. She'd have to stop as well, so they could catch up.

She ran them through a great thicket of scrub and mesquite thorns and the posse got torn to pieces. She wasn't more than thirty yards from them at the time, but they couldn't even see her. She made certain they could hear her, though, and she taunted them as they cried out like little school girls when the sharp stickers got them.

At one point, she was afraid she'd gone too far. One of the men, the young one who commented about Buffalo Bill's Wild West show, was blubbering, crying and having a little tantrum and Maria actually felt sorry for him. She could hear the pain and frustration and panic in his cries and decided not to do that to them again.

Some of the men fired in the direction of her voice and Maria laughed at them. They couldn't touch her and were nearly driven mad by her jeers. She was impressed when the colonel made them stop. He did not want the hare killed, only captured. She developed a little respect for him because of that.

She eventually left them to work their way through the little thorn forest and rode quickly to a high spot and watched them from a quarter mile away finally drag themselves through and regroup. They were disoriented until she called out. "Yoo hoo, boys. Over here!" She waved and gave them just enough time to pull their guns. She turned and rode over the hill and out of sight.

Finally, after five days with no progress, the loss of two horses to horrible terrain and not an insignificant amount of skin and blood from many of the gringos, they decided to send a scout out alone. They had a pretty good one. He was a former army scout, a Chiricahua, and he did a good job finding her. Maria watched him from her false camp, she'd made lots of false camps so they could track her, then she'd actually camp a distance away, in the brush where she could ambush anyone who tried to attack her.

The Chiricahua was fascinating. Maria had not seen one before. He was from up north. He was smallish but stout and wore a mix of army and white man's clothing. He had a scarf tied neatly around his head. He wore a kind of breechclout which would have covered his private parts, yet he also wore trousers. It all looked very odd to Maria. He had soft moccasins on his feet that extended up to his knees. Maria was impressed with him until he dropped his trousers. Nature had called and he defecated near her mock fire ring. She threw a rock and clobbered him and he sprawled on his back, lying in his feces.

She walked up to him and poked him awake with her foot.

He looked around and then spotted Maria and smiled. It was the first time he'd gotten a look at her in a week. She held out a water gourd and he drank. She wet a rag and placed it to the knot she'd raised up on his forehead. She wasn't worried about him at all, she knew he'd do her no harm or try to take her captive.

Maria smiled as she watched him recover. "And you call yourself an Indian?"

He smiled sheepishly. "You are a good rock thrower."

She sat down beside him, lit two cigars and stuck one in his mouth. "What's your name?"

"Joe."

"Really? I thought you'd have some long Indian name."

"I do." He looked at the end of his cigar. He was enjoying it. He pointed off in the distance. "They can't say it, so I'm Joe."

She held out her hand. "I am Maria. Welcome to my camp."

They smoked together a while and Maria went to her horse and dug some mescal out of her saddle bag. She offered it to him. It would make his head hurt less. He thanked her and drank.

"You know, Maria, they will stop chasing you if you give the rifle back."

"Hah!" She spit on the ground and smiled at Joe. "Anyway, this is too much fun. I don't want them to stop chasing me. They cried like little girls coming through the stickers. That was more fun than I've had in a long time, Joe."

She regarded him. "I hope you didn't get hurt."

He grinned. "I know how to travel in the desert."

"Well, what do we do now, Joe?"

He wasn't certain. He couldn't go back. He'd be dishonored and humiliated. He couldn't capture her and he didn't want to, anyway. He hated the colonel. Hated all of the arrogant bastards.

"I know." Maria grinned. "You will be my hostage, Joe. You can always say that your horse fell and it was on top of you and I was able to capture you. Then you will not have been captured by a woman and your honor will be saved."

He grinned at the irony of being captured by a woman. It was preposterous even if he had been. He was most certainly her captive.

He looked behind him and doubtfully sniffed the air. "First thing is to get the shit from my back."

They rode all that day and the next and Maria let Joe keep his guns and big knife. He respected her for that. She slept soundly but every time Joe moved, Maria would raise up, head resting on an elbow. She was a pretty good Indian herself. She'd watch him and determine what had awakened him and then turn on her side and go back to sleep.

As they rode, Joe had a thought. "We could run them through the worst of the Sonoran. We might kill a few that way."

"I don't want to kill any of them, Joe."

He regarded her. He didn't expect such compassion. She read his mind and shrugged. "I only kill bad men. These men were just rude to me."

He shrugged. "You have not heard of the Indian Wars."

They rode on. She took a deep drink and handed her gourd to him. He had another thought. "We could run them across the Rio Grande, way up east, near Matamoros. It's near the Gulf and I hear there are sharks in the river there." He bared his teeth and made chomping motions with them.

"What are these sharks?"

He smiled at her and wondered at her innocence. "The great fish with the sharp teeth. The posse would hate that."

"But they might get killed." She drank again and then lit two cigars. "Come on, Joe. You are wanting too much blood."

They rode on and then had to wait for the lumbering posse to catch up. Maria did like Joe's idea though and turned north. She'd not travel so far east, but she did have some ideas about the Rio Grande.

They'd slept another night as the posse had to bed down again and they didn't want the hapless men to lose their trail. Maria was getting tired of doubling back to leave enough clues so that they wouldn't get lost.

She made a fire in a low arroyo and they settled in for the night. Joe had killed a chicken and they added that to their meal.

"Who are all these men so worried over this gun, Joe?"

"Oh, the colonel, you know. He's a big ass. Was in the Great War, back east where the white men were trying to rub each other out. Then when that was done he came out here to kill Indians." He poked at a fire and Maria gave him some mescal. "Then there's the Russian. Kosterlitzky. He's a rurale and he's with the colonel. He was having a lot of fun watching the colonel get angry about you. He doesn't really want to catch you."

"What's this Russian?"

"A man from way on the other side of the world. He came here and now he is turning into a Mexican. He's very odd. Very smart, but very strange. He left his country, they say, because he loves this place so much." He looked around and wondered how terrible the man's homeland could possibly be.

Maria lay back on her blanket and regarded Joe. He was good company and he was not a bad looking man. He was tough enough. She noticed him looking at her differently this past day and was waiting for him to make his move. He didn't disappoint her and she was impressed with his boldness.

"Why don't you bed down over here tonight, Maria?" He looked her in the eye.

"Oh, that's a nice idea, Joe, but no."

He shrugged. "You don't rut with Indians?"

She laughed out loud. "Well," she held up an arm, comparing her complexion to his. "That would be hard to avoid." She got up and adjusted her blankets. "No, Joe. And it's not you, I just don't want to."

He let it go.


They had to wait nearly until noon to get moving and Maria hated the prospect of traveling in such heat. She'd surely kill some of the gringo posse now and she felt sorry for them. She and Joe traveled north and eventually made it to the Rio Grande. It was swift and deep where they finally crossed and their horses had to work a little to get through the moving water. They made it and rested and dried off on the other side.

Joe mounted up and she knew he was going to leave. She regretted it as she enjoyed his company. "Adios, Joe."

He was gone.

The posse finally made it to the river and began to cross. They eventually all made it. When the last man was on the bank, and they were all dripping and exhausted and taking inventory of their progress, they heard a voice, way off on the Mexican side. The pretty bandit was waving her sombrero. "Yoo hoo, boys." She turned and began to ride away. "What are you doing all the way over there?"

Some of the men drew their guns but the colonel ordered them to stop. He raised a white flag and called back. "Please, Señorita, don't run away. We have something for you."

With that, the youngest and fittest rider crossed back. He handed Maria a parcel and she opened it. There was a note which she read with difficulty. Handing it to the young gringo she said, "Read this for me, please."

"To the wild creature who we never caught. God be with you. C. Gibbs, Esq."

Maria held up a watch by the chain. She removed her sombrero once again and gave a deep bow. Kicking her horse into a run, she was gone.

Many years later, in his memoirs, Colonel Charles Gibbs wrote that if he'd managed to capture the beautiful wild Mexican who ran him through the hell of the northern Sonoran desert, he would have proposed marriage on the spot. No one was certain whether it was an attempt to make amends for all the Indians he'd slaughtered or to serve his own vanity. Perhaps he was actually expressing his true feelings. No one would ever know.

# Chapter XIII:  Alejandro del Toro

Maria sat in a great field, cross-legged and frustrated as she poked and pried and pulled on the fancy rifle. It was beginning to make her very angry and she decided that she might just as well smash it to pieces with a rock. The thing was nothing more than a fancy club. She raised it over her head and prepared to dash it to pieces when a kindly old voice startled her. "Temper, temper, little one."

She looked up, astonished that such a big man could sneak up on her so silently. She looked at him and realized he had her. She'd never been caught unawares and it was very confounding.

"Who are you?" She demanded and gave him a defiant look.

"Oh, that is my prerogative, little one. This is my land. I get to find out who you are first." He casually walked up to her and took the rifle from her hand. He looked it over and at the silver plate bearing the original owner's name.

"Maria." She stood up and wiped her trousers clean, watched him as he manipulated the rifle. He casually unscrewed the caps protecting the lenses on either end of the telescopic sight, looked through it and grunted in satisfaction. It was a finely made instrument. He handed it to Maria and now everything about the gun made sense.

"Ay, chingao. Look at that!" She pointed the rifle at a distant rock and it appeared to be right on top of them. She loaded the rifle with one of the big cartridges and fired. She missed.

"No, no, little one." He plopped down on the ground. "Give it to me, and a bullet." Maria complied. "You shoot off the bones, little one." With that he sat like a great overgrown Buddha. With legs crossed, he rested his elbows on his knees and looked through the telescopic sight. He squeezed the trigger and dust flew from the rock.

"Bravo!" Maria applauded. She loved the new rifle. It was thrilling. She could now kill bad men from a long way off.

He handed the rifle back and she tried it. Mimicking his actions, another puff of dust flew up, right next to the old man's mark. She stood up and kissed him on the cheek.

He bowed as he removed his big beaver sombrero. "Alejandro del Toro, at your service, Miss." He shook her hand gently then stood back, moved her around in the light so that the sun shone on her face. He removed her sombrero and, gently taking her hand, once again turned her in a circle. "Oh, you are magnificent, little one."

Maria felt a little tingly. He was a kind old man and did not intend to bed her. There was nothing provocative about him. He just enjoyed her, as he would a fine work of art. "You come with me, little one. I have a place, a lovely pedestal on which to put you."

They rode for nearly an hour and Maria was impressed with the rich man. He was obviously wealthy by his dress and by the fact that they'd been riding for so long and the land was all his—if he had not been lying to her.

Eventually, they made it to his hacienda and it was the grandest she'd ever seen. Many men came out to attend to them and take their horses. The big man took her by the arm and escorted her to his veranda. A table had been laid with a white linen table cloth, silver utensils and crystal. She'd not seen such opulence in her life.

"I hope you are hungry, little one. We dine in an hour. But before we do," he led her to a grand bedroom at the end of a breezeway off the courtyard. It was lovelier than the lady fence's garret bedroom. "You can get cleaned up in here."

She looked around as he left her alone and assumed this was his bedroom; the grand bedroom of the hacienda's Jefe and, in preparation for his return home from his morning ride, his servants had prepared a hot bath.

Maria wasted no time. She stripped and stepped into the hot tub and began to soak. It was heavenly. She reached for a cigar. An old woman handed her one before taking her outfit off for a good cleaning. She gave Maria a pretty dress to wear in the meantime.

After a wonderfully luxurious soak in the tub, Maria dressed for dinner and joined Alejandro del Toro on the veranda. She sat down and finished her cigar. The big man handed her a better one. "That thing you are smoking, little one, I've smelled better steaming dung heaps. Try this."

She did and it was heavenly, too. She sat, barefoot and cool and more beautiful than she'd ever been in her life. She was wearing the lovely dress and had just had a proper bath. She certainly was enjoying this Jefe and his hospitality.

"Jefe?"

"Uncle."

"Uncle?"

"Yes, you call me uncle. I am your uncle forever." They ate together and he began telling her the story of Alejandro del Toro but, more importantly, he told her the famous story of the beautiful wild creature who'd bested the gringos and Emilio Kosterlitzky, the most famous rurale officer of the time.

Maria was pleased. She did not know that she was famous and it tickled her to think that what she had done would make her that way. She found it all a bit of a lark. It was the easiest thing she'd ever done, evading and leading the posse on a wild goose chase, yet it seemed very important to the Jefe. No wonder he was being so good to her.

"Jefe, eh, Uncle?"

"Yes?"

"How does such a big man move so quietly? You are the first one to ever surprise me."

"Hah! My little one, I was a bandit before your mamma was born! I can sneak, run, shoot, and hide from anyone better than men not nearly so fat as me." He grabbed up a fistful of his paunch and shook it up and down.

"So, you are not a rancher?" Maria looked around and wondered if he'd slaughtered the real owners of the place.

"Oh, this is all mine. All mine. I built it from nothing, from stealing cattle and horses from the gringos. Ha ha!"

She was pleased with how happy he was to show off to her. He was remarkable as he did not take very much of it seriously.

He stood up abruptly. "Come with me little one." He held out his arm and she took it. He walked her to his stable. "This might be someone you know."

The vaquero from her village was there. He was Uncle Alejandro's chief groom. He nodded to Maria. "Hello, child." He held out his hand for her and she took it. "Remember me?"

"I do." She smiled and then looked on at her new uncle. "He told me to go after the bad men. He was the only one to tell me the right thing to do."

"We have something for you, Maria." With that he opened a paddock door and brought forth a wonderful surprise, a palomino filly decked out in Chica's tack. "Her name is Alanza."

Alanza stood at just over 14 hands tall. She had power radiating from her beautifully muscled body. It was obvious that she was descended from fine Arabian stock. Her eyes were huge and very dark, her ears tiny and tipped ever so slightly toward each other. Her muzzle was so small that it could fit in the palm of Maria's hand. Tipping her head as she pranced up to

Maria, her golden coat shone with dazzling highlights. Her mane, tail and forelock were a soft ivory and flowed in rippling waves. Four white socks reached halfway up her legs, almost to her knees, and her hooves were large platters; feet designed to travel easily on desert sands.

He smiled as Maria took the horse's soft muzzle in her hands and pressed the animal's face to her cheek. She looked her in the eye. "Hello, my Alanza."

"Alanza." The vaquero looked on at Maria. "Do you know the meaning of this name, Maria? It means ready for battle. She's the smartest animal I've ever known, Maria. She'll be a good match for you."

Maria, in one motion was up on her back. She grabbed the reins and leaned forward, her body pressed seductively against the filly's mane. She whispered in her ear and tapped her sides. Even with Maria's bare feet, Alanza knew what to do. Maria needed no spurs and they rocketed down the paddock aisle and out into the late day sun. They rode hard into the desert, she and the animal as one. Alanza was just as happy as her mistress. Maria knew the horse and the horse knew and immediately trusted Maria. She was light and balanced and knew how to sit in the saddle, knew how to hold on and move with the creature. They both wished for something to jump.

They came back lathered and happy. Maria jumped down and ran to the Jefe. She reached up and kissed him on the neck. "Thank you, my uncle. Thank you."

She turned to the groom and held out her hand. "Thank you." She pulled him in close and kissed him on the cheek. "You are a good judge of horses. I will treasure her for the rest of our time together on this earth." She looked back at Alanza who was now being walked around by one of the men, cooling off and shaking her head periodically from side to side.

She looked especially pretty in Maria's tack.

# Chapter XIV: Deutsch-Mexikanisch

Maria endeavored to make her first foray into the United States. She was well equipped with her many gifts and supplies from her new Uncle Alejandro and Alanza was the perfect companion. She decided to speak only English to Alanza as practice for when she mixed with the gringos. She was excited about the adventure into the new land and felt confident since her meeting with Joe the Indian and the gringo posse and American colonel. They surely couldn't all be assholes en el Norte. But it was a rich land, according to Uncle Alejandro, and Maria thought she could do some good marauding and stealing up there. The gringos would not be likely to miss anything as, according to the Jefe, they had so much.

She had time to think and did not even have to do much with Alanza. She'd point her pony and the animal seemed, as if by telepathy, to know what her mistress wanted and where she wanted to go. The weather was good and the new land added to the adventure. Maria had never traveled in this part of the country.

She had time to think about what had happened to her over the past many months. She had encountered many new ideas and people. All this gave her a renewed confidence, especially as it regarded her war with God. Maybe she didn't have to fight with God. Maybe the old padre did have his set of beliefs, but so did the lady fence with her ideas of reincarnation, and the prospector. Even Joe, the Indian, had his personal philosophy, though Maria never did get to ask him much about it. But he did have a faith and it wasn't the padre's. It was Apache faith.

So, perhaps they were all of the same purpose and maybe it was not necessary now for her to fight with

God. She could live with God and God with her. She'd do and act as she saw fit, and not worry over what Commandments she broke or didn't break. She knew—was convinced—that she had a pure heart and her intentions were always the best. She knew that breaking the Commandments were not always necessarily bad.

Like killing, for instance. It was perfectly acceptable to kill, she knew that. Some people just plain needed killing and Maria would oblige. She knew that it was not a problem or a sin.

And then there was stealing. Again, if someone had so much that they could get along without a few pesos or some cattle or a fancy rifle, then it was not so terrible to steal from them. It was just adjusting the imbalance, like in nature. When things start to get out of hand, nature balanced them out.

And then there was this idea of being with men, or women, really. She grinned about the lady fence kissing her and the whore washing her a little too enthusiastically. What could be the sin in all that? There was none. Of course, no one as yet had struck her fancy. The women were out of the question, it just didn't suit her to be with women, though the lady fence's kiss was the most tender Maria had ever known, it just did nothing for her. And Joe the Indian asking her to bed down with him was nice, but she didn't fancy Joe, or the old prospector, she could tell he'd fallen in love with her too. But all in all, what sin could there be in bedding down with another when not married? She didn't want to be married, but she certainly wanted to do the act again. It was good when she did it with Crisanto, and she knew she wanted to do it again, some day.

She thought more about all the hearts she'd broken already. She hadn't tried to do that, but she had. She was just simply too beautiful, inside as well as out. She got a little flutter at that thought. She was special. She knew she was special and she thought that she should be thankful to God for all that. He had created her and He made her beautiful and intelligent and a good rock thrower and she could shoot well and ride as if she and Alanza were one creature. Now she had the fancy rifle from the colonel and could kill bad men from a long distance.

So, even if the prospector was correct, that God kind of kicked this all into motion, but then left us alone, gave us free will—which made good sense to her—it was still God who'd given her the basic materials for her magnificence. This made her very happy and she resolved to be a good steward of this perfect being. She was magnificent and would not squander what she had been given. She would still do her marauding and stealing as she planned. Still make things right in the world that were wrong and still redistribute the wealth as she saw fit, but she'd do it in an honorable way.

She stopped to light a cigar and smoke. In the distance, to the east, something caught her eye. It was a queer sight as there did not seem to be any form of human life in the area. Certainly this was not a campfire, it was too big. It was also too big to come from a homestead and it was too concentrated to be a brush fire.

She decided to investigate and Alanza quickly obliged. They were upon it in short order and Maria was sad to see another bandit attack. Bodies were strewn about and the men who'd killed them made certain to add to the carnage by defacing and defiling most of the poor victims. They were all men except for three old women and Maria could see by the path left behind that the bandits had taken hostages. This is why the homesteader's corpses did not include young women or children. Maria surmised that it was likely the work of Sombrero del Oro or at least some of his men, as he was a famous slave trader from way back.

She surveyed the site and resolved to drag the victims to the burning wagon. The bandits, in their blood orgy, killed the horses pulling the wagon, so it could not be taken as booty and the black hearts ruined it instead of leaving anything of value behind. Maria lacked the ability or inclination to dig so many graves but thought burning the corpses preferable to having them picked apart by scavengers.

As she moved amongst them, she saw a corpse appear to be moving. She investigated and saw an infant, barely alive, under an old woman's body. She apparently died trying to shield the babe. Maria grabbed the infant up and held her and the child awoke and began a terrible loud cry. She was dehydrated and hungry and would likely not have lived another hour had Maria not discovered the terrible site.

She made a camp upwind of her makeshift pyre and thought hard about how to get something into the infant's body, as the child was yet too young to do anything but suckle. Maria soaked her scarf and placed it into the babe's mouth and the child sucked it with abandon. This worked and she continued this way for more than an hour. At least now she was hydrated a little, but Maria knew the child needed milk. She needed to get her to someone who was nursing or at least to someone with goat or cow's milk.

She looked up at the sky and figured she still had a few hours of daylight. She thought hard about what to do. She'd seen no one in the past full day. Uncle Alejandro's ranch was too far. She looked at the little one who was so exhausted from all the work at extracting the water from the scarf that she had fallen back to sleep.

There was nothing for it and Maria soon realized that the bandits were the only hope, the only salvation for this little one. She walked Alanza down the trail, after the bad men. Judging from the fire and how much it had consumed of the wagon, she figured they were not more than ten miles or so away. The captives were likely traveling on foot and this would slow them significantly.

Maria pulled a rebozo from her pack and fashioned a sling. The babe rode across her chest, her tiny face pressed against Maria's breast. She could feel the baby breathing; it was a good feeling. She could not help but remember her own dear Rosario who'd not made it so far. She wondered at that. Wondered if this is what it would have felt like, what it would have been like if her own little one had lived.

The babe awoke crying and Maria was impressed with how loud such a little package could scream. This would not do. It would not be possible to sneak up on the bandits with a crying baby and she thought hard about what to do. Maria had nothing for a baby. She had water and mescal to drink. She had beans and jerky and a few tortillas to eat. She had many good cigars from Uncle Alejandro, but she had no milk or nipples or nursing bottles.

She had a thought and offered her a breast. The child took it and worked at it like a ravenous little beast and Maria immediately had her doubts. It was as if a rattler had taken hold of her nipple and she was not certain any of this was good for either one of them. But eventually the poor child settled down and resolved to suckle for comfort rather than sustenance, as if the little one knew this was the best her savior could offer for now. They both were able to relax, Maria riding a little more quickly and the babe quietly falling into a world somewhere between slumber and wakefulness.

Maria leaned forward a little in the saddle to ensure that her sombrero shaded the child in the late day sun. She, too, became a little dreamy, drifting off as she let Alanza take them to the bad men. She was now in a world with her little Rosario, the suckling babe triggering the primordial bond, the longing and the ache deep in the pit of Maria's womb, the instinctive happiness only known by a mother with her suckling babe.

It would be dark soon and Maria looked a little odd, a scout peering from the scrub in her vaquero outfit, wrapped in her red rebozo with a babe latched to her bosom.

She hauled out her fancy rifle and looked through the telescopic sight. She could see them all well enough. There were four women and three girls. There were four bandits. She moved and the baby became unlatched and began to cry. Maria ran back to Alanza. This would not do. She could not kill all the bad men in this state and she could not leave the infant alone. Something would have to be done.

When it was fully dark she snuck up on the camp. The bandits had the hostages tied together in a group. They tied them with rope at the neck and had kept them without food or water. This was done to make them more easily controllable.

Maria picked out the infant's mother immediately. The poor woman was in a daze. She stared at nothing. Her dress front was wet, her leaking breasts adding to her discomfort and pain.

Maria looked at the bandits having a good time. They were getting drunk now and paid no attention to the hostages at all. They knew that the desert was a perfect prison. Escape was futile.

Maria moved fast. She snuck in and cut the rope from the woman's neck. She held her finger to her lips and commanded all of them to be quiet and they complied. She grabbed the woman by the hand and pulled her along. Once they were a hundred feet away, she pulled the baby from her breast and handed her to her mother.

"Here, lady. Take your baby. She's a little beast!" She smiled and tucked herself back into her blouse. "Ay chingao, she has eaten them, I think."

The woman looked at Maria and then at her baby. She was convinced that the child was gone into the Great Beyond, and seemed unable to fully grasp what was happening. She pressed the infant to her breast and the child went to work. They made it to Alanza and sat down.

The woman looked at Maria, who did not look much different from the bandits. She was afraid of her and did not speak.

Maria lit a cigar and gave the woman her water gourd. She handed her some jerky and the woman ate. "Danke." The woman bowed her head then regarded the baby. She switched breasts and was feeling better as the pressure was finally relieved.

Maria looked the woman over. She did not understand her strange words. She resolved to ask her questions in English. "You are not an American?"

"Deutsch." The woman hesitated. "German. I, German."

Maria considered her. She was a big woman with pale skin and brown hair. She did not look like any person Maria had ever seen. Maria smoked and watched the woman with her baby and thought it a good idea to give her a little mescal. The German took it and drank, coughed a little and smiled. "Gut. Danke, eh...thank you."

And now Maria had a chance to try her English some more. "Lady. Tomorrow, we will get the rest. You sleep now. It will be all good tomorrow. I promise."

The German understood and settled down to rest, the infant cradled in her arms. The baby was content and quiet and, as Maria drifted off, she could hear the woman softly crying. Maria was happy. She shifted a little and reached inside her shirt. She held her hand up, certain it would be full of blood. Her nipples were sore, but intact. She smiled and muttered to herself as she shook her head, "Little beast."

The first bandit's head came apart and even Maria was impressed with the rifle's awesome power. She quickly worked the next bullet into the chamber and hit the next man a little low, tearing a hole through his throat at the Adam's apple, shattering the vertebrae and making the man's head tip as if he'd fallen asleep. He dropped down next to his mount.

The other two finally realized they were under attack and took up defensive positions. The shooter was too far away to see and they did not know where to hide. She hit the next man in the back and his breastbone exploded, but the shot did not kill him outright. Great gouts of blood squirted with every beat of his heart. He sat and watched it until he died.

The last one had had enough. He threw himself on his horse and rode as hard as he could into the desert. Maria was right behind him on Alanza. She'd put the big rifle away. She quickly caught up with the man, who was completely panicked and firing his six shooter wildly over his shoulder. He just wanted to get away.

Maria was amused by this and equally angry. There was no sin worse, to her, than to abuse a baby or a child and she resolved to make the bad man pay. She galloped up alongside him and he pointed his six shooter at her. She was so close that even a scared bandit couldn't miss and he pulled the trigger as Maria smiled at him.

"Hah, no more bullets, muchacho." And this was true. The bandit yanked on the trigger again and again and heard nothing more than the click of the hammer falling on spent primers. He turned away from her, looked forward and urged his mount on, trying to get his horse to outrun her. But this was impossible. Alanza was more fit and carrying less weight. Maria continued to ride alongside.

"Careful, muchacho. You might fall." She taunted him and he became angry. He pulled his big knife and began slicing the air in her direction. He didn't know her game and was uncertain what to do next, but Maria soon allayed his anxiety. With a quick movement, she drew one of her six shooters and held it toward the man's head as they rode side-by-side. Suddenly she lowered the muzzle and fired into the bandit's spine, just below his jaw. He flopped over like a ragdoll onto the desert floor, cart wheeling end over end as his horse continued on at a full gallop.

She rode up on him. He was lying on his side, doubled over and unable to move. Maria got down and stood over him. With some effort, she pushed him hard with her foot and he flopped over onto his back, the morning sun beating down mercilessly on his face.

"You are in a lot of trouble, muchacho." She lit a cigar and blew the smoke at him. "Want one, muchacho?" She pointed at the cigar and he nodded yes. She knelt down beside him so that her face was now just a foot away. "No, sorry. Don't have many left. None to spare." She grinned.

His eyes rolled about; the pain was too much to bear, her bullet making it impossible to move anything else. He breathed in unsteadily and waited.

Maria reached over and stuck a finger in his vest pocket. She tore downward and found some money there. She went through the rest of his pockets and got a couple of rings and a necklace and one pocket watch. She put these in her pocket and then, reaching down, removed his gun belt. He cried out in pain.

"Oh, sorry." She shrugged and continued to strip him. She removed all his clothes until he was naked, sweat pouring from his face. The clothes had no value, they were essentially rags, but she did not want him protected from the sun.

"Well, I have to go now, muchacho. Bye."

"No, no." He cried out weakly, plaintively. "A bullet."

"Oh, no muchacho. I will not waste another bullet on you." She got her water gourd and opened it, took a long sloppy drink with much of the water running down her chin and neck. She looked up at the sun and then down at the man who was already starting to burn. She lifted the gourd and dumped the remaining contents over her head until she was soaking wet.

"Ah, that feels good." She reached down and, opening her shirt, exposed her breasts to him. She looked down at herself. "That little baby, she tore them to pieces, muchacho. Look at them."

He did and could say nothing.

"Muchacho, I want you to make sure to see me. See that I am a woman. A woman did this to you, muchacho. A woman." She breathed in and spit a huge gob onto his forehead. "There's a drink for you if you get thirsty later, boy." She wiped her mouth. "That's more than you gave the little one, isn't it?" Turning her back, she mounted Alanza and rode off.

The hostages were working on the corpses when she returned with the bandit's mount. They'd gotten their valuables back and all had a good cry. They were a resourceful lot and would soon have everything in order. They wasted no time.

Maria was proud; she'd never saved anyone before. It was overwhelming to see the people relieved, given another chance at life. They were a remarkable bunch in their resolution and hard work and Maria enjoyed listening to their strange language. It was fascinating.

They all regarded her and the woman with the infant brought the others together to greet Maria.

"Danke," they all announced in unison and bowed respectfully to Maria.

She smiled, "De nada." She looked at the sleeping infant. The child would be fine. She'd eaten on and off since being reunited with her mother and now they were both much better.

Maria put her hands on her own breasts, "She is a little terror, no?"

"Ah, meine Dame, when there is milch, eh milk, it is much easy."

Maria set up camp and took an inventory of what they had. Everyone would have to double up on horses, but they would all be able to ride. The bandits had a fair amount of food and water so they were pretty well provisioned. The women needed little direction in putting things in order and Maria soon realized that she was being waited on hand and foot. She must have had a puzzled look about this as the woman with the baby approached her, then looked at the others of her party.

"They are all very taken with you, meine Dame. They are thinking you are not real, perhaps, eh, a creature from mythology, ah, not human."

Maria smiled and felt herself blush. She looked herself over and realized that she must have presented a very strange sight, indeed. These women were used to frontier life, but by their own appearance, it was abundantly clear that they did not take on the garb of the land. They dressed in their mother country's style and in this Maria looked very different.

"Tell them I am just a human but I am not like the others in my land. They will not see more like me anytime soon." She lit another cigar and offered one to the spokeswoman who graciously refused.

Maria was not certain what to do now. These women and children were in the middle of nowhere with little left of their personal belongings and most of their party dead. They couldn't be left out here alone and the spokeswoman, seemingly on cue, began to talk.

"Meine Dame, we have very much long travel to go. We are going all the way to south, to Soconusco. Do you know this place?"

Maria had not heard of it. Had never been south of Mexico City. "I do not."

"Would you take us to this place?" She regarded her party. "They have all discussed it. They asked me to ask you. They will do whatever you say. We will care for you and pay you well if you will take us."

Maria smiled. She could get used to this. "Yes, we will go to this place. I will be happy to take you."

They stayed at the camp for the rest of the day and through the night. Maria watched them; they kept to themselves and spoke in hushed tones in their strange language. Maria was amused when she noticed them looking at her whenever they had the chance. They were a very formal and shy people. The little ones were slightly bolder, intrigued, but they still kept their distance. They were still a little afraid of the woman who looked and acted like a bandit man.

They had a meal and Maria could see that they were Catholic. This surprised her. They were not like the padre, yet were another group from another land. She'd been told that en el Norte there were many different kinds of people and she guessed that they were yet another bunch, these Germans. She'd never known of such people. She liked them. They doted on her and would let her do nothing and it reminded her a little of how things used to be with Juana, when they were living in the cave. Maria liked everything just so, and Juana would sit back, like a little princess and Maria would do all the work. These people were like Maria back then. They seemed to be driven, compelled to work all the time. No work was ever finished. They were efficient and, much like Maria, did everything just so.

The lady with the baby approached her again, just before everyone bedded down. "Mein Dame, they want to know, will it be permitted to go back to the attack place? We would like to bury our families."

Maria thought about it. She regarded the woman and then the others and thought about the horrific site. It would be difficult for them. She'd arranged the bodies respectfully but knew it would be an ugly thing to see. "As you wish, but

I did give them a good funeral. I am Catholic, like you, and I did a good prayer for them. They are safe from the wolves and in a good resting spot. It would be better to move on, but as you wish. We will do what you want."

She left Maria and conferred with the others. When she returned she said, "Mein Dame. We will move on tomorrow. We thank you." She'd been crying and Maria felt compelled to continue. They'd suffered in her country and at the hands of her countrymen.

"I am sorry, lady. There is much sorrow and cruelty in this land but please know, it is not all like this. We Mexicans, we are not like those men." She watched the woman breathe deeply and regain control of her emotions. "Was your husband one who got killed?"

She nodded. "And my father and grandfather and grandmother, mein Dame." She smiled weakly and looked down at her baby, clamped to her breast. "But this little one has survived." She looked at Maria and tears ran down her face. "Thanks to you, this little one is good."

Maria walked up as the German woman finished her prayers. She nodded and gave the woman a smile.

"Do you pray, mein Dame?"

Maria blushed. "Only for others, not for myself."

The woman sat by the fire and Maria offered her a cigar. She waved it off again. She did not take tobacco. "Would you have more of that drink you gave me before?"

Maria got out one of her bottles and poured the mescal. "Gut Schnapps." She held up the cup in a toast and drank. "Mein Dame, may I know your name?"

"Maria."

"Ja." She nodded. "I see that." She drank again. "I am Ulla."

They sat and drank for a while and regarded the sleeping camp. Maria liked her new friend and felt a certain bond since they had each lost so much. She wanted to talk. "I have been fighting with God."

"I see."

Maria regarded her. "I have had, like you, many bad things happen. I have only stopped being mad at Him, but still do not want to pray to Him." Maria watched for her reaction and continued. "I don't ask God for anything. He's..., He does not seem to listen and He..., He lets bad things happen. Things without reason."

The woman smiled and took another drink. Tears were running down her face and she wiped them with the backs of her hands. "I do not know, Maria. I do not think He plays any part in the badness of the world. I just do not know."

She was like the prospector in this and Maria was a little surprised as the woman had lost nearly her whole family. Before Maria could speak, Ulla continued.

"One could say that God sent you, just as easily as they could say that God sent the bad men." She took a deep breath and her voice was quivering. She was remembering the attack. "But, I do not think that God has so much time... so much time to do for us... do for us or not do for us. I do not think that it works in such a way." She smiled at Maria. "I do not think that reason is a part of any of it. It is just a great mystery."

Ulla stood up and approached Maria, held out a cup and Maria poured. "But I am glad you found us, Maria. We are all glad we found you."

They drank into the night; neither was tired and they were enjoying each other's company, the spirits, and camaraderie.

Maria continued on the subject of prayer. "I never did get anything I prayed to God for."

Ulla smiled. She was quite drunk now and had stopped crying. "He is not a genie, Maria."

They both laughed at that.

"Then what do you pray for, Ulla?"

She became quiet and her eyes filled with tears. Maria was sorry for asking. Ulla looked Maria in the eye and then at the dying fire. "I just give thanks. I just give thanks."

Maria slept late, well into daylight and was treated to the German's hospitality again. They had all prepared for the trek south and had Alanza ready and Maria's traps packed and ready to go. They had her breakfast, including hot coffee, waiting for when she awakened.

She sat up and stretched and had begun to eat when she felt a light touch behind her and looked around. The smallest girl was standing behind her, stroking her long raven-colored hair. The child was beautiful and exotic. Maria had never seen such lovely hair on anyone. It was like corn silk or spun gold and the little one looked over at her mother. "Ist sie unser Schutzengel, Mutter?"

Her mother smiled as she worked and looked on at Maria reverently. "Ja, mein Liebling, das ist sie."

Ulla came over and smiled at Maria. "She wants to know if you are our guardian angel. And, she loves your hair."

Maria turned and held out her arms. The child came into them and sat on Maria's lap. She was about the age that her little Rosario would have been now, had she lived. She breathed in the scent of her hair and then held it up next to her own. She took a handful of each and braided her hair with the child's, "Like night and day, little one."

The child nodded, "Ja, mein Dame, ja."

Maria reached into her saddle bag and pulled out a good hairbrush, the one Uncle Alejandro had given her as a gift. It was made of fine bristles with a tortoise shell handle. She handed it to the child. "Would you brush my hair, little one?"

She pantomimed the brushing motion and the child understood. She nodded gravely, stood up and did a proper job. She worked diligently and soon Maria's hair was neatly brushed. She looked into her bag again and produced a matching mirror. She looked into it and nodded. "Good job." The child was pleased.

"Now, my turn." She took the brush and worked on the child's hair, glorying in the many shades of gold. It was the most beautiful and exotic thing Maria had ever seen. She patted the girl and kissed her on top of the head. "You ride with me, my little one."

The child beamed and looked at her mother for approval. Soon she'd be in the saddle with the beautiful schutzengel.

As Maria rode, she taught her new charge many words. The little one was a sponge and Maria was determined to give the child as much of a head start as she could in her new homeland.

Maria learned from Ulla of the hatred for Catholics in these peoples' home country and marveled at that. She could not understand how, if they were all of the same purpose, especially as they were all Christians, it could be that one group of believers in Jesus could hate and persecute another.

She regarded these new people. They were so queer. They were intelligent and resourceful and always working. They were so serious, especially to Maria, and they treated her as the peons used to treat the padre, as if she were some superior creature. She was simultaneously flattered and put off by this. Maria did not want to be treated as a superior creature. She was happy to use her gifts in battle and happy to have saved the people but she didn't want special treatment for this.

Ulla told her, as they rode along, about how the family had to leave their homes in Prussia and at first they were very excited to come to America, to try their hand at making a good life in Texas, where there were many of their kind. It was all working; slowly they were making headway, amassing some manner of wealth and success—much more than they could have ever achieved at home—but it was constant labor. Many of them missed their homes: the climate, the camaraderie, the familiarity of the food and the kinds of food the land produced. It was a bittersweet immigration.

And then her uncle, her father's brother, who'd left Germany many years before and made his way, first to Texas and then, finally, to Mexico, called them south. He'd taken advantage of Porfirio Díaz's call to foreigners to help modernize Mexico. He had a growing coffee plantation and they were all to meet him down there to help make it a success, live as a German community on the Mexico/Guatemalan border. It was a great and wonderful adventure, until they were attacked by the bandits.

They had a big meeting about it. They knew so little of Mexico. They knew it would be good to be Catholic in Mexico, as the overwhelming faith was Catholic, and they might enjoy continued freedom there. But Texas was not a bad place to be Catholic, either. There were many Mexican Catholics in Texas, and the non-Catholic Texans left them alone. They were, as Germans, left alone as well. No one bothered them and it was a good life. Ulla cried a little at the thought. She looked over at Maria and shrugged. "There was really no reason to leave Texas."

But they had left and now they were partway to their new homes, with Maria as their protector and guide. Ulla, as if she were somehow clairvoyant, in her shy, German way gently suggested that Maria stay once she'd gotten them to their new home. "You would be welcome in my home, Maria. You would be welcome by us all."

Maria blushed and held onto her tiny charge a little more tightly. The child looked up and smiled and patted Maria on the hands as if she understood everything her aunt was saying.

Maria entertained the idea of staying with this group of hard working, kind people. Perhaps she could. She'd never been so far south but she'd met a few Guatemalans in her time. They were very poor people, but they were kind and decent. They spoke in a strange dialect but were nice enough. Maria thought about all the Germans. They might be fun to live amongst for a while.

She'd been so content lately, wandering, not worrying over any of it. She was not ready to settle down, yet the little child in her arms felt so good and natural and she knew, deep in her heart, that one day she'd be a mother. She wanted to have a baby but the thought of finding a man, someone who could match her in intellect and nerve and zest for life seemed a daunting, perhaps even, an insurmountable task.

Would she find a nice German man? That might be interesting. She had not yet met a German man, but the women were lovely and she liked them. She liked the way they liked to work, as Maria liked to work. She'd enjoy making a home and keeping things in order, providing for her family and clan. She'd fit in with Germans. She thought about the vaqueros on Uncle Alejandro's ranch. So many of them ogled her. They weren't bad, there wasn't anything bad in it, and any one of them would likely be pleased to marry her, but she just did not know. She could not see herself living as a vaquero's wife. She could not see herself spending all her days in a kitchen making tortillas and preparing food and constantly washing and cleaning while her man was out on the open desert, having all the fun. She smiled at that thought. That was the problem. Maria liked to wander and none of that seemed compatible with having a baby and a husband.

She thought that she might do some more marauding and some gambling and turn this into a nest egg and buy her own place. Why not? She was a good gambler, the old man had taught her well and she had a good memory for numbers and counting cards. Most of the men she gambled with were very stupid or left everything to chance and she always beat them.

Uncle Alejandro had done it. He was a bandit and saved up his booty from the bandit life and turned it into a nice ranch. Why could she not do this? She could then hire women to help with the chores and the babies. She could be like the wealthy hacendadas who even had wet nurses so that they didn't have to feed their babies. Her womb contracted at the thought and her nipples ached. She might just as well not have wet nurses, she'd like to feed her own babies, but she could have cooks and women to clean. She could have a family and still be free to go and roam when she wanted. That would all work well.

But what kind of man would have this? So many men were weak and proud. They would not let a woman pay the way, or let a woman go off and roam when she wanted. This was a conundrum. Maybe she would have a man, keep him like a bull for breeding. She could have him as an employee and use him like a stud horse when she needed to become pregnant. She smiled at that thought. She remembered the old man telling her about the Arabs, the people of the desert all the way over on the other side of the world and the old woman got mad at him for telling Maria about the harems of the old sheiks. She could be the same way, except the other way around. She could have a harem of men, and she'd have them impregnate her as she saw fit. If any of them gave her any grief, she'd just fire him, send him packing.

She chuckled at her naughty thoughts. It would really make God angry, at least the God of the padre. She thought on that a bit. The Arabs had their God, and they had a harem, and they didn't anger their God with the harem, so perhaps she could do this without angering God.

By the third day and with little progress made, Ulla approached her new trail boss. "Maria?"

Maria looked up at Ulla and smiled. "They have decided that they want to take the rest of the journey by rail. Will you take us?"

Maria stopped and had Ulla bring them all together. They'd eat at this spot and make a plan. Maria dismounted and held the little one who'd fallen asleep. She kissed her and put her down in the grass. They were upon her immediately and Maria smiled as she was never able to do any work. The Germans had it all under control and this brought her back to her memory of mimicking Uncle Alejandro's past. She thought that she would pursue this dream. She'd amass a fortune and have servants. Perhaps she'd hire only German women as they were perfect in this way.

She looked up at the sun and remembered that the main rail line ran, like a spine, right down the middle of Mexico. If they turned hard west they'd hit it likely by midday next.

She told Ulla of this and she conferred with the others. They agreed upon the plan and in another day were on a train from San Luis Potosi heading south to Vera Cruz. After that, they'd wire for someone to fetch them from the plantation.

Maria was sad now. There was no reason for her to go with them on the train. Her work was finished but she didn't want to leave her new friends. She actually wanted to travel overland, escort them, get them to the plantation, even if it took the better part of a year. She wanted to see what it was like down there near Guatemala, see what a coffee plantation was all about. She remembered Ulla's offer and it didn't seem so difficult when she was going to ride Alanza all the way down there, but a train? She didn't need to ride along on the train; it would be safe enough without her.

She felt anxious about this and was giving herself a headache over it. She held her little charge in her arms and kissed her often on her pale cheeks and neck. The child was just too precious to resist.

Ulla read her mind again. "Maria, you must come with us. We will pay the passage for you and your pony. We must have you with us until we get there."

Maria smiled self-consciously. Ulla was sweet to her. She didn't know what to say, had nowhere in particular to go. "I..., okay, as you wish, Ulla."

# Chapter XV: Tapachula

When they finally arrived they were surrounded by Germans. They all had heard of the attack and the brave bandida who'd come to the rescue. They took turns shaking her hand and bowing formally to Maria. It was all overwhelming and her head was fairly swimming when a familiar voice called out.

"Are you still good at throwing rocks?"

It was Juana and Maria thought she would fall over from the shock. Juana saw this and was upon her, grabbed her in her big arms and held Maria tightly, nearly suffocating her. She pushed Maria back, at arm's length and looked her over. "You have gotten beautiful, just as I expected you would."

Juana had gotten bigger. She was near three hundred pounds now and sported yellow hair, like the whore back at Nuevo Casas Grandes, but Maria could see her, recognize her little bandit friend. "I know. You thought I was dead." She took Maria by the hand and led her to her home. She was the mistress of the plantation, Ulla's uncle's bride and Maria was somehow not surprised.

They sat and had American whiskey and Juana produced some good cigars. The parlor was magnificent and looked like no other place that Maria had ever seen. It was decorated in the German style, as was the entire house. It was what one would expect to see in the Bavarian Alps rather than the southernmost tip of Mexico. It exuded wealth and Juana did not actually look out of place sitting there.

Maria had a good look at her. Juana now dressed like the Germans and kept her hair in the German fashion, parted neatly down the middle, the ends curled tightly underneath. She looked so odd with her dark Indian skin and blonde hair, but from a distance she looked no different than her Teutonic family.

Maria drank the first whiskey down and Juana refilled her glass.

"I, I, Juana, that day, your burro came back covered in blood."

"Yes. Well, Maria, first, I am sorry that I never found you. I am sorry for that, Maria. I've known all these years that you thought I was dead but I could do nothing about it. I'm sorry, Maria."

Maria waved her off. "How did you..., how did it happen, Juana?"

"Well, that day, I was riding along and the man who attacked us, remember the one with the thing on his face? He was after me again. He grabbed me and I scratched that big ugly growth on his face. I don't know what that was, but he bled like a stuck pig when I did that." She laughed. "But he got really mean with me then and beat me. I kept running around and around the burro, and he'd reach over and take swipes at me. It was kind of funny, really."

She took a puff from her cigar. "Not at the time, but now it seems funny. And he bled everywhere. The burro was bloody, he was bloody, and I was bloody. Then the burro ran off and he finally got me and knocked me senseless."

She poured for them both again. "And then he took me way south, down beyond Vera Cruz and just kept me." She laughed. "He used to want me to do things for him, wash, make him food. You remember me, Maria, I am not the working type." She grinned broadly. "I used to do everything wrong, I'd scorch his shirts with an iron, I'd burn his food, mix shells in his eggs. Not cook meat all the way. I swear, I fed him more raw pork than anything. Bet he had worms." She laughed and continued. "I'd break things, piss in his coffee." She smiled at Maria's reaction. "I did, Maria, I used to piss in everything he drank. He always wondered at how I could ruin all the food, it tasted horrible. I'd even mix shit in his food. One time I made a stew and used chicken guts and didn't even clean them out. It was a mess. He got angry about that." She laughed.

"How long were you with him?"

"Not really that long, about a year. He just died one day. I came in, and I swear, I didn't poison him, at least on purpose, Maria. But, he was stone dead in his bed. So, I took everything and went farther south. I found the Germans and they liked me. I'm a terrible worker, Maria, you know, and these people are like you, always working, like back at the cave. But I am entertaining and I taught them Spanish and soon got a job in the house, taking care of the children." She smoked again, "Well, not really. I just played with the children, everyone else took care of them, did all the work."

"And how did you get to this?" Maria held out her hand and waved it across the room.

"Gerhard." She smiled. "He's Ulla's uncle and he's the partner of the people who employed me. He's a monster, Maria. I mean to look at. He is hideous: big, fat, old, and he is just the ugliest man in the world and he is madly in love with me, Maria. He, well, you'll see."

She stood up and took Maria by the arm. "I'm so pleased you are here, Maria." She kissed her cheek. "When we got the wire, I knew it was you. I knew it was my friend, Maria. Just felt it in my bones."

They were interrupted by a booming voice. "Schatzi! Where is my darling Schatzi?"

Gerhard Falkstein burst through the door and nearly ran them over. Maria regarded him and Juana had not exaggerated. He was a phenomenon of ugliness. He was heavier than Juana by a hundred pounds; he was old, red faced and pock marked. He had an enormous nose under which hung a gigantic, full-lipped mouth.

He looked at the two women and smiled broadly. "There's my darling." He kissed her sloppily on the cheek and regarded Maria. "Oh, you are the famous lady." He bowed at the waist and held out his hand. Maria extended hers and it was engulfed by his giant fist. He shook her hand energetically.

He suddenly began tearing at the tie around his neck, "Come, come, ladies, we must get ready. Go get ready, we are to have a great celebration." And he was gone.

Maria smiled and watched Juana watch her husband march out. There was love and care in her eyes and Maria was happy for it. "You see, I told you he was a beast."

"And babies, Juana?"

She shrugged. "Not yet, but it's not for lack of trying." She winked at Maria. "He is a good lover, and his sausage is very strong!" She smiled and led Maria into a guest room. "You get cleaned up and ready. Gerhard has a big party planned for you."

And the party was like nothing that Maria had ever seen and was exclusively in her honor. She could not keep her seat as one after another, the people of the community were compelled to honor her with a bow and a firm handshake. She was overwhelmed and, finally, Ulla came to her rescue. They sat together and watched the spectacle unfold. There was food Maria had never seen before: bread rolls and potatoes made in many different ways, noodles, sausages, pig, lamb, rabbit, and everyone continued to offer it to her.

She watched Ulla take it all in and the widow's eyes were wet with tears. Maria, distracted by all this hero worship nearly forgot that most of Ulla's family were now gone. She looked at Ulla solemnly and patted her gently on the shoulder. "I am sorry, Ulla."

"I have my little one." She watched as a band had started playing and several guests began dancing. Over on the other side of the room, bachelors milled about.

They were too shy or reserved to approach Maria and not certain if the appropriate time had passed for Ulla. "Look at them, Maria. They all want to be with you."

"And you." Maria regarded them. "This is not like my land, Ulla. Peons and landowners and hacendados do not mix."

Ulla nodded knowingly. "It is the same in our land, Maria. That is why we are here. We were, as you say, peons, in our land. Now Uncle Gerhard is a plantation owner. It is," she swept her hand around, as if to take them all in, "not this way with our family. We treat everyone with respect and they are all welcome."

"And no one was concerned about him marrying Juana?"

Ulla grinned. "Juana is a force of her own, Maria. No one can *not* love Juana. She is the opposite of us, we Germans. She is dark, she has a, how do I say this, she has no inhibitions." She looked at Maria. "I cannot say there was not some murmuring, but that was because of the difference in age, not the difference in race or social position. Uncle Gerhard is nearly fifty and Juana, well, much younger. But anyone with a heart can see how happy she makes him, and how, at least we hope, Juana is happy as well."

And, as if on cue, the lord and lady of the manor entered. Juana spotted Maria immediately and grabbed her by the arm, "Come on, I've got some nice sausages for you to meet."

# Chapter XVI: El Norte

Maria finally took leave of the Mexican Germans, despite Juana and Ulla's protests. She remembered Ulla crying and Juana with her little impish grin standing by, waving, as she rode off. She also waved to another new friend, a tall skinny Irish woman named Bronagh. She stood proud and gave Maria a resolute look as she rode off. It was Bronagh who did not try to keep Maria from leaving. Maria thought about Bronagh as she rode along.

Bronagh had married one of Ulla's cousins and, as with so many marriages between the Germans and the Irish, it was a complimentary union. It seemed unlikely, like mixing water with oil, but the resolute, hardworking, serious Germans and the wistful, dreaming, wandering Irish often made for good marriages.

She remembered Bronagh's words, in her lilting accent, "Go on with ya, girl. Get the wanderlust out of yer system, then settle down." She looked at Ulla and Juana, "The child's got the Irish in her, I swear it. The lass has Irish blood." And Maria was struck by that. Why did she want to move about so? The people, Juana's people wanted her so badly to stay. She could have had any of the eligible men, and perhaps, even if she were so inclined, some of the not so eligible men. They were a handsome bunch and so sincere, serious, even grave, yet she could tell that they had a deep respect and admiration for her.

She decided to take the coastal route and visit the lady fence. She had the gringo Colonel's watch and really had no use for it. Maria planned her day according to the sun and the moon, not a timepiece and she thought it would fetch a good price. She also had the bandits' guns and she'd gotten three gold teeth out of them.

She rode along and was overwhelmed by the beauty and vastness of the Pacific. It felt good with the constant breeze from the sea, and she wondered why more people did not live here. She thought about how difficult life was in the desert with the old woman, and now, near the sea, it seemed one would never go hungry; there was so much bounty from it and along the shore. She resolved to perhaps someday live somewhere along the coastline.

She made her way through various sleepy villages, ate her new favorite, fish, and traded with the locals. She stopped in Acapulco de Juárez and made a little fortune gaming there. She was getting better reading men who played cards or shot craps or generally spent their time gaming and she was especially successful at the ones that did not involve chance.

Maria hated chance, hated games of luck as she'd never had much of it in her life. She thought again about the old woman and the mirror. She stuck with games where the outcome could be determined by her intellect and skill, not by the toss of the dice or the turning of a wheel. It all came down to the only one in the world she could truly rely on: Maria.

And so time passed and weeks stretched into months and Maria slowly made her way north. She was in no hurry and had no intention of taxing Alanza. Her lovely horse was to be preserved and, as she'd brought along an extra mount, a nice dapple grey gelding, the three never got too tired in their travels.

She arrived at the lady fence's store on a late afternoon and was surprised to see it staffed by a pretty Chinese woman. The woman bowed to her and Maria asked about the lady fence. "I will get her, Miss."

She looked happier this time and she was pleased to see Maria. She presented her new assistant and gave Maria a knowing squeeze of the hand. Now Maria understood her happiness. "I am glad for you, lady. I am very glad."

They conducted business and Maria added to her bankroll. Soon she'd have enough to buy Uncle Alejandro out, if he were ever inclined to sell. They dined and then swam at the familiar spot and Maria watched the lady fence in love and it was a relief to see. Her companion was very sweet and Maria learned that she was from the states, from San Francisco, and was traveling south when she stumbled upon the lady fence's shop. They were immediately compatible and now inseparable.

After a time, the young woman went off to bed, leaving Maria and the lady fence alone. She regarded Maria as they shared another bottle of the French wine.

"You look tired, Maria."

And she was but not overly so. Maria looked older, more wizened, more cynical, more mature since the last time she'd visited the woman, and this is what the lady fence was now seeing in Maria. It made the fence a little sad. Maria was old beyond her years the first time they met, and now she was like a grizzled war veteran to the lady fence's way of thinking.

That night Maria slept alone in the garret as the lady fence and her new love had a proper bedroom on the first floor, next to the kitchen. The bed and sheets were as lovely as ever, yet Maria felt a little let down. She was saddened by the fact that she would not be sharing her bed with the lady fence. This was ridiculous as she was not emotionally or sexually attracted to the woman, but some human contact would have been nice. It was one of the things she'd hoped for, looked forward to as she approached the store that day.

She was lying in her bed and thinking of all the people she knew and wondered what they were doing at this very moment. Juana and Gerhard, probably making love; the lady fence and the Chinese woman below her, probably the same. The padre, praying. Ulla, nursing her baby, dreaming of her husband, making love perhaps to a new suitor? She hoped the latter. Bronagh, praying, perhaps just finished making love, or perhaps ordering her German husband to do something, some final chore before bed, then making love.

She snuggled deeper into the sheets, pressed her back against the soft mattress and remembered all those years ago with Crisanto. That was the best gift she'd ever given anyone in the world and she liked it, enjoyed it as well. She wondered when she'd find a man. It wasn't a matter of if, it was when. She wanted a man, she was sure of it. She didn't want just a rutting bull, either, or a harem. She wanted one man, her man who would love her and help her raise a family and give her all the love he had to give. She wondered what he'd look like.

He'd not be one of those in the saloon, she knew that. She didn't like any of them in the saloon. Even the ones who were good at cards did nothing for her and she wondered at that. Why not? She smoked and drank mescal and gambled, yet she found no man who lived that way at all appealing.

She thought about the men who she liked in her life. The old man was really the only one. He was the kindest to her. He taught her to be so good with everything that was useful and important; how to ride, shoot, gamble. He taught her all of it. She liked... she loved him as one would love her father or grandfather. Maybe that is what her husband would be like. It probably would.

Thinking about the old man got her out of her mood and she was no longer lonely. She was tired now but wanted to be cozy under the warm covers. She got up and opened a window and looked at the moon over the Gulf of California. It turned everything silver and the wind off the gulf blew in over her, through her, and she felt a great chill.

She hopped back into bed and scooted under the lovely sheets and the heavy covers and fell into a deep sleep.

## The Cage

Maria arrived in the states on a clear afternoon, surveying the town of Bisbee. It was one of the bigger towns she'd been to and it would be good for gaming. She had a nice bankroll and planned to double it. After that, she thought she'd move north. Someone told her of a town way up north called Flagstaff where there were lumbermen and she was also told that lumbermen were not good gamblers. She didn't know if this was true, but thought it would be a good adventure and this is what Maria wanted.

She rode along the bad part of town, which was substantial at this time in Bisbee, and looked for the most ornately decorated saloon. She came upon one that featured a giant gilt bird cage hanging from a fancy scroll bracket at the corner of the building. The sign read simply The Cage, in elegant gold-painted script. It was inspired by the success of the Bird Cage Theatre up in Tombstone where the whores had little cubbies along the walls hanging from the ceiling. This is where they plied their trade.

The owner of The Cage, a wily consumptive and alcoholic showman, decided to take it up a notch and hired a local blacksmith to make giant, human-sized cages which were painted gold. These he hung from the ceilings about the place and his girls would sit or stoop or stand in them and put on a little show. The big joke about The Cage was that you'd never take a meal sitting directly beneath one for fear of things falling down. Mercifully, the whores would take their customers to more private facilities to consummate the business at hand.

Maria regarded them and it made her feel as she had when she met the yellow-haired whore. It was just another example of the inhumanity one person or group of people could heap upon another and Maria decided to look away. She cast her eyes around the room and was immediately admonished by the barman. "No guns, Chica. No guns."

Maria eyed him and looked at the six shooters on her belt. Before she could respond a drunken man called out. "Awe, Hank, it's Annie goddamned Oakley." He leered at Maria; she did not know the joke.

"More like Anita goddamned Oakley. Don't give a damn if it's Carrie goddamned Nation, no goddamned guns in the saloon."

A raspy voice came into it over her head and Maria looked up long enough to see a skinny woman swinging in one of the cages. She was wearing underclothes like the yellow-haired whore, yet she wore nothing on her bottom. "Leave her alone. A lady needs a gun in this shithole. God knows you bastard men have 'em."

"That's the wrong kinda gun." The drunken man beamed at his own cleverness.

The woman laughed and began coughing uncontrollably and Maria could now feel a light mist of spittle strike her face and neck The skinny woman reeked of sex and sweat and body odor, her pudenda hanging there like a beacon of depravity, naked and thick with matted hair only inches from Maria's face. She was the most pathetic creature Maria had heretofore seen, yet she was somehow fascinating in her ugliness. Maria regarded her as she removed her guns and pointed them at the man menacingly, "I'm no Chica, gringo."

The drunken man laughed. "Come on over here, darlin', I've gotta gun for ya." He was bold now that Maria was unarmed. He reached out and grabbed her by the wrist.

Maria smiled at him and did not pull away. She leaned in close, so close that her breath tickled his hairy ear. She whispered, "Gringo, if you don't let go of me, I'll cut your balls off and shove them up your ass." She stood up as his face and grip slackened. She smiled at him and wiped her wrist clean, as if it had just been subjected to a dung heap. She walked on.

By this time Maria had amassed a rather impressive vaquero outfit. Her gun leather was even more ornately appointed with conchos and silver dots. She wore men's trousers and a pretty print blouse that unbuttoned down the front, displaying all the gifts given her by the Almighty. Even without her six shooters, she looked mean, tough, and this was remarkable for a beautiful woman who stood not much beyond a height of five feet. She was turning heads.

She finally settled on a table with serious men. These men did not ogle or comment about her appearance. They were businessmen and their business was cards. Maria watched them. One man was especially successful, as evidenced by the pile of money to his right. He was a severe looking man and Maria could tell that he was dangerous. She would play him and double her money as quickly as possible.

She sat down without asking and they all regarded her with contempt. "Whores don't sit at table, woman."

"Good, gringo, I will tell one when I see her."

"This is a thousand dollar table."

"Oh, I will settle for that, I guess." Maria pulled out a wad of bills, more than two thousand dollars, and laid it on the table. She lit a cigar and waited. She was dealt the next hand.

She bet conservatively until she could get a feel for what the players were about, what cards they had, what they had face up. There were many players at the table and Maria soon had a good grasp of what hands could be left for her adversaries to play. In short order she had a successful run and in two hours had increased her bankroll significantly.

She was becoming comfortable now and a little complacent. She did not follow the old man's rule to quit when she'd achieved her goal; the cards were good and her opponents mostly bad. The Cage was beginning to intrigue her and the whores were giving her some attention. They liked to see a woman besting the men.

One whore was especially attentive and kept Maria in good supply of drink and cigars. Maria refused liquor and sipped only beer. She did follow the old man's advice in this always. Never get drunk when gaming. It would affect the mind and she'd not win.

Soon it was down to the severe looking man, his friend and Maria. Most of the severe looking man's pile was now on Maria's side of the table, as were the bankrolls of her other opponents. This made the severe looking man very brusque. He still retained his poker face.

In another hour Maria was finished. She had amassed over six thousand dollars. The men were not ready to let her walk away. A crowd was gathering and finally, with the barman standing close behind her, the severe looking man announced, without looking at Maria, that she was a cheat.

Maria grinned as she rolled up her winnings. She pulled her blouse down to expose a little more bosom, just to throw them off a bit. It worked. She deposited the pile of money there and looked up at the gringo through the smoke of her cigar. "Gringo, you are like a little boy who lost his marbles at the school. Why don' you just take it, like a man?"

The pair leaned forward and the severe looking man's partner hissed in Maria's face. "We know you had a fellar planted behind us. He was signaling."

"That's a lie." One of the whores spoke up and Maria nodded to her without taking her eyes from the men. She should not have won so much, she thought to herself. She should have heeded the old man's advice, but what was done was done and now she'd have to deal with it, she'd have to move fast.

"Gringo. The only thing I did was count some cards, play a good game. If you are too estupido to do the same, then you needa make a better living doing something else."

"Count cards! Hah, never seen a pepper belly could count beyond ten." He leaned forward and Maria could not see his hands. Patrons began to move away, out of the path of any lead that might fly.

The severe looking man finally spoke. "You just go ahead and put that money back, Chiquita. You can keep what you brought to the table, but leave the rest. We'll see that those other fellows get theirs." He looked at his partner. "Lou's right, never seen a Mexican yet can count, never seen a Mexican yet who wasn't a cheat."

Maria stood up and leaned forward. She pressed her silver hideout gun against the severe looking man's nose and cocked the hammer back. "I know how to count to five, gringo. There are five bullets in this gun but I only need one to send you to hell." Maria glanced over at the whore who'd come to her defense. "Lady, go get my six shooters, bring them here." The whore quickly, happily, did as she was told.

Maria holstered one and now had the other cocked and pointed at the severe looking man's partner. "I don' play for fun, boys. If you don' wanna lose money, you maybe should play with matchsticks or beans. Tha's how I learned." She called out behind her. "Gringo barman, get aroun' here where I can see you." He did and now Maria slowly backed out of the bar. She made it past the skinny whore swinging above her in the cage, who was grinning broadly at the outlaw Mexicana. She kissed her palm and then blew it at Maria, looking on in delight.

The men were not finished with Maria. One of the bouncers appeared, a big ten-gauge pointed at her head. She looked him over. "Don' do this, gringo. They don' pay you enough." The man didn't move. "Please, gringo, don' make it so you go to hell tonight." He remained unmoving and Maria regretted having to kill him.

He did not really want to fight, she could see this in his eyes and he shook like a dog passing peach stones. He did not even have the presence of mind to prepare the gun; the hammers weren't even pulled back. The poker players and barman were making their move and Maria fired, punching a hole through the bouncer's head. She fired next at the severe looking man's partner, hitting him once in the chest; the barman took a lead pill to the neck. The smoke was thick and patrons were scrambling for cover. The severe looking man stood, stubborn, not going for his gun and not trying to hide. Maria hesitated. She did not want to kill if she did not have to.

"Finished, gringo?" She could see it in his eyes. She could see that he could not be left behind. He'd give her trouble and she remembered the vaquero's warning, "Never hesitate, Maria, never hesitate." And, as if on cue, the severe looking man went for his gun. Maria killed him with one shot.

She ran for the door and was quickly outside. Alanza was not where she'd tied her. She looked up and down the street. She'd have to escape on foot.

"Lady! Lady!" It was one of the whores who'd preemptively prepared Alanza and was waiting in an alley. Maria ran up and in one motion was on her beloved pony. She reached down and touched the woman's face. "Thank you, lady."

The whore blushed as she'd not been called a lady in a long time. Maria reached into her blouse and grabbed a handful of bills, thrusting them into the prostitute's hand. "Here's for you, lady. Get out of this business; get away from this terrible place." And she was gone.

She rode north through the night and at daylight stopped to check on her winnings. She had over seven thousand dollars and was thrilled. The American money was worth a lot more than the pesos. She would very soon be a wealthy hacendada.

As she rode she thought about the whores and this made her sad. The Mexicans were not really much better, but the Americanos were horrible to the women. Putting them in cages, like wild beasts, was probably the most upsetting. It was demeaning and it was humiliating when the gringos made fun of Maria. She knew she dressed strangely, like a vaquero, but does every woman who is outside of the norm have to be considered a whore? It made her angry. The thought of the Americanos being so mean to her for being Mexicana made her angry, as well. Maybe Juana was right, maybe the Americanos truly were all assholes.

She rode on into the desert and found an abandoned ruin on the side of a high hill. It reminded her so much of her cave-home all those many years ago. She hobbled Alanza and resolved to explore in it for a while. It was fascinating in its similarity to her old home in Mexico and this was something that made her realize how small her world really was. The US was not really a different land. It was the same. The desert was much the same, the Indians from all those many years ago were likely, more or less, the same. They built the same way with the same T-shaped doors and wall construction; all pretty much the same. It made her think hard about it all. She wondered at how similar it was before the white people came. Was it better then? Did the white men bring the greed and ugliness? They brought the guns and the horses, the old man told her that. Before the guns and the greed and the horses, was it better? Probably not. The old man told her the stories of the old Indians. They had the same weaknesses, the same cruelty, the same selfish aspirations, the same lust for gold. It was just being human and humans had a huge capacity for wickedness.

Maria thought some more about the gaming men. When she was in Mexico, the men she'd beaten weren't so cowardly. Of course, she'd not played for such high stakes. A man can lose a little and swallow his pride, but a man can't lose a lot, particularly from a Mexican, and a woman, and walk away so easily. She thought hard about that. She'd have to be careful.

She evaluated her performance at The Cage. She did well, but she'd blundered twice; first, by being too greedy herself. She had her goal and should have quit when she'd reached it. And, she'd hesitated killing the severe looking gringo. She should have just shot him and been done with it. But all in all, her fighting was good. She did not shake or get scared or nervous. Her vision was clear and her aim deadly accurate. She decided that it was a grand success and resolved not to make the mistakes again.

She camped at the ruin and enjoyed it. There was good water there. The place was phenomenal as it was so intact. Just like her cave in Mexico, it looked as if the inhabitants had moved out only the day before. Someone had been mucking around it recently, though, as there were ladders of recent construction about. Maria figured it had been visited recently, probably by travelers like her, too intrigued to pass it by.

She bedded down in one of the little apartments looking west and watched the sun go down. It cooled off and she needed a blanket. She stared at the stars and thought a lot about where her life was heading. She was content to be alone; liked the adventure. She was pleased to meet the whores and was sad for them, as she possessed a primordial revulsion to prostitution. She was no prude and did not have disdain for it because of the implications of sin. She had decided that was just another of the silly rules created by the padre to keep everyone under the church's control. No, it was the demeaning nature of it that she found so offensive. Many of the men who used whores were ugly about it. They did not treat the women with respect. There was no tenderness or love in any of it. And, added to the lack of respect and treatment of the women, she learned from Juana and the old man that many of the men brought horrible diseases to the whores. They, in turn, passed the diseases on and soon, many people were afflicted and eventually some died or were driven to madness.

She thought about the skinny woman in the cage. Who'd willingly put themselves in a cage? And she was there on display for all the world to see. Her most private part, set out like meat in a butcher's window. It made her very sorry for the whores but she didn't have disdain for them. She didn't blame them. So many had to do it to survive, they had no other recourse.

But it angered her to be labeled as one of them. To Maria, being a whore was kind of like giving up, and she'd never, ever give up. She'd fight, scratch out a living, survive but she'd never resort to that. She loved making love but being a whore was not about making love. It was, to her mind, giving up a part of yourself, the most important precious part of you, the part that made babies, made life and it was just giving up and letting that part be poked and prodded and inoculated with diseases and degradation. She would never ever be a whore and she resolved that men who called her whore would pay for it one way or the other.

## The Red Rocks and the Indios

Maria wandered further north with Flagstaff as her ultimate goal. She loved this land of Arizona. So often she could travel for miles and never see another human being and this suited her well. She was happy to be alone with her thoughts and was happy with how things were going in her life. As Bronagh said, she needed to get the wanderlust out of her system and this is what Maria was doing. She was a wandering Irish Mexicana and this suited her well.

She made it to a small settlement and was told that money would be paid for deer or elk. Although she didn't need money as her bankroll was now huge, she thought it would be fun to hunt for a bit. Maria liked industry, liked to have a purpose or task and she thought a little market hunting would be a good way to pass the time as she meandered further north.

What she did not expect was the fantastic, almost mythical, land of the Red Rocks. Nothing in her life had prepared her for this. Maria was certain that the place must have some kind of special aura about it. It simply felt different, as if there was some sort of cosmic or magnetic pull on her very soul.

She decided to camp here for several days, glorying in the strangeness of the place. Oftentimes, she'd ride Alanza into a canyon or to the base of a magnificent mountain and just sit, listening to the nothingness of the desert and wondering if she had not found her final place, the place where she'd live out the rest of her days.

At one point, the wind picked up and she and Alanza took refuge in a cave system. There she found petroglyphs of elk with Indians hunting them. It was prophetic and she felt even more tied to the land. Wasn't she an Indian, really? She was called a Mexicana, but her dark skin, the little village where she lived, the way she grew up, scratching out an existence, making baskets. It was all a very strange realization, as she'd not thought of herself as an Indian. The Indians were the Apaches and the Sioux and the others from el Norte, the ones who wore paint on their faces and feathers in their hair. But the more she thought on it, the more she wandered about, the more evidence she saw; the drawings on the rocks, the ruins in the mountains, the pottery shards on the ground, all these things led to her identifying herself as an Indian.

She looked at the stick figures stalking the elk. They had no weapons, but if they had, would they be spears or throwing sticks or bows with arrows? She considered her fancy rifle. It was really the same thing when she thought about it. They hunted to survive, and she hunted to survive. They likely hunted for pleasure, for community, just to show their gods that they could do it. Show that they could and would make it in this unforgiving land. And wasn't that what Maria was doing? Making her way, showing her God that she could do it, that she'd survive in the most unforgiving land on the planet, without help, without a man? She'd thrive; flourish in this land or in the most horrible saloons or the most desolate mountains, wherever she found herself, she'd survive and flourish.

When the wind died she was able to hunt. She would recreate the act that was played out over the past many hundreds, perhaps thousands, of years. She leaned forward and patted Alanza. "They didn't have you back then, my darling." Alanza snorted and tossed her head.

She settled on a young mule deer and in short order, was dressing it out. She sensed a presence and retreated, hid and waited and was surprised by the diminutive figures standing around the deer carcass. The children could not have been more than four or five, alone in the middle of nowhere. Maria approached them and nodded. They nodded back and then regarded the deer on the ground.

They had no Spanish and Maria did not speak the language of these Indians. They knew a few English words and through some rudimentary speaking and much sign language, Maria learned that they wanted the offal, which she happily gave up.

They all worked together and Maria resolved to bone the animal outright and gave the skin, head, everything but the meat, heart and liver to the children.

They were pleased. They were so excited to bring something better than a rodent or rabbit or hare back to their families. This would make a feast.

Maria watched them. They were getting everything red with dirt and she imagined what a mess it would be by the time they got back home. She signaled to them to bring her along and soon they were amongst a group of lowly hovels made of natural materials and a few sheets of discarded corrugated metal. This is where the children lived.

There were only women here and they regarded Maria with a solemn nod of the head. They were guarded, strangers invariably caused some sort of stress and trauma. No one with good intentions, it seemed, ever visited the Indians.

But soon they were disarmed by the pretty woman's charm and Maria resolved to give them the entire beast. She was rewarded with a bed in one of the Hogans and a festive dinner that evening. Maria was humbled and thrilled by these acts of kindness.

By sundown all the children were around her with the smallest ones resting in her lap. She kissed them on the head and sang and spoke to them in Spanish. They loved the queer language and mimicked most everything she said. One came out with Maria's things and this she found quite astonishing. They did not seem to have a concept of ownership or privacy of things.

The child found Maria's old mirror and was looking it over. Maria called her over, pulled her down onto her lap and held it up so the child could see herself. Maria smiled and looked, pointed at the image in the mirror, "This is the only one in the world you can truly rely on, little one. The only one in the world. You remember that."

The child looked at herself and smiled. She did not know what the pretty woman had said but it didn't matter. To her it sounded like magical birds singing in her ear.

The next morning, she was up first. Everyone was tired from the late night celebration and gorging on the fresh venison. They were not accustomed to eating so much, nor so well. Maria got Alanza tacked up and rode out again. She'd kill them an elk this time.

She rode out onto a plateau that opened up to a surreal view; red sky and red land. This morning the sky was the color of the rocks all around and she had difficulty determining where one ended and the other began. It was beyond comprehension and she waited and watched as the day unfolded. She patted Alanza again. "Is this the most wondrous thing you've ever seen, my darling? It is, for me."

And then, as if her whole body had been consumed by a tidal wave of emotion, she realized she was happy and filled with contentment. She felt the familiar flutter deep down in the pit of her stomach. She was truly happy and nothing, no matter what, could happen to her in the future that would ever compare to this feeling, this emotion of being in the moment, here and now, taking in all the natural beauty of this desert. It was one of the happiest moments of her life.

They had good luck and Maria killed a young cow. She marked the spot and rode back to the little settlement. Her band of helpers would soon have it broken down and back home. They all worked diligently and the youngest ones, the ones too young to really work with any level of effectiveness, played and sang and kept everyone entertained. Maria watched the workers to make certain they did a good job. She did not want red dust in the meat this time.

She stayed with the Indians a long time, every morning when she'd awaken, resolving to move on, the children would do something to keep her. One day slid into the next and before she knew it, weeks had passed. This did not bother her one bit.

The women loved her. They fussed over her constantly and Maria was like a princess. She could do nothing for herself as she was the huntress and kept their bellies full. The least they could do for her was keep her clothes clean and her Hogan in order. She was beginning to like this kind of living and it reminded her of the Germans.

In the evenings the women worked on the hides and Maria entertained the children. She taught them games, how to play cards, singing songs in Spanish and they taught her words in their tongue. They'd laugh when she spoke with her native accent and then mimic her and run away.

The end of the day was always the same. Three or four of them would cram into her Hogan and comb her hair. Maria had to count out three hundred strokes or they would never stop and she'd ultimately have to shoo them from her little room. Invariably, one or two would end up back with her and she'd awaken in the morning with a child pressed tightly against her back.

Eventually the wanderlust once again took hold of Maria and she headed north. Everyone stood in line and bid her farewell the morning of her departure. The children laughed and waved and some of the women cried. Maria would not forget them. They were on her list, the list of good people who'd done her a kindness and she'd be back with prizes and gifts, toys and candy and things to make their lives a little easier. She turned and smiled, "Adios, my lovelies, adios."

## Canyon del Muertos

Maria arrived at the settlement of Canyon del Muertos early one evening. It was the worst place she'd ever visited in her life. The place was like a deadly mushroom, doomed, slated for disaster from the time the first tent was erected.

Like a festering disease, it spread its malice and depravity over several acres.

It was named after a canyon that had to be spanned by the railroad and it seemed that one incompetent act, one blunder followed another. This was how Canyon del Muertos came to be. Even before the white man came, it seemed to be cursed. Legend had it that hundreds of years before, a tribe of Indians was caught at the bottom of the canyon as a flash flood swept through, wiping them all out. An enterprising settler with a Spanish flair gave it the name and that is how the place became known as Canyon del Muertos.

The reason this place was doomed was that there was no reason for a town to exist here at all. The place was the result of a comedy of errors, yet there was nothing comedic or funny about it. The railroad was being built and progress was swift, except for a mathematical miscalculation. The bridge built in Chicago and shipped down was short by just enough to cause a delay. While everyone waited for a replacement bridge to be built and shipped, little shacks were thrown together. As if by invitation, all the miscreants in the territory were drawn to the place.

In a normal town there was some reason for it to exist: mining, or ranching, lumber, or some sort of commerce. But there was nothing in this godforsaken place to attract normal, hardworking people. It was just the opposite; it was a place for the morally bankrupt, lazy and deceitful. It was simply doomed. Like carrion drawn to a rotten corpse, all came to Canyon del Muertos.

Maria was excited. Shots were fired up and down the street. Bad men walked up on her and leered, looking for an opportunity. Nearly every stranger who came to town offered some promise of capital. No one was safe and the town was known for devouring lawmen. More than twenty had been appointed in the first year and were all retired by gunplay.

She rode and calculated. Alanza was not safe, nor was her saddle or traps. She certainly couldn't ride her pony into a saloon. She thought about what to do when a boy caught her eye. He was a little vagrant, not more than ten, and he reminded Maria of Juana a little. He was quite fat for a boy living on the street. She called for him to come over to her and the lad complied.

"Little boy, where can I keep my horse safe?"

He nodded. Maria could see that she was casting her spell. The boy grinned. "Not at the livery stable, all thieves there." He spit tobacco juice at Alanza's feet.

"Okay, you are a clever boy. You have told me where not to put her, tell me where to put her, boy." She picked through a pocket, found a coin and tossed it to him.

"Follow me."

He ran through an alley and Alanza followed, past a small row of shotgun houses. They eventually ended up at the back of a brothel where a big woman was squatting, having a pee. She did not stand up as the boy approached, but eyed Maria indifferently.

"This lady needs to keep her horse somewheres that it won't get stole."

The prostitute shook herself a little and pulled up her bloomers. She was agile for a big woman. "A dollar a day."

Maria handed her five. The prostitute stuck this in her bosom. "For another dollar, I'll give ya a room, long as you don't mind the banging." She nodded with her head at the bordello behind her. "Some of these boys try to drive us right through the wall." She was warming up to Maria as she watched her dismount and take her fancy rifle and Winchester from Alanza's saddle. "You ain't lookin' for work I guess, honey?"

Maria didn't respond. She did not take it as an insult but she nonetheless didn't respond. The woman continued. "Don't get many Mexican gals up this way. You're sure a good ways from home, honey." She took the fancy rifle in hand, looked it over doubtfully.

"Where is the best gaming, lady?"

The whore pointed her in the right direction and Maria started walking. She decided to carry her Winchester as everyone in the little settlement seemed to be armed. She'd have better luck with the extra bullets and long barrel of the rifle in the event there was a shooting. Maria was counting on it. She looked back and smiled. "You take good care of my things, lady and I'll make you rich."

The whore shrugged and looked down at the boy, his mouth full of tobacco. She then spoke to no one. "If you live through the night."

The place was lively, as decadent as The Cage but not nearly so polished or rich. Maria knew she would not find thousand dollar tables here. She looked around and several men ogled her. Suddenly a giant of a man loomed over her. He was a Negro, the first Maria had ever seen and she was fascinated by him.

"He fancies you." Maria looked on at a scrawny man with rotten teeth, not much older than she was and she wondered how anyone could destroy teeth in such a short time. She looked at the man as she lit a cigar and the big Negro stared down at her.

The Negro was a powerful man; he'd spent his life working on the railroad. He stood well over six feet tall and had very dark skin, darker than any Mexican she'd ever seen. He wore an eye patch over his left eye but it wasn't big enough to cover the hideous wounds he'd received. Around it could be seen significant scars. He wore a green plaid work shirt with a large checkered pattern, accentuating his impressive mass. Maria could tell that he was not fully in control of his mental faculties and she smiled at him. "Hello, Mister."

The Negro turned his head, like a dog intrigued by a whistle. He responded with a sound similar to a huffing voice, "Yeahuh."

The scrawny man spoke up again. "He can't talk to ya. He got a tampin' iron drove through his head, Miss. He can only say 'yeahuh.'"

"I see."

She held out her free hand and the Negro took it. "What's your name, Mister?"

The scrawny man spoke up again. "He ain't got one; he's just called Big Black."

"Come on, Big Black, you sit with me." He followed like a giant trained bear and Maria noticed that everyone gave Big Black a wide berth. She should not have to shoot her way out of this saloon after winning.

She laid her money out and the dealer gave out the cards. It was another big game, which Maria always liked as she had more cards to count. Winning came easy this night, easier even than at The Cage. Most of these men were pretty thick. She wondered if lumbermen were as stupid as railroad workers. If so, she couldn't wait to move on to Flagstaff.

Suddenly a man reached over and grabbed Maria by the arm. He was not angry or aggressive, just excited to recognize her. "I... I know you! You shot up all those hombres down in Bisbee."

Several men looked the diminutive Maria over and then looked at the man. They liked a good story about shootings. Big Black noticed the man's hand on his new mistress and jerked his head a little sideways, grunted "yeahuh," and the man knew to get away.

"Sorry, Miss." He looked afraid of Big Black and this amused Maria to no end.

"God damn, I hearda that." The scrawny man with rotten teeth continued. "Goddamn, lady. That was sompin'."

The dealer continued and enjoyed watching Maria play. The saloon was so violent that every table had to have a dealer as the patrons could not be trusted to work it out for themselves. The dealer not only ran the game, but acted as enforcer and nursemaid. This dealer was an especially violent and hateful man, but he was enjoying Maria. He was not evil, just hateful and mean and tough.

He was hateful as he'd had a belly full of this place but could not move on and he enjoyed watching his regular customers lose all their money. He was sick of them, tired of their inane conversations and poor playing. He was tired of the senseless violence and tired of watching these animals kill each other. He was simply tired and now found something, someone, in the form of Maria to watch and enjoy and to break up the monotony.

He turned at one point and sniffed the air with a sour look on his face. "Goddamn you, I told you to stop that."

The man next to him smiled sheepishly like a scolded child. He passed wind as a hobby and was very good at it. Everyone hated him, he was disgusting. He tried to look at his cards and ignore the dealer, but just couldn't contain himself and started to giggle uncontrollably, like a little boy.

"Enough! Jesus Christ, you're stinking up the place worse than Hedor, there." He looked at the scrawny young man with rotten teeth who'd now clamped his lips tightly together and did his best to breathe through his nose. The dealer regarded Maria. "Can't you see there's a lady present? Jesus man! Show a little goddamned respect, a little goddamned self-control."

They played along some more and Maria was clearing the table faster than any farting man could ever hope to do. Few were left with enough money to ante up and now she was with Big Black and his rotten-toothed friend, the dealer, a gambler, and the windy man. They played for a while and Big Black gazed at Maria adoringly.

At one point the game was interrupted as the dealer suddenly lost control. The windy man had been farting for some time. Everyone just accepted it, but the dealer had reached his breaking point. Maria's presence was likely the catalyst. She'd cast her spell on him and the vapors unraveled him, the thought of a lowlife leaking the poisons from his body in the presence of such a beauty was simply too much. He turned; face red, veins bulging and his eyes as wild as a roped mustang. He looked at the man. "I swear, you son of a bitch, if you do it one more time, I'm putting a bullet in you."

The man suppressed his grin and sat, chagrined. He did not look at the dealer or anyone at the table. Maria tried to settle everyone down. She spoke into her cards. "Let me light another smoke, dealer, that'll help." She did and blew a big cloud in the direction of the windy man. "If that don' do it, we'll get the boy here," she pointed at Hedor, "to blow his breath around, it might improve the air."

They all laughed but the dealer was not amused. He had such rage these days and nothing seemed to help. He stared at his hands and continued to fume.

She won a big pot and couldn't help herself. She reached over and grabbed the Negro by the arm and gave it a squeeze. "How's that one, Big Black?"

He turned his head a little sideways. "Yeahuh."

Maria was ready to call it a night when the dealer suddenly stood up. His face was now beet red and he pulled his six shooter. He fired and killed the windy man.

The scrawny man leapt from his chair in horror, "Sonofabitch, you are a tough one!" He quickly shut his mouth to avoid offending the dealer further, then muttered under his breath, "Shootin' a man for fartin'. This is a goddamned wicked place."

Big Black and his scrawny companion escorted Maria to the whorehouse. The young fellow was a bit smitten now, as well, but knew that Maria was out of his league by a mile. He also knew that Big Black would kill him if he tried for the Mexican beauty. He walked along and talked incessantly, mostly about the town and Big Black. He had known the man the longest and knew what happened to him.

"He used to be smart, lady. He was settin' charges and had his face over a tampin' iron and the charge went off, blew the damn iron right through his head. He flopped around like a gill hooked fish and damn if he didn't live after they pulled that steel from his head. That's what happened to Big Black. Now he can't talk 'ceptin' that one word. But he's all right. He knows what's goin' on."

They arrived at the brothel and Big Black stood by, awaiting orders. The scrawny man looked the place over. He'd known it well enough, though the whores were so put off by his rotting mouth that they'd never give him any commerce.

"You can't stay in here, lady. Come on with us. We got a good place, me and Big Black. You stay with us."

And she did. It was one of the shotgun shacks she'd passed when she followed the boy down the alley. It was a wreck but had a good bed. It was Big Black's bed and he offered it to Maria. She took him up on it and she slept well. Big Black took a chair outside her door, like a faithful hound.

She stayed with them for a week and extracted as much as she could from the hellhole. Eventually, no one would give her a game. The place was beginning to wear on her nerves; it was evidently a magnet for stupid men. Everywhere, men were behaving badly, getting drunk, falling over, and vomiting great gouts in the street until the place reeked of it. The sound of shooting guns was incessant and sometimes made it difficult to sleep. One man died under the window of Big Black's bedroom, gut shot, but not before wailing for more than an hour. Maria resolved to put a bullet through his head, just to get some sleep. As she'd gotten up, he had a sort of fit and mercifully died on his own. She could finally settle down and have a few hours rest.

She was up early this day and had gone down to the brothel to fetch Alanza. The scrawny man was sleeping and Big Black was at his job, which was to collect beer bottles from all the saloons and deliver them to a small brewery at the end of town. It kept him in food money.

Early in the morning, Canyon del Muertos was at its least horrible. Those who were awake were too drunk or sick to cause trouble; everyone else was generally passed out. Alone, she tacked up Alanza, even the little tobacco-spitting boy wasn't around.

She had everything in order and led Alanza down the main street, known affectionately as hell street by the inhabitants, and on toward Flagstaff. She didn't want to talk to her two companions. They'd fallen in love with her. They weren't a bad sort, but there was no sense in getting too caught up in goodbyes. There would be no profit in it for any of them.

She was preparing to mount when she saw the men behind her. She knew they intended trouble and thought it might be better to fight on horseback. Then, reconsidered, the stupid men might shoot Alanza. She continued to walk.

They'd been up all night but hadn't had much to drink. They were planning an early morning robbery, and Maria was simply in the wrong place at the wrong time. They'd been hoping for a swipe at her for the past several days and here was their big chance. She'd taken money from two of them playing cards, the third one just wanted to rob her.

They wasted no time and went for their six shooters. They didn't mind shooting someone in the back and Maria was famous for the Bisbee incident. They were fairly terrified of her. She wheeled and ran toward an alley; she did not want Alanza in the line of fire. She had her Winchester ready, pointing at the closest man when Big Black appeared out of nowhere.

He knocked her back and Maria flew like a rag doll several feet down the narrow pathway. The bad men now had their guns trained on the big man. They all fired and Big Black stood like a mountain, absorbing bullet after bullet, closing on them, doggedly, without hesitation. He smashed a bottle over the head of the first man and dropped him. The second, now dumbfounded by his ineffective fire, tried to retreat and Big Black hit him hard on the nose, dropping him to his knees. The third man continued to fire, too unnerved to shoot well enough for a killing shot and too petrified to try for an escape. He too went down.

Maria was on them, watching as Big Black finally crumpled, first to his knees and then falling face down, like a great dark giant, into the dusty street.

She pulled at him with all her strength, turning him over onto his back.

He looked up at her and nodded, "Yeahuh."

She looked at him. He had been hit with more than a dozen bullets in the abdomen, most meant for Maria. She held him gently in her lap and cradled his great head. Bending down, she kissed him gently, on his bloody lips. "Tell me your name, my love, tell me your name."

"Yeahuh...Henry."

She held him and watched him expire. "You go on to heaven, my love, my Henry. I will see you there soon." Big Black was dead.

Maria retrieved her Winchester from the alley as the men began to stir. She emptied the rifle into them, pulled her six shooters and emptied them. No one would be able to identify them when she was finished, that was her intent. She finally mounted Alanza and they rode off.

Hedor followed her and caught her when she was halfway to Flagstaff. He'd been crying over Big Black, his face and eyes puffy and red. Maria finally stopped so that he could catch up. She waited for him to speak.

"Lady, I..., I."

"You may not come with me."

"I don't know." He looked at the reins in his hand. "I don't have nowheres else to go, lady. Can't go back there. Can't."

"You go home, boy. Go to where you were born, go to your mother, boy, and live. Don't go to such places again. Go home."

He was crying and Maria moved Alanza close to him. She offered him a wad of bills but he wouldn't take it. She shoved the money into his dirty shirt pocket and patted him on the chest. "Go on, boy. Take this and go."

She wheeled and suddenly pulled up. Looking back, she said, "Muchacho, his name was Henry."

Flagstaff

Maria felt drained. The death of poor Henry and the ugliness of Canyon del Muertos had put her in a funk and she now rode along wondering why she'd put herself in such a place. The big man died for her. She hadn't wanted this to happen, never intended to put him in danger and was a little put off by it all, as she didn't need his help. She could have killed the men easily had he not intervened, she knew that. She was ready with her Winchester and she was certain they'd lose their will to fight once she dropped the first one. The others would have been easy to finish off, then. And anyway, she'd put a good bit of distance between herself and the bad men. She'd never seen a bandit yet who could shoot a six shooter better than she could with a

Winchester, especially at that distance. She'd had the upper hand.

Poor Henry. At least he died well. He died in her arms and, like Crisanto, died knowing love in the last moments of life. That was a good way to die and Maria was glad she could give him at least that much.

She thought more about these gringos. The further she moved north, the less she liked them. They all seemed so greedy, obsessed with gaining wealth without working for it. At least in Mexico, it seemed, most of the people were resigned to their fate. They'd be poor but make the best of it without resorting to low living and murder.

She thought about the bandits who killed the old woman and old man. Maybe the bad men were the same everywhere. She was so tired now and she'd given herself a headache over all this thinking and worry. She counted her money and had added only a thousand dollars to her bankroll after expenses and after giving Hedor some of her cash. She hoped he'd take her advice and move on. She liked him and felt sorry for him. He was too decent a fellow to live such a life.

When she hit Flagstaff her spirits lifted a bit. It was a nice town and much cleaner than the hellhole from which she'd fled. Flagstaff had industry. It had the timber trade and the railroad and ranching. It had a decent, hardworking citizenry. She saw a nice hotel and decided to change her strategy a bit. She rode into a well maintained livery stable and boarded Alanza there.

The people were kind to her, an old couple not unlike the old man and old woman who raised her, and they willingly stowed her traps. She removed her sombrero and vest, gun belt, pulled her trousers out of her boots and hid the ornate Mexican stitching on the tops. She now looked relatively benign.

She sauntered into a ladies shop and was greeted by an older white woman who looked her over doubtfully. Maria expected such and laid a wad of bills on the counter. "I need a nice dress, lady."

The woman picked the money up and counted it. She looked at Maria and smiled. "You've come to the right place, my dear. But first, a bath."

Maria, now dressed properly, like a lady, proceeded to the Bank Hotel. It was the finest place she'd stayed in since her visit with Juana. The lady had dressed her in dark grey and this muted Maria's complexion enough to allow her to blend in, at least a little. She'd decided that she did not want to make a statement just now. Her fame at Canyon del Muertos was flattering, but it did nothing to add to her bankroll and this was foremost on her mind.

The clerk greeted her with deference. Maria was learning that if she waved enough money around, it almost always resulted in respect or at least, civility. People liked the color of green and were invariable not so put off by a dark complexion when enough of it was involved. She was soon registered and settled in for the night. The room was cozy, the bed soft and comfortable.

Maria had surveyed the place when she arrived. It had a grand lounge and dining room, with a small gaming area in a corner for the more well-to-do patrons inclined to such activity. It made it possible for them to lose their money without leaving the place, and this is exactly what the proprietor had in mind. He'd brought in a card sharp from San Francisco, a good looking man who dressed well in silk vests and fancy striped ditto suits. He had dark hair and sprinkled it liberally with some sort of treatment which made it shine like a new penny. Maria eyed him as she sat at a table. He was soon standing beside her and introducing himself.

"Traveling alone?"

"Sí, ah, yes, my padre, eh, I am sorry, my English, not so good. My father coming to see me here." She pointed doubtfully at the floor and gave him a shy smile.

She was magnificent and he snatched glances at her without being too obvious. She offered to let him sit down. "You are a game man?"

"Yes, ma'am. I run the tables here. Come from California but been here since last year. Not a bad place. Money's good and you don't have to duck bullets." He grinned and liked her response to his suggestion that he'd seen much danger. He looked as if he knew she was impressed. "Do you play?" He was convinced that such a sheltered young woman had not and wanted to impress her further by showing off his knowledge of the games.

"Oh, no. Padre would not like." She shifted in her chair and looked down at her coffee cup. "He, well, he teach me one game, call in our language veintidos, I think. I think that is what it mean, eh, what it called."

The man grinned. Her broken English was charming; she was simply delicious. "Veintiuno, twenty one."

"Ah, sí, that is the name, Twenty-One." She grinned. "I have played this game." She looked away, a little shy about being around such a handsome man. "But we have play for only button. Never money."

He eventually pulled himself away. He had to work and she promised to visit him at the gaming table that evening. She smiled coyly and waved goodbye, promising to visit. But Maria had other plans. She went to her room and resolved to stay away from him for the rest of the evening. She'd work on him over the next day.

At around nine she approached the desk clerk and asked him to keep some money for her. He was a young man, bookish, and not comfortable around women. Maria worked her magic and had him stuttering and stammering. He became pale when she produced her stack of money.

"We, we can't keep that much, ma'am!" He held up his hands as if to ward the money off.

"But, you are called the Bank Hotel, no?"

He stammered again and summoned the proprietor who sauntered over to offer assistance. His eyes widened at the sum, "Go on, lad, put it in the safe for the lady." He grinned uneasily at Maria. "Safe and sound, ma'am, safe and sound."

She returned to her room and ordered a bath, got it, and requested half a dozen other things a woman of means would want, as much as she could imagine. It was all a lot of fun. She was beginning to enjoy this civilized living and wondered if sleeping on the desert floor would start to get uncomfortable.

She slept soundly, well into the morning and then prepared, making herself especially pretty for the dealer. When she arrived at the dining room for breakfast, he wasn't there. She joined a couple, an older man and a woman in her early thirties. They were very friendly for gringos but Maria knew that there was something about them that was not quite right.

The man stood up and shook her hand gently. He sat down and introduced himself and his companion. "Name's Hodgins, ma'am, and this is my daughter." They nodded a greeting and Maria ordered something to eat.

"And what brings you to Flagstaff, ma'am?"

Maria hesitated a moment and pretended that she was having difficulty finding the English words, she played up her accent again. She thought that if she was going to make up a story, she'd make up a big one. She remembered Ulla telling her about Porfirio Díaz and how he was interested in foreign trade. It was a good story and she was going to have fun being a rich timber merchant's daughter.

"My padre, eh, my father, he is coming to buy timber for the presidente, eh, Díaz, our presidente." Their eyes widened. "And you, what is your business?"

"Oh, my daughter and I, we just travel, travel and do a little gaming for fun. Passes the time. We heard the fellow here, he's pretty sharp, from San Francisco."

"Ah, the cards. Sí, he told me about the cards. He says he will teach me."

"Oh, you don't know cards?"

"Oh, a leetle. We use to play at home, in the hacienda, with the servants. We'd play for beans and button." Maria watched the woman eat and mimicked her actions. She had no use for fine dining or the implements or courtesies they entailed, but she was aping the lady's actions well enough to get by.

"Oh, then you must try."

Maria grinned and looked a little self-consciously at the table. "My padre, he say I can do as I will with my money, to buy things, or whatever make me happy. Maybe I can try this gambling."

The woman smiled. "Just as long as it's for fun." She was very nice to Maria. "You never want to spend money that you need to live on for cards or gaming, that's for certain, but if you have, say a few thousand..." her companion coughed and shuffled under the table. "Well, not so much really, a few hundred to spare, you can have a fair evening of entertainment."

"Oh," Maria brightened. "I have more than seven thousand, and in your American dollars, I don' need that much for dresses or things.

The man choked a little and coughed. Maria leaned toward him, "Are you okay, Señor?"

"Oh, fine." He was distracted by the dealer walking past the dining room. He looked at his companion and grinned. "Think his feelings are hurt?"

The woman smiled. "Oh, he's gotten a little rusty since California. These rubes have dulled his mind."

They got up and shook Maria by the hand. "We hope to see you at the table tonight, Miss. We won't be too hard on you, but we give no quarter."

Maria looked up at them. "Que?"

"We don't give chances, Miss. You're swimming with the sharks now, and we don't give any breaks. Be warned." The woman pulled her dress front straight, she smiled warmly at Maria.

"Ah, sí, I unerstan', lady. It is all in fun. If I lose, I lose." Maria blew through her lips as if the money was made of newspaper. It did not matter how much she won or, more likely, lost.

The dealer approached Maria and watched the couple leaving out of the corner of his eye. He looked hatefully at them, then smiled at Maria. "I missed you last night." He held her hand and kissed it. He sat down and poured some of the coffee left by Maria and her companions. "What did they have to say?"

"Oh, they are very kind." She looked on at him as he scowled.

"That's not the word I'd use for them. Be careful with them, Maria. They cheat at cards. Knew them in San Francisco. They got run out of the whole state of California, and that's a big state."

Maria looked shocked. "I, they said they just play for fun, they say they are travelers. The man's daughter seemed..."

"Daughter?" He scoffed. "So, that's what he's calling her these days. More like his whore." He looked on at Maria, embarrassed. "I'm sorry for using such a term, ma'am."

Maria looked a little embarrassed, afraid of the rough characters she had been with.

"Maybe you should stay in your room until your father arrives." He looked concerned as Maria seemed to be ready to faint, seemed that the whole thing was overwhelming her to distraction.

"Oh, no. No." She fanned herself a little with her hand. "It is all, very, how do I say, exciting." She reached over and grabbed him by the hand. "If you will look out for me, I am sure to be save, eh, safe."

They were all playing when Maria arrived. The dealer was tense, as Maria had expected, and the couple was very pleased to see her. Maria had, just that afternoon, been coached by the dealer and she at least held her cards properly, but had to be prompted to bet at the appropriate times. She suddenly remembered something, "Ah, I got the chips, but," she dropped a wad of several thousand dollars on the table. "I can get more if I need them."

They played a few hands and Maria watched them all. They were good, they were good cheats and pretty soon she was down by half of her fortune. She smiled, embarrassed. "I am not so good with this game, I think." She took the next hand and fumbled with a card, dog-earing the corner badly. "Oh, I am sorry. It is a ace, now everyone know what it is." She shrugged and the dealer took all the cards back a little perturbed at the pretty señorita. Maria grinned as if she did not know why.

He turned and retrieved a new deck, showed them all the seal was unbroken and opened the pack. He dealt the next hand.

Now it was Maria's turn and she played all the tricks the old man had taught her and a few more that she'd picked up over the years. Now that the marked deck was out of commission, the cheats had a bit more difficulty pulling off their shenanigans and this worked to Maria's advantage.

She palmed cards, added ones she'd stolen from the previous deck, shorted the pot, and watched the dealer distribute cards from the middle and bottom of the deck. When this would happen, she'd knock a glass over and drench the table. The man was becoming very angry at the bumbling Mexicana.

And on top of this, Maria was counting cards. She could tell before the couple or the dealer really had any time to review, when she had a good hand and, more importantly, when they did not. They were careless. They were convinced that the pretty señorita had more money than brains. They could not imagine what was going on in her mind. They were becoming more frustrated by the minute when Maria suggested the other game, the veintiuno. They all agreed as the young woman was getting on their nerves.

"I don' know about this game, you know what they say about Mexicans, we can't count to more than ten." She grinned sheepishly.

She smiled at them and looked at the pile of money. "I lost almost all my money and now look," she dropped chips from a height and let them clatter all over the table in front of her. "I have the most now!"

She looked on. "I have a good idea. Let's play with many deck."

"Many deck?" The dealer was not laughing.

"Sí, you know, we put out five deck, that is what the old hand Pablo used to say. When you play veintiuno, you play with many deck. It is more fun."

The dealer and the couple actually liked this idea. There'd be less chance of the hapless girl winning so easily. They soon had the five deck game going and within an hour Maria had most of the chips. She yawned and stood up. "This is very fun, but I am tired. I am going to go to bed."

They stood up and wanted to make her stay but thought better of it. They nodded and bid her a good night.

Maria added three thousand to her bankroll and looked at a clock on the mantel. She could leave now, but eyed the bed. It was so soft and she was enjoying it. She decided to leave in the morning. She was just about to undress when she heard the knock on the door. She thought about not answering, knew who it was and didn't want to deal with him this night.

He knocked again and tried the handle on the door. This made her angry and she pulled it open quickly, startling the dealer and making him jump a little. She smiled innocently. "Oh, hello." She looked up and down the hall as it was not appropriate for men to visit a young lady at such an hour.

"Miss, I need to talk to you." He looked back and forth as well and took the initiative, pushing his way, gently, but firmly, into her room.

She moved to the other side of the room and sat down at a writing desk full of her winnings. She'd made certain to change the chips to cash and there was a significant pile in front of her.

The dealer eyed it lovingly, like a dog after a new soup bone. He looked back at Maria.

"Miss, you've made a bit of a mess for me."

"Que?"

"Oh, let's stop this, the both of us. I know what you are, and now I'll tell you what I am. I'm in with that lot. We were going to rob the house and take off, then you came in. We thought we'd get your money too."

Maria reached over and pulled out a cigar. There was no reason to hide from him any longer. "So?"

"So...," He looked her over. She was especially captivating now that she was working on the cigar. "Why don't you throw in with me? How'd you like to live in the best hotels, we could go east, we could see the world. Ma'am, I've never seen anyone who could count cards like you, and with that dumb Mexican act, we could rule the damned gambling houses of the world."

He was misty-eyed and Maria had him. She regarded him through the smoke. He was a good looking gringo, that was certain. She could get used to looking at him, and maybe even do some other things.

She thought about him trying to cheat her. He couldn't and that bothered her on two levels. First, she could never trust him and secondly, he was too stupid to pull it off. She was smarter, more talented than him. Why would she need him? He wasn't really a very good player. She decided to keep these thoughts to herself.

"No, gringo. I am going back to Mexico." She decided not to say any more. She didn't want to waste time and he wouldn't listen anyway. She watched him get angry and prepared herself for action. He did not disappoint.

"Well, what if I tell you I could have you arrested, locked up and thrown in jail? You'll never see Mexico again."

Maria stood up and got close to him. She looked into his eyes and reached out, squeezed his cheeks together gently. "You are a nice boy, but you are in, ah, over your eyes, ah, in too deep water. You are in too far and I'll forget that threat, but you have to go now, gringo."

He stood, not certain what to do. She wasn't afraid and not in the least intimidated by him. In fact, it was the other way around. He put up his hands in surrender. "All right, but you're missing a plum opportunity, a plum opportunity." He turned to leave. "Just one kiss?" He gave a look more confident than he was.

Maria looked at him. He was bold and a little drunk. She decided to humor the poor fool and kissed him gently on the cheek.

He was on her and threw her at the bed, missed, and they both landed on the floor. Maria was angry and tore at his face with her nails. He recoiled and screamed like a child. He fell back on his backside and held his bleeding face. "Goddamn, why'd you do that?"

She got up and found a rag and fresh water. When she turned he was pointing a little gun at her, a two shot not unlike Maria's own. She dropped her shoulders in disappointment. She was not in the mood for this nonsense.

"What now, gringo? Are you going to shoot me with that little gun?"

"No, eh,... yes, if you make me. You're going with me. We're going to become a team, like that old bastard and his whore. We're going..."

Maria had her own gun out now and pointed at the gringo dealer's head. She stared him down. "This is what is called a Mexicano standoff, gringo. You shoot me, I shoot you. We both go to hell together."

"If that's how it's got to be." He fired and Maria obliged, her bullet passing through the man's left eye, dropping him like a ragdoll.

His bullet was small, a little thirty one and Maria took the shot just above the nipple of her left breast. It felt like a bee sting and she sat down for a moment to think things through. People would be beating on the door soon and she had to decide what course of action she would take.

She pulled her dress down and looked at her back through a mirror. The bullet had not gone through. She breathed deeply and it was difficult to get her breath and this made her cough. She tasted blood. She was lung shot and knew it. She looked down and watched the blood seep out from the hole. She packed it with a washcloth and put her dress back on. She had to get to Alanza and out of there.

She gathered her things and barred the door with a chair. She stepped over the gringo dealer, looked him in his good but lifeless eye and grinned. "See you in hell, my gringo friend." She opened the window and was gone.

She woke up the liveryman and his wife to fetch Alanza and her traps. The old man tacked Alanza up and worried over Maria. He could she was in no fit state to ride and her dress was now quite wet with blood. She ignored his protests and the man's wife resolved to at least clean and dress Maria's wound as best she could. She did a capable job.

"Adios, people. Thank you for your help." She rode off, swaying a little in her saddle and the man was certain she'd fall before getting to the edge of town. They were good people and not used to patching up bullet holes in Mexicanas, but did not want to cause the girl any more trouble so they closed up and extinguished all the lights as soon as she was out of sight. They waited and watched, and sure enough, two riders came through, stopped momentarily at the stable and looked around. They continued in the direction Maria had ridden. The man's wife gave his arm a squeeze. She'd been with him more than thirty years and could read his mind. He wanted to help the señorita. "It's not for us, Dad, it's not for us."

Alanza galloped south as Maria went in and out of consciousness. By daylight they were at the edge of the red rocks, near her Indios, when she finally fell off. She slept heavily in the desert and began to dream of the couple she'd beaten at cards the evening before. The dream was vivid. She could hear them talking but she could not move or even wake up.

"She dead?"

"Not yet. Lost a lot of blood. I've got it."

"Should we take her traps?"

"No. Someone could make a connection, just get the cash."

"It's, it's a lot."

"How much?"

"More than we lost, a lot more."

"I pity her. Look at her. She was a card playin' little bitch."

Maria dreamed of the Indios and the red rocks and of Alanza whinnying at her. She dreamed that a dog was pushing her with its nose and then the dog became Alanza.

She was hot and soaking wet with sweat and blood. At one point she felt beneath her head and thought she was resting on a comfortable pillow like at the lady fence's house. It was a big goose down pillow and she put her hands up to feel it, fluff it a little, enjoy the coolness of the underside with her hot hands and her pillow was now little Rosario and her baby was hungry. She put her to her breast, the one that was shot and it hurt, ached all around her breast like when the German infant was nursing on it.

Then she sat up, too close to a fire ring. Juana and Ulla and Bronagh were all at the fire, but Juana was ten years old again. She was eating and Ulla pointed at Maria, signaling to everyone that she was finally awake. Bronagh chastised them, "Now, don't be gettin' on your high horse. She needed to go a wanderin', it was in her blood."

Juana pointed at Maria with a drumstick. "Look at the state of her. She'll surely die, then where will we be?"

Ulla reached out with an ointment and now she was the yellow-haired whore from Nuevo Casas Grandes, "Put this on your nipples, Maria, it soothes them."

She sat up, leaning on an elbow and looked at the fire. She was too sleepy to speak or take the ointment and soon dropped back down. She could no longer find the pillow or Rosario but she was just too tired to care. She turned to face away from the fire and felt liquid hitting her face. The man, the shop owner, the dirty bastard Sanchez was there with the coal oil and was splashing her all over with it. He'd come back to burn her up. She sat up sputtering and felt the coolness of the rain. She was awake now and getting cold; the rain was coming down hard and lightning bolts were illuminating the sky. She had to get off the mesa.

Alanza knew it, too and was not far away. She'd been trying to wake Maria for most of the day and steadfastly waited nearby for her mistress to stir. She walked over and pushed her with her muzzle, as if to force her to mount up.

Maria did and they rode to an arroyo and waited at the edge, out of lightning strikes and away from the impending flood of water. She felt better now, drank some and ate a little dried beef. This she immediately vomited and resolved to drink only sips of water. She'd worry over food later as vomiting pained her in the breast terribly.

She was tired again and leaned back into the muddy bank, drifting between wakefulness and sleep. A thunderclap woke her and she looked around. Every time the lightning flashed, it illuminated a face in the bushes. Over there, the old man and old woman who raised her at the church, at another spot the old padre, looking as glum as ever, then the lady fence and her companion, and finally, all the Germans. They were in a group, the Germans, as if they'd formed a choir, were planning to sing at a Mass, but they never did. They just stood there, silently, watching her, waiting.

She shook herself and finally came fully awake. She was freezing cold and knew that she had a fever. She needed to find shelter fast.

The Indios finally found her after she'd fallen from Alanza again. She was sleeping at the base of a slot canyon, not more than a mile from their home. Alanza was a good scout and seemed to know the trail, seemed to know where to take Maria to get the help she needed. The Indios had little trouble getting them to Maria's special Hogan. She slept there another five days.

When she finally woke her fever was gone and she could keep food down. The Indios had cleaned her wound and it was beginning to heal. She could breathe better now and it did not pain her so to move about. She'd keep the bullet as a souvenir, lodged under her shoulder blade for the rest of her days, and whenever the weather was changing, Maria would know by the ache from the little lead slug.

She smiled at all the faces peering in at her when she was finally with them once again. They loved and admired Maria so much and could not bear the thought of losing her.

She had no fortune now, but at least she had all her guns. Her vaquero outfit was still good and the Indios had cleaned it and readied it for her, so she was not in such bad shape. She looked through her things and found a small roll of cash in one boot, then another; in her gun belt was a slot and she kept cash there, there was more in her war bag and under her saddle skirt.

The old man taught her well. She remembered his story as she looked over the cash she now had. He told her an old story of a man who'd been shipwrecked, Robinson Crusoe was his name, and he had gunpowder from the wreck. He had hidden it in little caches everywhere in the event that, if lightning should strike it, not all would be lost. This is what the old man told her to do with her money. Never keep it all in one spot. So she had some seed money, a few hundred dollars, with this the fortune could be remade. It didn't bother her so much at the time, she was lucky to be alive.

She stayed with them for nearly a year and was eventually as good as new, perhaps even better than she was before being shot, as she had no mescal or cigars or bad places to go and gamble to wreck her health. She was becoming a fixture with the little band but knew she'd eventually have to move on. This was not her home; this was not how she wanted to spend the rest of her days. The wanderlust had once again taken hold.

## Chapter XVII: The Mule Tamer

Maria spent the next two years crisscrossing the desert. Making her fortune and becoming a hacendada no longer seemed so important. She just wandered and looked for adventure, looked for a game. She was a little lost now as the games and small skirmishes just did not pay off in entertainment value as well as they used to. She was drinking more mescal these days and it was becoming difficult to get a good game. She'd developed a reputation in Arizona, the incident at The Cage, then at Canyon del Muertos where she'd shot up the three men and even in Flagstaff, where she was famous for killing the dealer, had made it difficult for her to get by. No one wanted to gamble with either their money or their lives with the beautiful wild Mexicana.

This is when the gringos started to make her angry. They were hypocrites. They could gamble, fight, kill, but when there was a chance they'd be bested by a Mexican and a woman, they'd run the other way, like a cur with its tail between its legs. They liked to look at her, liked to try to bed her, but they would not play cards with her and soon she was run out of the bigger places in the territory.

She soon developed a remedy for this lack of cash source. She became an excellent thief. She'd steal anything that was of value, portable and not tied down. She was careful about it; she'd never steal from the poor or from honest working men. But she would steal from big companies: mining companies or the railroad or the stagecoach lines. She'd steal from other thieves or anyone who insulted her, just as she'd done with Colonel Gibbs when she'd taken his fancy rifle.

Whenever she was run out of a town or settlement or refused a game, she took the same path, a habit she'd formed. It went along the lines of stealing whatever she could, downing half a bottle of mescal, then galloping Alanza up and down the street, emptying her six shooters into the saloons and brothels on each side. This is how she became known as the beautiful devil.

The loot always made it to the Indios, in one form or another. Most of it she'd turn into cash and purchase foodstuffs for them. Sometimes she'd splurge and get the little ones candy or toys. For the women she'd buy coffee, tobacco and sugar. It was the one thing in her life that gave her some satisfaction and made her a little happy.

She went to visit the padre. It was bittersweet to see the place at the church where the old man and old woman raised her. A new family had taken over and the padre introduced Maria to them. They offered her a meal and it felt so queer as nothing had changed except the people. The chairs and tables and plates and stove, all of it was exactly as she'd left it when the old folks were murdered and she ran away from God and the church. They let her see her old room and this was different; they had three small children living in it now. It was nice to see children's things and she did recognize the chamber pot that had caught her little Rosario when she was born.

She rode out to the desert and visited Rosario that day. She found the spot where she amputated Crisanto's leg and then, a little farther on, she could see the remains of Rosario's grave. Her bullet wound suddenly ached and she had to leave. She had to ride on to the west and visit the lady fence. There were only good memories there and she needed some now. She should not have visited the padre.

But the lady fence and her companion were gone when she arrived. The store and the house behind it were shuttered and the place looked as if it had not been occupied for some time. This was mostly

Kosterlitzky's doing, as he'd been tough on the bandits in the region, thus the lady fence had no real commerce any longer. She'd moved on with her companion and Maria was truly heartbroken to find them gone.

She broke into the home and climbed the stairs to the garret. The bedframe was there but the mattress was gone. She opened the window and let the sea breeze in. It felt good on her face and she closed her eyes and remembered back to the first time she'd visited. So much had happened to her in all that time. She remembered Juana, her chubby little body pressed against hers in bed, how she was always eating, it seemed.

She thought about Juana. She missed her and hoped that she had babies by now, hoped that she and Ulla were happy down south with the Guatemalan workers and the coffee plantation and the Germans. She suddenly felt like she would cry and she didn't understand why; this had always been such a happy place for her. Her bullet wound ached again.

She took Alanza down to the beach and they camped by the surf. She didn't want to be alone up in the garret and Alanza always comforted her.  She was always nearby watching over her, ready to sound an alarm, to give her own life for Maria if that was what was required of her.

They ate and Maria had half a bottle of mescal and listened to the lapping of the surf. She went for a swim and sat naked next to the fire to dry. She felt good being naked. She thought of men when she was naked and considered that maybe this was what was lacking in her life. She liked men. She loved making love, at least the one time with Crisanto, and imagined it might be better with a partner who was not mostly dead.

By morning she was ready to travel again. She wanted to see the Indios. She'd gotten some money and would buy them some things. It was when she was with the Indios that she was happiest and it made her feel like it would be possible, perhaps someday, to have what they had. To have children to nurture and love and this made her bullet wound ache again. It went all the way down to her womb and she wanted to cry again. It seemed that she wanted to cry almost all the time now. The only way for her to keep this from happening was constant travel and mescal; lots of mescal.

So she rode with purpose to the Indios and stopped off to see Uncle Alejandro, who was thrilled and begged her to stay. He worried about her. Maria did not look well. She looked haggard and worry-worn and just not as pretty as she once was.

"Please, child. Stay. You will never want for the rest of your days. We have good men here. Find one, find the most handsome boy and I will make you queen of the hacienda. I will make all your troubles go away."

She felt like crying at his words and her wound ached. She smiled weakly. "I know, Uncle. I know this thing and I thank you for it. I must make one more trip and then I will return."

He nodded sadly and Maria thought she could discern just a hint of a tear in his eye. The old man loved her and did not want to lose her. He feared what the next trip would do to his precious charge.

Maria made him this promise and had every intention of fulfilling it. As she rode off, she looked back at the old Jefe. "I will be back, Uncle. I promise you, I'll be back."

She rode into a small hamlet and was furious to be, once again, denied a game. Now even in the little places she was known, or at least not given any respect or consideration. This bunch was especially disrespectful: rude and angry and self-righteous. They would not give her a game and told her that gamblers and tramps and Mexican whores were not welcome in their town. They stood back, not willing to fight, none of them even armed, yet they talked like tough men, they talked and Maria got angry and stormed out.

She found some shade and sat there until dark. She had three bottles of mescal and downed two. She was completely drunk and looked for something to steal. She could find nothing here. The little settlement was just too small, the people too resourceful and hard working. They did not have time for the frivolities of the cattle or mining towns. There was no fun here, only hard work and severe and boring people. It was totally civilized and Maria did not like it much.

She dozed a little and by midnight was ready for some action. She mounted up and galloped Alanza up the street. She surveyed the place and the people, more people than usual were milling about. She wheeled and pulled her six shooters, firing wildly at each side of the street, scattering the offensive inhabitants of the town. This was a little bit of fun and she stopped to reload. Suddenly, she was pulled off of Alanza and everything went black. She was out.

She awoke in a little shack to find a man fiddling with her guns. She sat up slowly.

"Ay, chingao!" She glared at her captor. "Pendejo, what are you doing?"

"Waiting for you to wake up." He placed the gun back in its holster and set the rig down, out of her reach.

"Ay, look at my clothes." She took a damp scarf and began brushing herself off. "Did you wipe me down, Pendejo?" She looked at him suspiciously.

"I did. But not anywhere I shouldn't."

"What?"

"Not on your private parts." He smiled at her. "Are you trying to get hanged, or are you just stupid?"

She rubbed a knot on her head with her scarf, then looked at it for blood. "Ay, my head is sore." She looked at him again. "What are you talking about, gringo?"

"Do you not know of the troubles?"

"No." She was trying to focus. "Are you some kind of law, mister?"

"No." He pulled out a cigarette and lit it, offering her one. She refused it and pulled out a cigar, leaning forward so that he could light it. "So you don't know about the murder of the family outside of town?"

"No, I know nothing of any murder. Ay, you really hurt me, Pendejo." Rubbing the back of her neck, she looked around the room. "So I am not arrested?"

"No."

"Where is my horse?'

"Beats me. Tombstone by now, shot dead, not certain. It ran off like its hind parts were on fire, heading south. Heard lots of shooting, so the towns' folk were probably shooting at it. What kind of stupid stunt was that anyway, shooting up the town?"

She rubbed her head then picked up her hat. "I don' know, Pendejo. When I drink mescal, I do some things." She stood up and stretched her back, blew smoke at the ceiling of the shack. "I really gotta go, Pendejo. Will you let me go?"

"Not without a horse." He looked at his watch. "I tell you what, let me go find your horse and you stay here. Don't leave, understand?"

"Sí, I understan'." She reached for her gun belt and looked for his reaction. He allowed it.

She waited until he was gone and then began looking around her little hideout. This was a strange gringo. He was dressed too well to have such a shop, the shop of a laborer. This could not be his shop; he was dressed like a gentleman. She wondered at his game. She started looking through drawers and broke a lock on a desk. He came in and discovered her.

"Hey, stop that!" He pushed her away and began straightening up. "So, you're a thief as well as a drunkard?"

"I need money, Pendejo."

"Has working or getting married or doing something honest ever crossed your mind?" The man continued to put the place back in order.

She spit on the floor. "I don' need to work and I don' need a man. I take what I want, Pendejo, like you gringos take and take from the people who have been here for hundreds of years. You are just as much a thief as me."

He laughed. "Well, you have a point there."

She looked him up and down. "You are a strange gringo, Pendejo. You don' look very much like, like…"

"Not very tough?" He smiled. "I know, I know. I've heard that before."

"Why are you not so mean to me, Pendejo? Most gringo white men don' want nothin' to do with me. They avoid even to look at me."

"I think you're funny." He smiled. He looked at his watch again. "You'd better beat it out of here."

"Why so secret, Pendejo?"

"What's this 'Pendejo'?"

"Oh, I don' know, it just seem to fit."

"It wouldn't be good if the people around here caught you. They'd likely string you up, just for good measure. A bandit gang of Mexicans and Indians killed a whole family just outside of town. It was pretty bad. The leader wears a gold sombrero. Maybe you know him?"

"Ay, chingao, sí, I know him, Pendejo. He is mal puro. One day, I will meet up with him and kill him, but he is like smoke, he is hard to catch."

"We're meeting up in a couple of hours to go after that gang."

"You, Pendejo?" She chuckled. "You better not go after bandits or they will be digging a grave for you, especially Sombrero del Oro."

He took her by the arm and Maria was surprised and a little impressed with his resolve. "I appreciate your concern, Chiquita, but I'll be just fine. How old are you, anyway?"

"Guess, Pendejo." Maria eyed him devilishly. She liked the attention he was giving her.

"Sixteen?"

"Hah! I have twenty-six years, Pendejo."

"Well, you won't have twenty-seven years if you keep this up. Now, get on your horse and ride. Don't stop." He tossed a half-eagle at her. "And I don't want to hear from you or see you in these parts again."

She turned to leave, then grabbed him and kissed him hard on the mouth. She thought for a moment and kissed him again, harder this time. "You kiss good, Pendejo."

She got on Alanza and rode past a couple of mules and realized they belonged to the pendejo. Another odd thing about him. Mules. Who rode mules? Mules were good animals but they were made to bear heavy burdens, pull great carts or plow fields and tear stumps from the ground. They were not made for riding, that was the purpose of a horse. She thought hard about the strange gringo. He was a very odd one.

She could not believe her luck. She rode on. She had a lot of money from the man and he had let her go. She even lifted his watch and she believed that maybe he even knew it and let her. She could not understand that. He let her go. It was confounding enough that he captured her. Maria had only been bested once, and that was by Uncle Alejandro. Now she was bested by a gringo who looked for all the world like a complete alfeñique.

She thought about kissing him. She liked that. Of all the men over all the years, he was the only one she'd ever kissed, ever really wanted to kiss, with the exception of Big Black, but she only kissed him to send him off to heaven. She didn't like to kiss him really, he was such a mess and all bloody and dying. She just did it, just as she'd done to Crisanto, to send him to a happy death.

But this one, she wanted to kiss him and did and liked it.

She rode aimlessly, without giving where she was going much thought. She headed north until she got to the Indios and was distracted by thoughts of the pendejo the entire way. They were happy to see her as always and accepted her gifts graciously.

She stayed with them for a week and enjoyed their company, but the gringo kept intruding into her thoughts. It was ludicrous. What could she ever do with a gringo rancher? He was likely married, anyway, and she had no interest in married men.

She could not get him out of her mind and finally rode back to the little town. She needed to know more about the man who rode on mules.

She reached the town on a clear morning and found an older Mexican woman working on some washing next to the shack where the gringo had briefly held her captive. The woman had an indifferent look on her face as Maria approached her. She dismounted and tied Alanza, then sat down near the woman and lit two cigars. She handed one to the woman without speaking and the woman took it and clenched it between her teeth as she continued with her task.

"Lady, I need to know about a man who lives around here." The woman was listening, but did not look up. "He is a gringo and he rides mules like others ride a horse."

"I know this man. Señor Walsh. He has a mule ranch not far."

"Is he a good man?"

The woman finally stopped and looked at Maria. She liked Maria, despite her manly dress. She could tell that Maria didn't have bad intentions. "He is the best of men."

Maria felt a flutter in her belly and a pain at her bullet wound. She started to speak when the woman interrupted her. "He and his uncle are good men. They are good to everyone but they are extra good to us and the Indians. They have a good ranch and it is very grand, but they take care of their people on the land. There, people are treated with respect, paid well. They are a good pair of gringos."

"And the one who is not the uncle, is he... does he have a woman?"

"Not him. The uncle, though. He's got Pilar, the bitch." She spit on the ground when she said the woman's name and Maria was amused by this.

"This is his wife?"

"Hah! No. She is a Mexicana, like us, but she is the lady of the manor, or at least she thinks so. She is a housekeeper and gives the old man one every so often. She thinks no one knows. Hah! Everyone knows. She thinks she is better than everyone because she had an aunt who was married to a shopkeeper once, and that was a long, long time ago. Now she runs the ranch like it is hers. Old slut!"

"And the other one, this Walsh. He has no woman?"

"No."

She took her leave of the washerwoman and rode on south. This was interesting news. She felt good again, felt a flutter in the pit of her stomach. She didn't go to him, though. She wanted to go then thought better of it. She needed to ride south. She needed to see Uncle Alejandro but was not certain why.

She returned to the hacienda and her uncle was pleased, as usual. He was also happier at the way she looked. She appeared to be happier, more rested; not so haggard. She was distracted, though, and Uncle Alejandro could read her mind.

"You are in love, little one."

Maria blushed. It was the first time she'd ever been embarrassed in her life. She looked at the Jefe and grinned. "He is a gringo."

"I see."

"You do not think this is bad?"

"Not particularly."

"Do you not think all the gringos are assholes, Uncle?"

"No. Just most of them." He smiled. "But Maria, most Mexicans are assholes, as well." He got cigars for them to smoke and continued. "This world is full up of assholes, Maria."

She grinned and thought of something to say, but he continued. "Most all people in the whole world are assholes, no one country has the monopoly on them, Maria."

"This man, he captured me, as you had. He is, not, how do I say... He's not very much like you, though. He is very fair, very fine, like a boy."

"I see." He grinned. She was fairly gushing about the man. "And how old is this fair boy?"

"Oh, he is no boy. He is, actually, quite old, I think. I think maybe not as old as you, but much older than me."

"I see. And why, my dear, are you here and not there, with him?"

She became self-conscious again and tilted her head slowly from side to side. "Uncle, this is a silly thing. He would not be so interested in me, I think. He is a hacendado up there in Arizona. He is quite a gentleman. Such a man would not have any interest in me."

"Then he is either stupid or crazy or a eunuch. Is he any of these, Maria?"

"I don' know. I don' think he is crazy. I know he is not stupid, but I do not know this eunuch, so I cannot tell you this."

He laughed. "He is not, child. I am sure he not a eunuch. He is a man and any man who loves women would love you. Go, child, and get him. If you want him, get him."

She woke and sat up in Uncle Alejandro's bed. A lamp was lit in another room and Maria got up to investigate. Juana was taking a bath. She was full grown now and she smoked a cigar and her enormous breasts poked out of the bathwater like two perfectly matched islands. She picked up a tortilla and ate it and spoke with a full mouth. "I didn't think you'd get an old one, too."

"I didn't get anything." Maria pulled up a chair and watched Juana eat. She was such a pretty woman and Maria now realized she was even prettier naked than she was wearing clothes. She looked beautiful with her blonde hair done up in the German style.

"Oh, this mule man. You'll get him. I know it."

"How did you know he had mules?" Maria was suspicious of Juana. She seemed to always know everything.

Juana shrugged. "I don't remember. But you'll get him all right and then you'll have babies."

"Have you had babies yet, Juana?"

Juana shrugged again.

"You don't know if you've had babies, Juana?"

"I've forgotten." She stood up and water splashed out onto Maria and now she was cold.

"Why is it that you never remember anything I ask about, Juana?" She was a little perturbed.

Juana shrugged. "I never forget to come see you when you have a problem, though."

Maria could not argue with that. Juana was faithful in that regard.

"You know why you've fallen in love with him?"

"I don't know that I have."

"Oh, you have. It's because of the old man. The old man who taught you to play cards and shoot. You got a man like him. And he was old."

"That's ridiculous. You never had an old man raise you, yet you got an old man."

"But I didn't love him. Do now, but I didn't."

"Why'd you marry him?"

"Because he's got a lot of money, of course. Why do you think?"

"I don't know." She looked at Juana. "Do you suppose I really do love him?"

"Sure you do." Juana eyed her. "Go find me a towel, Maria."

When she returned, Juana was gone.

But Maria could not make herself go north for more than a week. She felt so queer about this; she was always confident and in control. She never put anything off that she wanted to do. She wondered if nearly dying had anything to do with it. That took a lot out of her but she hadn't hesitated since then. Whenever she had a showdown with a rude or potentially bad man she was as calm as ever, not afraid, she'd not hesitant.

It was true that she hadn't had to kill anyone since then, but she knew, deep down in her bones that she could if she needed to. No, she was certain it wasn't that. But every evening it was the same, she'd go to bed with the resolution, the determination that tomorrow she'd be on her way. She even had trouble falling asleep because of her excitement.

She'd take the advice of Juana and Uncle Alejandro and go see this mule man, as Juana called him. And her feelings hadn't wavered, either. She still thought of him constantly. Why? She'd been with him for less than half an hour, but it was enough time for her to know that he was something special, that he was someone she could love.

And the washerwoman, she called him the best of men. She was obviously a woman who did not mince words; Maria could tell that by watching the woman work. She was resolute in everything she did. She certainly would not call a man the best of men if she didn't mean it.

And he liked Mexicans. She'd heard of gringos who liked Mexican women, that was not such a stretch. Mexican women were some of the most beautiful in all the land. Anyone with a brain, as Uncle Alejandro said, would be a fool not to find Maria attractive. She knew all these things in her mind, and in bed at night she'd remind herself of them. But every morning she'd get up and waste time, have two hour breakfasts with Uncle Alejandro, go curry Alanza, play with the vaqueros' children, have a two hour lunch and then take a nap. She would finish the day by spending more than two hours over dinner and the day would be gone. This would go on, Maria feared, indefinitely. She simply could not shake the procrastination.

Then, finally, on a clear Thursday morning, she awoke to find Alanza tacked up and tied to the hitching rail outside her bedroom door, standing quietly in the veranda's shade. Uncle Alejandro was waiting for her. He smiled and nodded at Maria's pony. "Time to go north, little one."

She looked at him and her stomach fluttered. She took a deep breath. "After breakfast, Uncle."

"It is made, it is in a sack hanging on the saddle horn, child." He handed her a tin cup of coffee. "You can drink it as you ride."

There was nothing for it now. She had to go. Uncle would not let her dally any longer. She smiled and saw his eyes get all teary, like a proud father handing his daughter over to her new husband. "You go. You are getting too old for this wandering, Maria. Soon, you will be too old to have babies and every young woman should have the gift of babies. It is the way."

He grabbed her in his great arms and hugged her and kissed her on the top of the head. "You go. Go to him and then bring him to me. I have to make a good speech to him and tell him how precious you are. I must tell him how he has to be good to you for the rest of his days."

He was becoming overwhelmed at his own sentimentality. Uncle Alejandro, despite his toughness, was a romantic at heart. He moved her, physically, to Alanza, nearly picked her up and placed her on the saddle. She was suddenly looking down on the man. He looked smaller to her, old and frail, and she did not want to make him unhappy. She gave him a weak smile. "Okay, Uncle, but you did not have to push the bird from the nest. You could have just told me to go."

"Ah, Maria, I know a procrastinator when I see one. Now, go. If he is worth a centavo he will know what is good for him, go." He pointed a big finger north. "Go."

She felt better now. It had begun, this great journey north. She did stop in some of the little saloons on the way, on the Mexican side, to visit friends. These men were not bad men and they would never play cards for much money, just for the enjoyment and camaraderie and they all loved and respected Maria. She'd go easy on them when she played and would typically turn around and either buy drinks or leave her winnings on the table for them to take back.

They were also the best of men. They worked hard for their meager income, worked hard to keep their families alive, scratching out a living in the rough country to the north. They were always pleasant to her and every one of them felt a certain responsibility for her, a father's responsibility. They hated to see her go.

As she rode she talked everything out to Alanza and practiced her English. She needed to make a plan regarding the mule man. "Alanza, I think I need to be a little tricky with this mule man." Alanza bobbed her head, as if in agreement and Maria patted her on the neck for it. "I think I will show him the worst part of me, and then if he likes that part, he'll like the nice part of me."

She was excited at this prospect. She was like a school girl who had not yet developed the skills to seduce a boy, awkward and a little silly. She'd be this way to the mule man. She'd tease him with her womanly offerings, seduce him, vex him. She'd leave him and come back just when he'd think she was gone from his life for good. She'd make him beg her to stay, and only then, only after he begged, or at least demanded it, would she stay. If he could fall in love with her after that, then she'd know he was her kind of man. If he got insulted, or found her revolting, then she'd know to move on.

This excited her. She would play a part because, in reality, Maria was no trollop. But the mule man didn't know that. All he knew of her at this point was that she took mescal and smoked cigars, rode up and down the streets shooting her pistols, and that she kissed him when she'd not even known him for an hour. It had been a good kiss, not the kind of kiss you'd give your mother or father. It was a very good kiss.

And he liked it. She knew he liked it and liked her. But that was what was so nice about him. That was what intrigued her about him; he hadn't judged her. He did call her a thief, but he wasn't disgusted by her. He was an educated gentleman and a gringo but he'd treated her as if she were an equal. That was the thing.

She urged Alanza along a little faster. The weather was good, not too hot. She wanted to get to the little hamlet and find out how to get to the mule man's place. She was ready now. She felt the little flutter in the pit of her stomach again and was ready to see him.

She made a nice camp and had some of the food Uncle Alejandro's cook had packed for her. She bedded down and talked to Alanza who'd drifted off to sleep. Maria could hear her rhythmic breathing. She didn't mind that Alanza had abandoned her. Her dear one had done her good service all day and deserved some rest.

Maria began to drift off and thought about what to do next. She wasn't sure but it would have to happen the next day. She'd be there by midday and she'd have to go ahead and do it, whatever it turned out to be.

She found the washerwoman who gave her directions to the mule ranch. She was pleasant enough but a bit odd, as if the washerwoman knew here was someone, one of her kind, and she'd kick the bitch, Pilar, out and be the new lady of the mule ranch. This pleased the washerwoman, so she was especially helpful to Maria.

Maria continued on her way and after a time saw the entrance to the ranch. It was a vast spread, more austere than Uncle Alejandro's, but a good ranch and obviously very rich. Maria could tell this was a rich man's place. She suddenly felt weak in the legs. She had never, even in battle, felt this way.

She stopped Alanza. They found an arroyo, out of view of any travelers who might make their way to or from the ranch. She got down and ate a leisurely lunch. Alanza grazed.

This was nice land, a little south of the red rocks, but she could visit her Indios babies easily from here. It also wasn't far from Uncle's place. She suddenly thought all this was preposterous. She was already thinking in terms of being the lady of the house, knocking the bitch, Pilar, off her little throne. How could this be? She'd never thought about things in this fashion, ever. Now she was planning on a grand scale. She had to have some mescal! This was making her insides shake and she did not like it. She did not like this feeling one bit.

One mescal led to another and soon she was sleeping like a newborn babe. When she awoke, it was fully dark and the moon was high. Off in the distance she could see silver moonlight shimmering on the mule man's hacienda. She stood up and was a little woozy. She drank a lot of water and a little more mescal and this steadied her.

She got on Alanza and felt better. This was actually the best of all possible things. She would not have to be presented to the bitch, Pilar, or the mule man's uncle, or any of the hands. The mule man would not have to be embarrassed that a wild Mexicana had come calling on him in the middle of the day.

She rode. Alanza seemed to know she needed to be extra quiet, like a great housecat. They were soon at the hitching post outside the rancher's door. It was grand and Maria was impressed. It looked to have a woman's touch and likely not that of the bitch, Pilar. More like a refined lady and she thought that the mule rancher or his uncle must have, at some point, had a wife. A woman had most definitely had a hand in all this.

She tied Alanza off and had a look around. She could see well despite the fact that no lamps were burning. Everyone was in bed for the night. She wandered to a big window and peered in. It was the mule man's bedroom and he was there, sleeping peacefully with his mouth agape. Now he looked about a hundred years old and Maria thought all this an idiot's errand. She watched him some more and he turned and closed his mouth and was facing her and no longer looked a hundred years old. Now he just looked like himself, old, but not so old as to be decrepit.

Maria pressed her face against the pane of glass, hands cupped on either side of her head. She could make out the bedroom and, it too, had been decorated by a woman. No man would have tassels on his lampshade, she thought. Uncle Alejandro's lampshades had no tassels. Uncle's room looked as a man's room should. It was masculine and this man, this mule man, was sleeping in a woman's room.

She now turned and looked the ranch over. It was well appointed and well maintained. She could see the bunkhouses for the ranch hands, and the barn and corral. It was all in order. She wandered around the perimeter of the house. It had a long overhang and would be cool in the summer. There was a veranda with table and chairs and she thought it would be good to eat and watch the mules in the corral. It was how they spent their days, breaking and training mules, and then coming out onto the veranda and having their meals. She imagined the gringo conversations here. They likely didn't differ from any of the vaquero or hacendado conversations. They likely talked of the same things.

She found the door and turned the handle. It was not locked and she entered the vestibule. It was cool inside. It smelled of mesquite fire from the hearth and the food from the last meal cooked by the bitch, Pilar, and candles and coal oil lamps. It was a nice smell of a nice home that was nicely maintained. It had a good feeling and Maria suddenly felt overwhelmed by it all.

She felt desperately that she needed to be here tomorrow, set up house, live here, spend the rest of her days here, but that could not happen so soon. She'd have to make it happen. She could not just tell the mule man that it was going to happen. She had to make him make it all happen.

She wandered through the halls, found the uncle's room and listened to him snore. He seemed to be a nice one, too. He was even more ancient in sleep than the mule man, but kind looking. The bitch, Pilar, was not in his bed. She'd likely fornicated and moved to her own room.

Maria thought about Pilar. Pilar would hate her. She'd hate her for her youth and beauty and manly dress and common manners, and charm. She'd be the one to win over. If she was at all decent, she'd protect her men as a mother bear would protect her cubs. Maria would have to be careful with Pilar. She didn't want to oust her completely; she needed the woman to keep the uncle happy and keep the place running. Maria had learned from Juana in this respect. Juana told her, as the head of a hacienda, you did not cook or clean or work. You managed the place and kept the men happy. And this is what Maria would do with the help of Pilar.

She now moved onto the mule man's room. He turned toward her and she thought she'd been caught. She did not want to be shot and this was a real possibility. Even alfeñique gringos kept a gun under their pillow. But he didn't shoot her. He kept sleeping and Maria was able to wander around his room.

The woman was there, in a picture, along with a child. Now she felt sorry for the gringo. These people were dead. It was the only logical explanation and it made her sad. She looked around for more things to see, more things to stall her but they just weren't there. She had to do it now.

"Pendejo... Pendejo." He had not dreamed of the Mexican girl. "Pendejo!" He felt a shove and sat up in bed. Maria stood over him with mescal on her breath. She was impressed that he was not frightened. He was completely calm and recognized her right away.

"Oh, hello." He rubbed his eyes. "Why are you in my room, standing over my bed?"

"I missed you, Pendejo."

"Oh, that's nice." He looked outside, realizing that it was dark. "Most folks come calling during the day."

Maria had to start the act. She began walking slowly around the room, looking at things, picking up pictures. "You have a nice place, Pendejo."

He smiled at the absurdity of having a young señorita in his bedroom.

"Who are these people, Pendejo?"

"That is my wife, and the little one, my daughter."

"They are dead, Pendejo?"

"Yes."

"That is sad." She put the photos back. "So... what are you doing, Pendejo?" She began fidgeting with the lampshade tassels by his bed.

"Well," He yawned. "I can tell you what I am not doing." He threw his legs over the side of the bed and sat at the edge. "I am not sleeping."

She grinned, "You are funny, Pendejo."

"What is your name, Chica?"

"Oh, I go by many names, Pendejo. Why don' you guess, and I will tell you what is right?"

"Jezebel?"

"No."

"Lorelei?"

"No."

"Ophelia?"

"No."

"Lucretia?"

"No. But I like that name."

"Chiquita."

"No." She grinned. "You called me that last time." She ran her thumbnail across her teeth.

"Diablo?"

"Now, you are being silly, Pendejo. And I would be Diabla."

"I give up, Chica."

"That is it! I am Chica."

"I doubt it."

"What is your name, Pendejo?"

"Arvel."

She laughed. "That is a funny name."

"I am a funny man."

She yawned. "You *are* a funny man, Pendejo. Why don' you get angry with me?"

"I don't know. I think you are funny, too."

"I am tired, Pendejo."

"Then you should go home and go to bed, wherever that might be."

"I am thirsty, Pendejo." She suddenly wanted him. She knew this would do it. Either she'd be in or out after this and it was just as well to get it over and done with. "Would you get me some water?"

"Oh, you are a lot of trouble." He stood up and reached for a robe.

"Ay, chingao! Wha' happened to your back, Pendejo?'

"I got blown up in the war."

"What war?"

"The great rebellion between the states. You know, the Civil War."

"Ah, sí, I know this war, the war where you gringos tried to rub each other out."

He grinned. "Yea, that war."

"Ay, you are a mess, Pendejo." She stretched, catlike, "I am tired, Pendejo, and thirsty."

"Yes, I know."

He sauntered out to get her a drink.

She acted quickly, shucking her clothes and jumping into bed, pulling the covers to her chin. She turned to the window and feigned sleep.

"Oh, you are a lot of trouble." He muttered under his breath as he watched her sleep. He curled up on the divan at the foot of the bed. He dozed off and began to dream.

She waited, then realized he was lying at the foot of the bed. She was beginning to wonder if he was not a stupid gringo. "Pendejo."

"What?"

"What are you doing, Pendejo?"

"Not sleeping."

"Come to bed, Pendejo. I am cold."

"It is sweltering, Chica."

"I am cold."

His mind raced.

"I am afraid, Pendejo."

He laughed. "You, afraid? I think not."

"You do not like me, Pendejo? No?"

"No... Yes, I like you Chica. Like I like a pit of rattlers." He sat up, then stood to face her. "It is not appropriate, Chica."

"What is this, appropriate? What does this mean?"

"Proper."

She knew now that she loved him completely. This was a man who did not take such things lightly. This was a man who'd not been with a woman for a long time, yet he was not weak. He did not jump on her like he was some rutting bull. He was a man who didn't run with the whores and this is what made Maria love him all the more. He'd be a good one and now she felt vulnerable and silly, naked under the covers. She took a deep breath. But it had to be. It had to be this way and she went forward. She played her silly game and went on.

"Ay, you are a fool, Pendejo." She looked into his eyes and pouted her lips, like someone who had not gotten her way. She hoped he would not see her trembling. She lifted the covers and scooted away from him, making room for him in the bed. Maria tilted her head, beckoning him.

"My God."

She awoke at dawn, her brown skin contrasting sharply against Pilar's crisp white sheets. She was the happiest she'd ever been in her life. He was good. He loved good and he was gentle and expert at it and it was a thousand times better than with Crisanto, which was not really Crisanto's fault because he was mostly dead. But it was better than Maria could ever have imagined it would be.

She stretched again, enjoying the comfortable bed, a bed better than Uncle Alejandro's and better even than the lady fence's bed because it had the mule man in it. He was good and she could not get enough of him. She looked up at him, her head resting on his arm, "Pendejo, why are you looking at me?"

He was fiddling with the earring dangling nearest to him, and then the bangles on her wrist. He laughed. "I was thinking of something funny."

"What, Pendejo?"

" 'And I will visit upon her the days of Baalim, in which she burned incense to them, and she decked herself with her ear-rings and her jewels, and she went after her lovers, and forgot me, saith the Lord.' "

She wriggled more deeply into the bed, turned on her side facing away and pressed herself against him. "You are funny." She fell into a deep and restful sleep.

The Mule Tamer

John C. Horst

# Chapter I:  Jezebel

Arvel Walsh had gone down early to meet the posse. He could not sleep and decided to head to town instead of lying in bed, staring at the ceiling. The story told to him by the chattering young hand about the slaughter kept him awake. By midnight he was dozing in a small room at the end of town. He leaned against some rope hanging on the wall of the cramped quarters, the air dense and still, rank with the odor of horsehair and rawhide and hemp.

He regretted his decision, now, as he recalled that old Will Panks had removed the bed just recently. Arvel had to try to get a little rest sitting on the dirty floor.

Will was a good man and a good friend whom Arvel had discovered living under the floorboards of the dry goods store's porch in the middle of town.  He was an utter wreck when Arvel first came upon him.

Most of the folks who'd come upon Will were afraid of him and thought him either an old drunk or addle-brained. Arvel learned that he was neither and had a mind sharper than most. He was a prospector trained in geology and civil engineering. One day, due to a slight error in calculation, he made a misstep and ended his career by breaking his back in the desert. He crawled miles and ended up, penniless and without means, in Arvel's little town.

Arvel set him up in the shack which was not, at the time, more than a lean-to at the very edge of town. Will was a proud man and would accept minimal help from Arvel and no financial aid, whatsoever. Slowly, with constant hard work, Will was able to regain control of his legs and now walked stooped over in a permanent crouch.

He earned his living making rope. As he got money he'd add a wall here and a window there. At some point he'd found an old rolltop desk in the desert, the discarded flotsam from a prairie schooner, let go by an overzealous traveler. He found a chair on a burning heap and rescued it and, until recently, had an old featherbed in the cramped quarters. It eventually became quite homey and kept Will out of the elements. As his health improved, his fortunes did as well and he now was able to live rather comfortably in the only boarding house in town.

Arvel was just drifting off when the barrage of gunfire jolted him to his senses. He peered through the cracks in the door. A rider, Mexican, judging from the saddle and sombrero, was racing up the street, firing in every direction. The miscreant stopped to reload, just feet from the shack's porch. Arvel grabbed one of the ropes hanging on the wall and slowly opened the door. When the rider holstered the first gun, Arvel stepped out onto the porch, threw his loop and jerked. The rider was pulled free from his saddle and landed on the ground, neck first. The horse galloped off and Arvel walked up to his prisoner.

The offender was a woman. Arvel picked her up and quickly threw her over his shoulder, grabbed her hat and rushed inside the shack. A Mexican would not be popular now. He eased her down onto the floor of the shed, tossed her hat aside, and began looking her over to see what damage he had done. She did not appear to be more than twenty. Her loose fitting outfit, despite its manly style, could not betray a well-proportioned frame. She wore a print cotton shirt, bright red scarf and striped brown vaquero pants. Her black boots were stitched ornately. Her gun belt carried a pair of silver-colored Schofields with fancy ivory handles. A matching vaquero dagger hung in a sheath in front of the holster on the right. The rig bore an abundance of polished conchos. Her tanned skin contrasted with the many bangles running up each arm.

Arvel smiled as a memory of his wife teasing him suddenly returned. When they made their forays into Mexico, the dark beauties never failed to turn his head and she loved to give him a hard time about it.

He suddenly regretted harming the girl. She was lovely and reeked of tobacco and spirits and human and horse sweat and earth. Like the whores in Tombstone, she was alluring and off-putting at the same time. He nearly forgot her transgressions as he watched her. He was right to stop her from shooting up the town. At least he did not put a ball in her.

Her face bore a peaceful expression as she lay there on the dusty floorboards among the bits of hair and hemp. It was a face formed by the centuries mingling Spanish and Indian blood. A small scar under her bottom lip added to her beauty and imparted a not insignificant suggestion of danger. She sighed as he removed her gun belt. The little viper would be more difficult to defang after she had awakened.

He removed her scarf, wetted it from his canteen and began cleaning the dust from her face and arms and decided it better to leave the rest. He turned his attention to her rig. He fumbled with the latch on one of the six shooters; they were a type he had seen only a few times. He never had much use for six shooters. The gun sprang open, ejecting cartridge cases into the air and clattering on the floor. The girl awoke at the commotion.

"Ay, chingao!" She felt her head and sat up slowly. She looked around the room, and then at her captive. "Pendejo, what are you doing?"

"Waiting for you to wake up." He placed the gun back in its holster, and set the rig down, out of her reach.

"Ay, look at my clothes." She took the damp scarf and began brushing herself off. "Did you wipe me down, Pendejo?" She looked at him suspiciously.

"I did. But not where I shouldn't."

"What?"

"Not on your private parts." He smiled at her. She amused him. "Are you trying to be hanged, or are you just stupid?"

She rubbed a knot on her head with her scarf, then looked at it for blood. "Ay, my head is sore." She looked at him again. "What are you talking about, gringo?"

"Do you not know of the troubles?"

"No." She was trying to focus. "Are you some kind of law, mister?"

"No." He pulled out a cigarette and lit it, offered her one. She refused it and pulled out a cigar, leaning forward so that he could light it. "So you don't know about the murder of the family outside of town?" He had not given it any thought, but was now wondering if she might have been part of it. She was unfazed.

"No, I know nothing of any murder. Ay, you really hurt me, Pendejo." Rubbing the back of her neck, she looked around the room. "So, I am not arrested?"

"No."

"Where is my horse?'

"Beats me. Tombstone by now, shot dead, not certain. It ran off like its hind parts were on fire, heading south. Heard lots of shooting, so the towns' folk were probably shooting at it. What kind of stupid stunt was that anyway, shooting up the town?"

She rubbed her head then picked up her hat. "I don' know, Pendejo, when I drink some mescal, I do some things." She stood up and stretched her back, blew smoke at the ceiling of the shack. "I really gotta go, Pendejo, will you let me go?"

"Not without a horse." He looked at his watch. The posse would be meeting up just before sunrise. "I tell you what, let me go find your horse and you stay here. Don't leave, understand?"

"Sí, I understand." She reached for her gun belt and looked for his reaction. He let her.

He walked out of the shed, onto the porch, and looked around for activity. Further down the street people were milling about. He untied Sally and mounted up; he rode south in the direction the horse had galloped. He passed several townspeople and no one seemed to pay him any mind. They had been through a lot, with the murder of the family nearby and now some crazy pistolero galloping up and down the street, shooting up the place.

They were all on edge and most were armed. Many had been drinking all day and into the evening and Arvel was certain if they found the young woman, they'd all be regretting their actions in the morning. He rode a quarter mile out of town and soon spotted the fancy saddle reflecting moonlight.

The girl's pony was an equine version of her mistress, beautiful and dangerous. She looked up from browsing as Arvel approached. He spoke to her calmly and she went back to feeding. He grabbed the reins and the filly willingly followed. Sally had a maternal influence on horses; they liked to follow the mule.

Back at the shed, the outlaw girl was prying on a locked drawer of Will Panks' rolltop with her big knife. Other drawers were upended, papers scattered on the floor and desktop.

"Hey, stop that!" He pushed her away and began straightening up. "So, you're a thief as well as a drunkard?"

"I need money, Pendejo."

"Has working or getting married or doing something honest ever crossed your mind?" Arvel continued to put the place back in order.

She spit on the floor. "I don' need to work and I don' need a man. I take what I want, Pendejo, like you gringos take and take from the people who have been here for hundreds of years. You are just as much as thief as me."

He laughed. "Well, you have a point there."

She looked him up and down. "You are a strange gringo, Pendejo. You don' look very much like, like..."

"Not very tough?" He smiled. "I know, I know. I've heard that before."

"Why are you not so mean to me, Pendejo? Most gringo white men don' want nothin' to do with me. They avoid even to look at me."

"I think you're funny." He smiled. He looked at his watch again. "You'd better beat it out of here."

"Why so secret, Pendejo?"

"What's this Pendejo?"

"Oh, I don' know, it just seem to fit."

"It wouldn't be good if the people around here caught you. They'd likely string you up, just for good measure. A bandit gang of Mexicans and Indians killed a whole family just outside of town. It was pretty bad. The leader wears a gold sombrero. Maybe you know him?"

"Ay, chingao, sí, I know him, Pendejo. He is mal puro. One day, I will meet up with him and kill him, but he is like smoke, he is hard to catch."

"We're meeting in a couple of hours to go after that gang."

"You, Pendejo?" She chuckled. "You better not go after bandits, or they will be digging a grave for *you*, especially Sombrero Del Oro."

He was growing tired of her impudence and took her by the arm. "I appreciate your concern, Chiquita, but I'll be just fine. How old are you, anyway?"

"Guess, Pendejo." She eyed him devilishly. She liked the attention he was giving her.

"Sixteen?"

"*Hah*! I have twenty-six years, Pendejo."

"Well, you won't have twenty-seven years if you keep this up. Now, get on your horse and ride. Don't stop." He tossed a half-eagle at her. He didn't know why. "And I don't want to hear from or see you in these parts again."

She turned to leave, then grabbed him and kissed him hard on the mouth. She thought for a moment, and kissed him again, harder this time. It was the first good kiss he'd had in five years. "You kiss good, Pendejo." She was gone.

* * *

Olaf Knudsen had come to the states twenty-two years ago. He was not married when he arrived and had only the clothes on his back and twenty one dollars. He worked in New York City for five years; seven days a week in a textile factory. After work, he went home and worked another three hours every night assembling ladies garters. His diet was salted fish and cabbage, not because he could not afford anything else, but because, by so eating, he could save more than sixty percent of his wages. He shared a bed with five other men. Two men shared one bed every eight hours. He dreamed of owning a dairy farm, and after five years, had enough money to purchase everything necessary to move west and pursue his dream. He picked up a nice wife along the way, and soon had a burgeoning family. They all had one purpose, and that was to make a successful farm. What took a lifetime of sweat and dreaming and toil was destroyed in less than an hour.

Arvel sat Sally and smoked. In the past twenty four hours his life and the life of everyone else in the region had been turned upside down. They had lived peacefully and uneventfully for years. No Indians, no miners, no gamblers, no Mexican bandits. The community had slipped into a quiet complacency, and that suited Arvel Walsh just fine.

He was working on five mules nearly simultaneously when the young man came riding up to his ranch, out of breath, flush with excitement, to tell him the news of the Knudsen family. He was amused by the boy, who was young and hungry for adventure. Arvel thought that he was not unlike himself thirty years ago, but now, well into his forties, hearing of this kind of excitement only made him sad. He was sad for the Knudsens, of course, but he was also sad that his mundane, complacent, normal life had been disrupted. He was getting used to the sameness of the days, and the only excitement that he now experienced was when a hand got kicked by an overexcited donkey or horse, or mule. Everything was humming along nicely for Arvel Walsh, until now.

### Posse Comitatus

The men Arvel had been waiting for gathered just before sunrise. Since no one had been taken captive during the previous day's slaughter, it had been pointless to give chase after sunset. Twelve men responded to the request by the deputy sheriff. The fellow in charge was a small man, no more than twenty five years old. He had been one of the deputy sheriffs for around six months and had proven himself in words only.

He had a fine Stetson and a fancy gun rig. His six shooter was bright nickel and the grip had a naked woman carved garishly on the outside panel. Many cartridges, more than fifty, were snugly fixed into loops across the front of his belt as he wore his rig with the buckle in the back. He had a giant knife, like an overgrown Bowie, with an ornate handle which stuck, menacingly, in front of the six shooter's holster. He looked uncomfortable and out of place in these clothes, as if he'd put them on to have his portrait taken. His scarf was a bit puffy and too tightly tied around his neck and tended to creep up over his chin as he moved. He continuously pulled it back into place.

His past deeds were difficult to verify. He had spent some time, by his own account, as a lawman in Tombstone and, supposedly, working for the Texas

Rangers. Judging by his blustery ways and fondness for hearing himself talk, everyone could pretty much agree that he likely hailed from Texas.

Dick Welles was there and Arvel was glad for it. He had known Dick since he arrived in Arizona. He was a good man, and a fellow veteran of the GAR, a rare thing in this part of the country as the land was populated mostly by former members of the confederacy.

Dick was a severe looking man with sharp features and blue eyes the color of a glacier. He sat, perched on his horse like a predatory bird, a dangerous hawk, ready to swoop down on his prey, looking on at the collection of volunteers. He looked terse, always; never cruel, but never friendly or smiling. He was the kind of man whom other men obeyed unless they were too stupid to know better.

His hair went white by the time he was forty. Once, his wife convinced him to dye it. So mortified was he at the outcome that he shaved his head, preferring temporary baldness to the hubris of such self-indulgence. He wore only brown or gray colored clothing of wool, as blue seemed too gaudy to him, silk was out of the question. He never wore black as he felt that this was the color reserved for undertakers and the clergy and he fit neither of those criteria. He was never without a cravat and waistcoat. He would wear a sack coat except in the worst heat.

Today he was dressed in his hunting clothes, which consisted of his older regular clothes that were deemed worn enough to get dirty. He was not a vain man, but proud enough to always be dressed properly. His hat was the only exception. He'd gotten it just after arriving in Arizona and it was once the color of honey. Now it was about as dirty as a hat could get and the grosgrain band was colored with a hundred different sweat stains. It was an exceedingly ugly hat and was incongruous with the rest of his outfit, looking as if perhaps he'd mistakenly picked up the property of a roper derelict, leaving a well-cared-for one behind.

"Bad business, Dick." Arvel extended his hand.

"Indeed. The girl said they tortured Olaf for better than an hour. She just escaped after they walloped her good on the head and left her for dead. They were in a state, whoopin' and hollarin', so busy with the blood orgy that she jumped up when they were occupied and ran like hell all the way to town."

"How many do you reckon there are?"

"She thought ten or twelve. Half Indians and half Mexicans, except for one white fellow, looked to be just running with them, and not all that connected with the gang. He didn't seem to take much part in the really bad business."

"It is all the same, lie down with dogs and get up with fleas."

The rest of the posse was made up of young ranch hands from the area, and a fellow from the Tombstone newspaper. Word traveled fast about this incident. Decapitation always makes for exciting news.

The young deputy was animated. He barked orders, strutted amongst the posse, commenting on what was lacking in each man's outfit. He was particularly concerned about the two elderly gents joining his expedition. He believed that fear was the best motivator. He eyed Arvel's kit doubtfully. "Sir, that mule is not going to slow our progress. We will be forced to leave you behind if you cannot keep up."

"Understood, Captain!" Arvel smiled.

"I am not a captain, Mister, and I'll thank you to take this a bit more serious. We're after some dangerous fellows." He looked on with contempt at Arvel's guns, consisting of his Colt thirty-six from his days in the war, and a Henry rifle, ancient by the standards of the well-equipped Texas lawman. Arvel wore his old garrison belt with the GAR buckle. It was so worn by now, that *Grand Army of the Republic* was nearly indiscernible. His big knife looked as if it had come from the kitchen. In fact, it had come from the kitchen and Dick Welles could swear it had retained the odor of onions.

"You have a cap-n-ball six shooter?" The young deputy sneered.

Arvel looked down at his revolver and smiled. He was enjoying this thoroughly now. The young man did not wait for his reply and began casting glances about in every direction, looking for evidence of even more incompetence among this group of volunteers.

The little fellow eventually wandered off, muttering something about having to nursemaid old-timers and kids. He lambasted a few other members of the posse, poking and prodding their equipment and generally making a fool of himself.

"Well, old-timer," Arvel winked at Dick Welles, "Let's do our best at not being a nuisance on this expedition."

They rode off, last in line, Sally with her younger brother, Donny, in tow. Arvel always took two mules on an expedition, as he had an abundant supply of the beasts, and thus was well provisioned in the event that things would go wrong. With the little general in charge, he was certain things would, indeed, go wrong.

They reached the homestead quickly; it was not far from town. As they approached, they were struck with the sweet pungency of burning human flesh. Tim Brown, nephew to the slain homesteaders, broke and galloped hard to the site, rifle in hand. What he hoped to discover or achieve by doing so, no one could tell. He was inconsolable when the rest of the posse caught up with him. The scene was disturbing, even to the most hardened war veteran, and most of these boys had little experience in such matters.

Except for the one girl who had escaped, every member of the family was lying about the yard. The house had been burned, only the scorched adobe fireplace and chimney remained. Dead livestock mixed with the corpses. Olaf's body smoldered in the dying embers of the fire-ring a distance from the home. The fingers of his left hand had been torn, rather than cut away, and they protruded from his gaping mouth. He had been scalped, evidently while still alive. His throat had been cut so deeply that the head was nearly off. The wife's body remained relatively intact. They looked everywhere for her head, but it could not be found. Two small children lay on top of her; from the amount of gore soaked up by their mother's dress, it was likely they died last, bearing witness to the terrible execution of their parents. The little girl, who was approaching her ninth birthday, had been defiled.

Tim Brown was of no good use to the posse. Aryel knew this would happen, and would not have permitted him to come along, if he had any say in it. He decided the best thing to do was to talk to the deputy as the young man was going to get himself and, perhaps, several others in a bit of trouble if he was allowed to go on. Arvel looked over at Dick who understood what he was thinking, and nodded in agreement.

"Deputy." He waited to get the man's attention and knew, from his countenance, that they were in for a bad time. He had lost color in his face and had trouble forming his words. He looked at Arvel, bewildered.

"Yeah, what is it?"

"I think we should send Tim Brown back to town."

The three of them watched the young man run from one body to the next, his actions defying logic. He tried to straighten the corpses' clothing, waving flies from open wounds. "That poor fellow won't be anything but a liability going forward."

The deputy pondered Arvel's words, then stood, stupefied. He began pulling at pieces of debris, and uprighted a bucket that lay on the ground at his feet. He removed his hat and began running his fingers through his hair repeatedly. He was trembling. "Well, I guess we'd better bury these folks and get that fire put out. I guess we'd better..." he began muttering incomprehensively.

Dick Welles intervened: "Deputy, why don't we get these boys mounted up and follow up on the bandits? The fire will cause no further damage, and the undertaker's already been alerted. He'll be along shortly to take care of these poor souls. There's nothing more we can do for them. But we really must take up the trail and get those black devils before they go and do any more harm."

"The trail is cold." The deputy spoke automatically, without emotion. "They could be anywhere by now." He rocked from foot to foot, fingering the brim of his hat.

"No, sir!" Dick replied. He'd seen men act like this in the war. They'd lose composure and direction. Giving them a task is the only way to get them out of it. "They went off due west," he motioned with a sweeping gesture of his hand, "and the only place for them to go is Potts Springs. They must take water there before heading into the desert. That's where we'll find them. It's not more than fifteen miles away. If they've moved on already, we can track 'em down and take them in the desert."

This brought the young deputy to his senses, more or less. He soon came around, more assertive and annoying than before.

"All right, you men, mount up." He looked down at Tim Brown, still fiddling with the headless woman. In a flash of clarity he instructed the man to stay at the homestead until the undertaker arrived. The young man did not hear him.

The bandits rode, just as Dick had surmised, to Potts Springs. They were well provisioned with spirits to celebrate their deeds and settled into the low mesa to take on a good drunk. They drank all night. Several of them wore the Knudsen's clothing. One Mexican was wearing Mrs. Knudsen's wedding dress. They lay nearly where they had fallen over in the early hours of the morning and were sleeping off a good drunk.

Potts Springs was the only logical place for them to go, if traveling west from the attack site. The reassuring thing about bad men is that they are almost universally stupid and this band was no different. It was easy enough to anticipate what they would do next.

The posse rode hard, too hard for Arvel and Dick's comfort, toward the bandit's camp. They knew that a brash attack would result in either an unnecessary loss of life or at least injury to members of the posse, and now they were down a man and outnumbered twelve to ten as the reporter could not be counted as a useful man. The two veterans knew well enough that it was always more dangerous to attack a position than it was to defend it.

Dick rode up next to the young deputy, trying to convince him to stop but the addled youth refused to listen and ran the posse to within a quarter mile of the spring. The dust cloud created by eleven men galloping hard would be a dead giveaway and was apt to give the gang time to prepare a defense.

The white man riding with the bandits was the first to stir. He had drunk hardily but was unable to sleep. The horrific images of the previous day's attack would not leave his mind. He was a pathetic man of twenty with bad teeth. He was known as Hedor for his mouth emitted a stench out to a distance of several feet. No one particularly liked him. He was merely tolerated. Like a rat, he seemed to be able to sense trouble before it happened and was therefore some use to the bad men. He had stumbled upon the bandit gang in late winter and, as he had no money and no cartridges for his rifle, his prospects were limited. He joined up as a temporary measure and hoped to drop out of their company when he got near enough to Tombstone where his fortunes would likely improve.

He stood on a high rock, relieving himself while scanning the horizon. He saw the dust and raised the alarm. Mexican and Indian bandits slowly roused from their drunken sleep but most were too hung over to move as quickly as they should. The bandit with the wedding dress cut it off himself with his big knife; he stood in his underwear, looking about for his gun belt and rifle.

Arvel saw the man on the rock. "Well, there'll be no surprising them now." He pointed, "There's one of them, right there, and he's raised the alarm." Arvel pulled out his Henry rifle and fired at the man, who dropped down instinctively, rat-like. The bullet parted his hair and started a stream of blood into his eyes, but he was otherwise unharmed.

The young deputy screamed at the posse. "No goddamned shooting until I give the command. We'll never catch the sons-of-bitches unawares now!" He glared at Arvel, then at Dick.

He stopped the troop momentarily and looked through his field glasses. Everyone waited for him to tell them what to do. The deputy looked bewildered. "Damn, I knew we shouldn't have stopped." He looked accusingly at Dick. "Come on, you men, let's ride." The deputy did take the lead, which impressed Dick Welles, even though he knew well enough that it was more likely due to the heat of the moment than pluck and courage.

The posse bolted forward to within a hundred yards of the gang and the shooting began. Arvel stood up in the saddle, placing the butt of his rifle on his right foot, and pulled the magazine spring up, working on replacing the cartridge he had fired as Sally galloped ahead, Donny in tow.

Dick looked over at him and laughed. "Jesus, Arvel, you look like a one-armed paperhanger trying to load that damned old rifle."

Arvel grinned. "You don't worry about me; just keep an eye on that deputy. You might learn a thing or two from him before this day is over." He got the cartridge replaced as Sally galloped on. He did not need to coax her. Sally knew what Arvel wanted, often before he knew himself.

The bandits' shots were high and wide and had no effect on the posse. They continued forward until they found themselves in an arroyo. They stopped there and dismounted. Bullets flew over their heads, buzzing past them. It was a sound Arvel remembered too well and one he had hoped he would not have to hear again in his lifetime. The deputy stood, fidgeting with his reins as the men took up shooting positions. The reporter curled into a ball, yanking his derby down over his eyes. He was acting more out of prudence than fear.

"Well, this is a fine spot." Arvel smiled at Dick as the man uncased his Winchester. "What do you say you flank left and I'll go right, and we'll see what can be done about this mess?"

"No, I think I'll  stay with you, Arvel. Those old timey guns of yours might get you in trouble. You might need me to take care of you."

They moved along the depression to the left, placing themselves between the sun and the bandits. There was an outcropping large enough to afford a good vantage point into the bandit camp. The posse began to return ineffectual fire which at least served to keep the bandits occupied.

Dick and Arvel made it to the high place. "There's room for just one shooter. Go on up there, Arvel. I'll keep the rifles loaded." He handed Arvel his Winchester and held out his hands, fingers laced together, to give Arvel a leg up. "Hold on, Cowboy, give me your cartridges, that relic of yours takes rimfires."

Arvel leaned Dick's rifle against the rock wall, pulled out a handful and pushed them into Dick's palm.

"What the hell are they covered in?"

Arvel looked down, "Sugar. Pilar gave me some pan de muerto," he smiled at the irony of his cook's food selection, "I guess they got covered in sugar. I had 'em in the same pocket."

"My God, Arvel, you are something. They're going to gum up your Henry." He stuffed the coated cartridges into his coat pocket.

Arvel grinned, "Come on, I've got ruffians to shoot. Lick 'em clean before you load 'em." He stepped up into the stirrup made by Dick's sugary hands.

Arvel slid forward on his belly, took up a steady position where he could look directly down onto the bandit camp. He placed Dick's Winchester beside him and proceeded to pour deadly fire into the group, first with his Henry, then with Dick's Winchester. Dick reached up and grabbed the Henry and worked on reloading it. The bandits, panicked, began to break from cover, allowing the rest of the posse to hit their marks. One bandit saw Arvel on the perch overhead. He turned, dropped his rifle and put his hands up, screaming to Arvel that he would give up. Arvel shot him in the forehead with Dick's Winchester, noting in his mind that it shot an inch high at that range. The man dropped as if he had fallen through a trapdoor.

When the shooting finally stopped all the bandits were dead except for Hedor. He lay, moaning and holding a loop of gut forcing its way through the gash made by Arvel's rifle.

"I am sorry for the low shot, son. You jumped up just as I was firing, otherwise I'd have killed you clean."

The man looked up at Arvel. He did not know what to say. He looked back down at his blood soaked hands and the gray loop of gut, like uncooked sausage, uncoiling from his abdomen. "Oh, that's all right."

He winced, cried out. He could not catch his breath. He watched as the blood flowed out onto the ground beneath him. "I ain't never been shot before." He curled his body. "I want to tell you boys, I didn't have no part in all that yesterday." He gritted his teeth. "I ain't tellin' you I don't deserve to be shot. I'm glad you killed me. I can't keep livin', seein' those folks go the way they did and ever time I close my eyes, that's all I see." He bent forward again, and let out a groan. "I didn't do anything for 'em, and shame on me. I will go to hell for it, sure enough."

"You a praying man?" the reporter spoke up. He looked at Arvel and Dick for approval.

"I, I guess."

"Well, you may atone for your sins and see where it gets you." He regretted, as a man who used words for a living, the inarticulate way he was stating it, but he was not certain what fate awaited the dying man. He felt better when Hedor seemed to take comfort at the thought.

The deputy pushed past them. "Get him on a horse; we'll take him back for trial."

Incredulous, Arvel replied: "IIe won't live another hour." The dying man begged for water, he looked down at the ribbon of gut, squeezing between his fingers. His eyes darted back and forth, first at Arvel and then to Dick.

"He's been gut shot, don't give him water, it'll only make his situation worse," said the deputy, with authority.

Arvel pulled out his canteen and gave the man a drink. He glared at the deputy. Hedor drank, but just barely, the color fading from his face. He cried out again.

"Get him on a horse."

Arvel faced the deputy again: "He will not be moved."

"And I say he will," the deputy put his hand on the grip of his six shooter. He hoped for some live prisoners. At least he would have one. He stared back at Arvel, who was no longer smiling. Arvel knew the man's game. He was driven by greed for recognition and any potential bounty. Arvel had no great compassion for the miscreant, he knew he would soon be dead, but there was no call to add to his suffering.

"I say..." Arvel was interrupted by a shot from Dick's Winchester. The bullet pierced the desperado's heart. The deputy looked at the two old-timers. He swore, and marched off.

"Well, there's an end to it," said the reporter from under his derby.

The deputy should have been pleased. All the bandits were dead. None of his posse suffered so much as a scratch. It was true that they did not get Gold Hat but, with his reputation, it was unlikely that he would have waited around for any posse to catch up to him. He was simply too slippery. The deputy was angry, nonetheless. More likely, it was because he was disappointed in himself. He'd lost his nerve. He knew the score, and he didn't like it much. The reporter did not help as he chattered incessantly about the two real heroes of the day.

As the deputy sauntered back to his horse, the little man encountered Sally, quietly resting among the horses. He pushed her on the flank, and when she did not move, thumped her smartly across the neck with his quirt. She hee-hawed and jumped aside.

"Whoa, there, cowboy," Arvel stiffened at his mule's cry. "You don't touch my mule, son."

The deputy's face reddened. He kicked the ground and jerked the hat from his head. He swatted Sally with it, then pushed her all the harder. "Then get this goddamned beast out of my way."

"Partner," Arvel softly said, "you molest that animal one more time, and I swear I'll put a ball in you."

The young deputy scoffed and continued to attack the mule. "I *hate* mules! They are worthless beasts!" raising his quirt. Before he could hit Sally again, Arvel pulled out his Navy Colt and shot the deputy in the toe.

Falling over, the deputy let loose a stream of obscenities. He held his foot, rolling about on the ground. "You son-of-a-bitch, you shot me!" He looked up at Arvel, fury and pain welling inside, and reached for his revolver. Before he could clear leather, Dick buffaloed him senseless, blood now pouring from the gash on his head as well as the hole in his boot.

Arvel attended to Sally, holding her face and speaking softly to her. He kissed her on the muzzle. He did not look at the deputy again.

By now the others had had enough of the young upstart, and they looked at him with disdain. No one blamed Arvel. They would not blame him if he'd shot the man dead. They admired his restraint. Arvel was a legend for his love of his mules. He'd even been known to buy mules back from people whom he thought did not deserve them, or who had misused them in any way. He often balked at selling them to the Army, as there was no guarantee they'd be treated properly.

"Well, I guess we can't just leave him here," the reporter finally said. A couple of the men threw water on the young deputy, who regained his senses. They bandaged his foot, now absent one toe, and put him on his horse. One of the young men rolled up the toe in the deputy's big scarf, stuffed it in his bloody boot and tied the whole affair with a piggin string onto their former leader's saddle horn. Half of the detail escorted him back to town. The other half stayed to arrange the corpses and collect their traps. They would later inform the undertaker who would bring out a wagon and retrieve the bodies.

Arvel and Dick stayed with this group, deciding it best to avoid any further dealings with the new amputee. Arvel thought of the Mexican girl as he looked amongst the dead men's belongings. He felt a little cocky. The evil Sombrero del Oro did not seem so difficult to beat. He was ultimately disappointed when he realized the leader was not among the corpses. The bandit leader had once again slipped away.

Dick talked the whole way back to town. It was how he unwound from battle. He liked to talk to people he liked and this was incongruous with his otherwise stoic demeanor. He laughed about Arvel's shot. He spoke of the good shooting, and teased Arvel about his Henry rifle, his old fashioned gun. "Guess those old-timey shootin' irons still work."

They rode a little farther, Dick continued: "Did you smell that white boy's breath? My God."

"I thought that was from his intestines, you did notice they were mostly in his hands."

"Nope, nope, that was definitely his breath. I definitely discerned breath."

Arvel was preparing to drink from his canteen and remembered giving a last drink to the dying man. He upended the container, draining it onto the ground, lifted the opening to his nose and sniffed doubtfully. He recorked it and put it back on his saddle horn. "I'll boil that later." He took it back off his saddle horn, "On second thought," he flung it into the desert. "I'll just get another one."

The posse met up at the saloon later that day. They convinced the two old-timers to join them in celebration. Most of the town folks and all of the inhabitants of the nearby ranches seemed to be jammed in the saloon and overflowing onto the streets. Even Miss Edna, the church organist, made an appearance, pounding out some happy tunes on the establishment's upright. They all were celebrating the end of the bandit gang. It would not bring the Knudsens back, but at least some solace could be gained from the fact that the bad men were all dead.

This was a quiet town which never attracted the rough company such as what was seen in Tombstone and Bisbee. No gamblers found it worth their time, no cowboys had business there. Most of the men were married, or well enough settled that whore houses could not be sustained.

But today, the townsfolk were giving the saloon good commerce and the beer and whiskey flowed freely.

The younger men talked and joked and backslapped their comrades. It was only in such a life and death struggle that one could form this kind of bond. Many of these men were tough, tough from living on the land, living rough, but few had experienced the sting of battle, as they were born after the war. Certainly they had been in the occasional bar fight or disagreement at the branding fire, but none had yet experienced mortal combat.

They all spoke excitedly of the two old-timers. They had never seen shooting like this. They each took up Arvel's old Henry rifle, which most of them had never seen before. The men began pressing the veterans about their time in the war. They wanted to know where they had fought and how many men they had killed. Arvel just smiled and told them that it was too long ago to remember and that Dick was the man with the most battle experience.

Finally, when everyone was sufficiently drunk, the reporter stood up and offered a toast: "To the great toe-shooter of the East. Boot makers fear him, chiropodists revere him!"

The younger men looked on silently. Most did not understand the joke and wondered if it was not an insult. Finally, Arvel began to laugh, and everyone cheered. He patted the reporter on the back. "Anyone who can weave a chiropodist into a toast has my undying respect, son."

As the drinking continued, and the conversation inevitably deteriorated, Arvel seized the opportunity to slip out. He headed home. He rode alone and began to feel a little melancholy. He regretted shooting the boy in the foot. He always regretted doing things out of anger. He did not mind killing the bandits.

Soon, he would be back to the mule ranch. He preferred the company of mules to people. He hoped that there would now be an end to the little excitement, and that he could go back to his simple uneventful existence.